For Owen

'Instantly one of those long arms glided

like a snake into the opening,

and twenty others were quivering above.

With a sweep of the axe,

Captain Nemo chopped off

this fearsome tentacle,

which slid writhing down the steps . . .

Seized by the tentacle and glued to its suckers,

the unfortunate man was swinging in the air at

the mercy of this enormous appendage.

He gasped, he choked, he yelled . . .

The poor fellow was done for.'

Twenty Thousand Leagues Under the Sea

by Jules Verne

A MESSAGE FROM CHICKEN HOUSE

Waking up on a giant jellyfish with the world gone to hell and ominous predators stalking the shore would be a bit rubbish . . . but you'd get used to it, wouldn't you? You'd probably even get a bit bored, after a while – I know the teenage me would. And whether you're on land or on jelly, there will always be issues. Like how to get off the jellyfish (and *not* get off with each other), avoid those bossy adults, grow your friendships, or stomach yet more raw fish . . . This surreal story by awesome debut writer Clare Rees is funny, thought-provoking and unbearably real (really).

BARRY CUNNINGHAM
Publisher
Chicken House

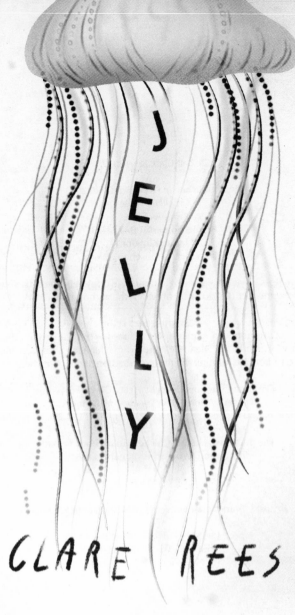

JELLY

CLARE REES

Chicken House

2 Palmer Street, Frome, Somerset BA11 1DS
www.chickenhousebooks.com

Text © Clare Rees 2019

First published in Great Britain in 2019
Chicken House
2 Palmer Street
Frome, Somerset BA11 1DS
United Kingdom
www.chickenhousebooks.com

Cover and interior design by Helen Crawford-White
Typeset by Dorchester Typesetting Group Ltd
Printed and bound in Great Britain by CPI Group (UK) Ltd, Croydon CR0 4YY

The paper used in this Chicken House book is made
from wood grown in sustainable forests.

1 3 5 7 9 10 8 6 4 2

British Library Cataloguing in Publication data available.

PB ISBN 978-1-912626-29-8
eISBN 978-1-912626-44-1

1

*P*itiful Pete was sitting right on the edge of the Jellyfish, facing out towards the far coast, and a few of us had gathered round to watch.

'What do you think your chances are this time, Pete?' called James. He bit into a piece of dried fish, ripping off the tail with an expert flick of his wrist. One thing about James is that he does eat disgusting foods in a non-disgusting way.

Pitiful Pete shrugged his shoulders, his eyes focused on the waves. He always takes a while to work himself up to it.

'Your problem's been with the tentacles in the past,' said James helpfully. 'If you can just get beyond those, you should be fine.'

'Your problem's with *your* face,' said Lana.

'My face is fabulous, and you know it,' said James. He puckered up his lips and gave a dramatic toss of his matted hair. His face wasn't exactly fabulous, if I'm honest. His eyes were grey like the sea on a dull day, and his hair was probably dark blond, though it was tricky to tell because it was so coated in dirt and salt. But there's always been something about James's face which makes you want to keep watching it. It seems to move more than other people's faces, as though he feels emotions more than everybody else, and most of those emotions are about being happy – even at times when that doesn't seem possible.

The tentacles of the Jellyfish were moving from side to side in their normal, irregular fashion. They might swipe over to the left with a swoosh, then waggle a bit, before swiping back to the left again. But then the next time they might do a waggle before swooshing to the right, or maybe a quick wiggle somewhere in the middle. It was pretty difficult to work out a pattern.

'Pete, why don't you come back from the edge?' said Kate softly. 'I can fetch you a nice cup of hot water and we could play bottle-top chess.'

Pete didn't respond.

'There's a lovely driftwood fire going over by the Big House,' she added, putting her hand on Pete's shoulder. 'And it's such a beautiful day. You've got so much to offer us here, and we'd be sad if you died. I'd really miss you.'

'Kate, what the . . . ?' James glared at her. 'The man wants to jump in. Can't he even do that in peace?'

'I respect everybody's decision,' said Kate. Lana rolled her eyes. 'But I'm just not sure that he's happy. I think Pete might feel more like himself after a nice chat.'

'I *think* feeling like himself is what's got him into this

2

situation. I *think* it'd be totally rubbish to be Pete,' said James.

I felt like I had to step in at this point. 'James!' I said. 'Rude!'

'It's true though, isn't it, Martha?' he said. 'The man's stuck on a giant jellyfish, for whatever mysterious reason. He hasn't eaten anything other than bony fish and seaweed for ages and he has to sleep in a crappy shack with a load of miserable, smelly people.'

Pete gave a big sigh and lowered his head.

'Some of those people are my best friends!' I said, loudly.

'The loveliest people in the world,' said Kate. 'Who care for you deeply, Pete.'

'Some of your best friends are complete losers,' said James to me. He took another large bite, picking out a couple of bones before he chewed. There was only the head of the fish left now. Its eyes were glazed and crusted over with salt.

Lana nodded. 'I know how Pete feels. Almost everybody on here is a loser, Martha. Especially you.'

'And some of your best friends are the smelliest in the shack,' added James.

'No!' I said.

'It's true,' he said. 'I pride myself on it. My farts last night were amazing.'

'Seriously, Pete,' said Lana, smoothly steering James away from one of his favourite topics. 'What's your plan?' Pete sighed deeply again, but didn't reply. 'I think if you stand up to do it, you'll get further when you jump in,' Lana said.

3

'Yeah, that's a good idea,' said James. 'And if you want to stand on my back, that might give you an even better chance? You know, if you say, *1, 2, 3, Go,* then we'd all push.'

Lana nodded. 'Or do a running jump?'

'No!' said Kate. 'You're not going to help him do this.'

At the other end of the Jellyfish there was a sudden burst of laughter, followed by a few shouts and calls. It sounded like the morning catch of fish was starting to arrive. It had probably landed on somebody's face again. It was always brilliant when that happened – there's nothing funnier than wet fish flapping in somebody else's face.

With a shudder, Pete stood up. His hair was clumped together and claggy with seaweed, so that it was hard to tell what was beard and what was hair. All the salt water made it stick up like the mane you'd draw on a lion when you were little and you'd run out of yellow crayons, so had to use the greys and browns.

'You can do it, Pete,' said James, slapping him on the back. 'This is your day. Come on, man. We believe in you!'

'There's still time to change your mind,' said Kate. 'We love you and think you're great.'

Pete turned and shook her hand, then offered it to the rest of us in turn. We all shook it.

'Guys!' I shouted over to the Big House. 'Pete's going to jump again.'

'Come on, Pete,' said Lana. 'Go for it!'

He took a few steps backwards and paused.

The tentacles slowed for a split second. There was a light waggle of movement, a lull. The breeze dropped too, and it seemed, for that moment, as if it might just be possible. Even the sway and pull of the waves seemed to pause. But then the larger tentacles swished sharply over to the left again, and the bits of jelly beneath them gave a roll, almost to show off.

'Good luck,' I said, and the others offered their goodbyes.

Pitiful Pete gave a nod in reply.

Somewhere behind us, the shouts and laughs came again. Nobody else was coming to watch Pete jump in.

He took a deep breath, looked once more up at the submerged houses and factories on the coastline, then took a step forward to launch himself towards them. He sprinted five paces, his ragged shirt streaming out behind him, and his bare feet slapping on the jellyfish mesoglea. He bowed his head and raised his arms as he reached the edge, before leaping off in a practised dive so smooth he barely made a splash.

There was another cheer from the Big House.

Then that lull again. The tentacles slowed. It was almost as if the world had stopped, as though time had paused. Lana looked round, eyes wide, and Kate put her hands up to her mouth. James raised his hands to keep us quiet.

None of us moved. I could see Pitiful Pete's dark shape sliding through the water. First one metre, then five, his arms scooping small trails of bubbles in the water behind him. He'd never got this far before.

There was a kerfuffle over by the fire again, and somebody

started to sing.

'Attention, attention!' Soldier John was shouting about something, probably trying to organize unwilling slackers into groups to gut the fish. There were the usual groans of complaint and more laughter. But at our end, we hadn't moved. We'd barely breathed.

Pete was still going. As he broke the surface he turned in confusion.

'Go,' I whispered, urging him on.

'Quick, quick!' hissed James, gesturing to him.

Kate covered her eyes.

Pete turned back again and started towards the coast. He was doing front crawl, his arms sleek and powerful like two diving seals. He was trying to go as fast as possible, but it's tricky to do that when you're also trying to avoid disturbing the water.

'He's past the tentacles, isn't he?' Lana whispered.

I'd been holding my breath. *There's still the longer ones underneath*, I mouthed back.

He was edging onwards, another metre, then another. He was into the open sea now, the waves higher and breaking against him, pushing him forwards. *Nobody* had ever got this far.

'You can do it, Pete,' I whispered. 'Come on!' I dug my fingernails into my palms to stop myself from shouting. But then it came, the same as always. A sudden, swift slither through the waves, the dark buzz of the powerful tentacle

6

cutting through the air, and then the thudding splash as it hit the water and scooped Pete out. He landed back on the surface next to us with a dull squelch, dripping and quivering.

'Did you see?' said Lana. She was so excited her hands were shaking. 'He almost did it.'

'Oh, bad luck, Pete,' shouted Soldier John. 'Are you still stuck here?'

'Yes, of course he is,' said Lana. 'But he almost friggin' escaped.'

And that was the start. That was when we started to believe we could do it. That maybe . . . we could escape.

2

The biggest problem with being trapped on a killer jellyfish isn't what you'd expect.

Once you get over your fear of death (basically because you start looking forward to it), and the smell of rotting fish stops making you gag, it isn't too bad, really. Boredom *is* an issue, yes. It's not the main one, though. The main problem is the other people trapped with you.

When I get sick of it all I go over to the back tentacles and sit in between the hard jelly ridges on the creature's muscle ring, looking out to sea. Sitting there means that the cold wind is blasting into your face, and the spray from the waggling tentacles hits you in the eyes. But it's still better than listening to Old Albert's Dire Warnings, or James's favourite diarrhoea stories. Again.

Sometimes the creature's muscle ring is the most popular place on the Jellyfish, and you arrive to find all of the ridges already taken. That's normally OK, though, because the people sitting there are going to be the quiet ones. And even if they did try to talk to you, it would come out as, '*Blugglerlp*' or something, what with all the spray flying into their open mouths.

The front of the Jellyfish – which I suppose might not be the front, given it's just a giant lump of wobbly flesh – faces towards the coast. We used to see people walking there almost every week. We would wave and shout, and if they weren't being chased by scuttling kriks – more about those later – they would sometimes wave back. It's like we were saying, '*Hullo! We're trapped on a giant killer jellyfish,*' and they were saying, '*Gosh, how interesting. Good luck, then!*'

In the middle of the Jellyfish is a load of splintered wood. We call it 'the Big House', which I think might have been somebody being sarcastic, but the name's stuck because a lot of the people here don't understand humour. It's made from bits of driftwood and rubbish all jammed in together and piled up to create walls. There are rows of plastic bottles, of course, and plastic bags are squeezed into every gap to try and block the wind – but they're mainly all faded and grey these days. We get super excited whenever we see another bit of brightly coloured rubbish floating towards us, because it means we can redecorate.

True story: Kate and Lana once stopped speaking to each other for a whole week, because Lana told Kate that putting all the blue plastic bags on one wall was, 'Stupid when they're not the same shade.' Even though they're friends again now, it still feels risky when there's a blue plastic bag amongst the rubbish. They avoid making eye contact when that happens.

We've gone for a tasteful selection of rags to decorate our corner of the Big House at the moment – me, Lana and Kate. They're mainly all different sorts of brown, of course, but we pulled them into strips and then wove them into a hanging which is supposed to look like trees in a forest. You have to use your imagination, because the background is also brown, just like the trees, so there are a few places where it's difficult to tell which is background and which is forest. Also, none of us could really remember what a forest looked like, so it might not be that accurate.

You do get sick of the people. Even the lovely ones. You get sick of never having any time to yourself, you get sick of hearing the same stories over, and over, and over again. You get sick of being able to tell what somebody is going to say before they even open their mouths.

This morning I bumped into James. Well, I say I bumped into him, it's not like there was anywhere else to go, really. He was standing in my way, and I diverted so we could have a chat about what had happened to Pete and how we might be able to get past those tentacles.

'Hi, Martha,' he said. He never normally calls me 'Martha' except when he wants something. It's normally 'Bucketface', or 'Idiotbrain', so I was immediately suspicious.

'Uh huh,' I said. 'What do you want, James? I'm busy.'

'Are you, Martha? Are you really?'

'No,' I said. 'You know I'm not. I was dropping hints that I don't want to talk to you right now. The polite thing to do would be to take those hints.' I put my hands on my hips to make it clear I was telling him off.

'Yeah,' he said. 'But I've got more important things to think about, Martha. We should all start thinking about repopulating the planet.' He grinned, and I swear his eyes gave an actual twinkle, though it could have just been light reflecting off the mesoglea.

'Right.'

'So are you up for it?' he said.

'I'm up for saving the world and the planet,' I said.

James did look surprised at this point, to give him some credit.

'Erm . . . good. Shall we get started then? In the Big House?'

'I don't see why not. Shall I invite some of the others?'

'Oh,' he said. 'Do you think that's appropriate?'

'The more the merrier, surely?' I said. 'Kate! Lana! Come here! James wants to repopulate the planet.'

From all over the Jellyfish, people started walking towards us. Old Albert was waddling faster than normal, Dr Jones put down her fishing rod, and even Pitiful Pete lifted his head to listen. It doesn't take much to get us all interested here.

'Oh, erm, that's not quite what I had in mind,' said James. 'I don't mind the girls, but I'm not sure about the others.'

'But if we're going to repopulate the planet, don't we need to involve as many people as possible?' I pointed out. 'Stinky! Dr Jones!' I called.

'Yeeessss,' James said. 'But I'm not sure . . .'

'Look,' I said, thinking it was time to get to the point. 'Does your plan for repopulating the planet involve taking off any of my clothes? Because if it does, there's no way that's happening. It's much too cold.'

He looked at my threadbare jeans for a few moments and I could see him working out the possibilities. 'Noooo,' he said, slowly.

By this point, almost everybody had gathered around us.

'Martha, I'm offering you the opportunity to have my children,' said James, styling it out. 'We could get started right now if you want?'

'Sadly I'm going to have to turn down your offer, James. I've got too much to do today.'

Old Albert coughed in his gravelly, phlegmy way. 'It probably wouldn't take him very long,' he muttered.

'Fine, then. Your loss. Lana, will you have my children?' called James.

'Get stuffed, dickhead,' said Lana.

'No need to overreact. You were only my third choice anyway,'

'Good. I wish I was your last choice.'

'It's a short list, Lana, but I'll add your name to the bottom of it, if that's what you want.' He smiled triumphantly as Lana made retching noises.

'Hang on,' I said. 'Does that mean I was your second choice?'

12

James shrugged nonchalantly. 'There're a lot of hot babes on board.'

'WHO?' I said, genuinely outraged.

'Well, you know . . .' he said, gesturing vaguely.

Dr Jones looked up at him expectantly, her fishing rod slung over her shoulder and the fish she was now gutting at her heels. Her hands were covered with the blood and there were scales all over her shoes, but despite that, she still looked mysteriously clean, like all she needed was a good shower and she'd be ready for normal life again. Her clothes had fewer holes than everybody else's and her blouse was still a shade which could truthfully be called white. Kate was trying to make her face look sympathetic to me, but also disgusted at James, so she was screwing it up into all sorts of weird positions. Right now, her forehead was all crinkled and her lips were pursed awkwardly. Her hair was a matted mess, but there were still the traces of plaits where she'd tried to keep it neat; and through the salt you could still see that her hair was glossy, a deep chestnut. On Kate's light-brown skin, the tan from the constant wind looked like a soft glow which enhanced her cheekbones and made her more beautiful, rather than making her look dirty or bruised like the rest of us. Staring Crone stayed where she was, of course, staring out at the coast. We don't know definitely if she's female or not, but she might be. There weren't many other options.

'Why was I not your first choice?' I asked. And I still think I was right to ask that, though I remember now that he didn't reply.

'Did you *want* to be his first choice?' said Lana. She asked it in a fake-serious voice, so that I knew she'd use my answer against me, whatever I said. That's a definite NO, by the way. That much should be obvious: one thing that's even less appealing than getting naked on a jellyfish is the thought of giving birth on a jellyfish. But at this point I got so distracted by the horror of that image that I basically couldn't speak, and so I didn't actually say 'No' quickly enough. But then I got in more of a mess, because I realized if I explained I didn't really want to be his first choice, but that there were so few eligible girls around I thought I should be at the top of the list anyway, then everybody would hate me. I'd then left it too long to say anything, so I blushed instead. I could feel my cheeks going all red, so I just made a quick spluttering noise which I hoped would confuse everybody.

'Pshaw!' I said confidently.

'It might have been the Jellyfish who was his first choice,' said Old Albert, nodding wisely.

'Uggh.' Lana screwed up her face in disgust.

'Albert, no,' said Dr Jones. 'I've explained this to you before, but maybe I need to clarify again. There are a number of reasons why it would be very difficult to breed with a jellyfish. If, indeed, this is a jellyfish. And if, indeed, it's female.'

'Yes, I think that would be very useful,' said Old Albert. 'I would like to know more about jellyfish breeding.' His eyes went all sideways then, but Dr Jones nodded enthusiastically, pleased at the chance to give another Biology lesson. I wasn't sure they had the same goals in mind.

'And if I could have babies with the Jellyfish – no offence, Martha –' James nodded at me, 'then would that mean that they'd be mutant jellyfish with the power to walk on land?'

'Well, erm . . . technically . . .' Dr Jones was planning where to begin. She had her hands up now, about to draw air diagrams with her pretend air pen. There were a few tuts from Staring Crone.

'James, that is such a load of rubbish,' said Lana. 'That's the worst idea you've ever had.'

'Was I on your list at all?' said Kate. 'I'd understand if I wasn't, but . . .'

And in between it all, with everybody now talking about possible jellyfish breeding, I could see James standing back, grinning at the chaos he'd caused.

3

*T*hen another thing happened that made us hopeful about escape.

'I think it's time to talk about mermaids.'

'Woohoo!'

'Hurrah!'

There was an immediate burst of clapping and cheering from the crowd in the Big House. Mermaids are always a super popular topic, and also sea serpents. We love stories about creatures from the sea, so we all settled comfortably, really wriggling nicely into the mesoglea to make a good seat, you know? I think we were all in a happy mood anyway after Pitiful Pete's 'almost-escape'– apart from Pitiful Pete, that is, but even he was sitting at the front vaguely listening, so he can't have been feeling too bad. In all, we were looking forward to a good evening.

There isn't much to do here, and sometimes, in the winter, it's really hard to tell the difference between night-time and daytime. All of those misty, dark days blend into the misty moonlit nights, and dawn and dusk can be so long and drawn out you can't tell when they begin and end. Even if you try to sleep for twenty-four hours, you'll find you can't – and believe me, we have tried. So we spend seriously a lot of our time telling stories, and it's something that's important to us. We all take it in turns and the rule is you have to listen. Sometimes they're not stories, they're maybe just rants, or something random somebody wants to tell us. But we always take it seriously.

Today it was the turn of Staring Crone. I don't remember ever having heard her speak before, though Kate has promised us 'she's a real sweetie'. The trouble is, Kate's not always reliable about that sort of thing; she once said Old Albert was 'absolutely lovely and had a great sense of humour', which kept the rest of us laughing for a week afterwards. So I'd never risked chatting with Staring Crone; she'd never exactly given the impression she'd reply anyway.

'Uh, we've heard a lot of mermaid stories, haven't we?' Staring Crone began. Her voice was creaky and quiet, like her throat was coated in rust. But it was a great start, so we all nodded enthusiastically.

'I hope she does *The Little Mermaid*,' whispered Kate.

'And they're lovely,' Staring Crone continued. 'We've got the idea that their upper body is normal but, uh, naked, and human, but their lower body is a powerful fish tail. I think there were some nice stories about hidden cities under the sea and happy adventures with songs and dancing fish.'

'Yes!' whispered Kate.

'But there are other stories too. From other places. Other countries have stories about mysterious sea creatures which can live on the land and under the sea. They're not all as nice as mermaids.'

'Like the kriks? They can live on the land and under the sea,' I whispered. 'And they're not very nice.'

'"Nice"?' James started laughing. '"Not very nice"?'

'Yeah, all right,' I said. 'They're ruthless killing monsters, then.'

'They're creepy bastards,' said Lana. 'Now shut up. You're being annoying.'

The Big House had gone unusually quiet. This wasn't the talk we'd been expecting. Staring Crone continued, her voice stronger now, louder and more confident. 'Many of those stories were violent, or were about the sea creatures killing humans. There are Greek Sirens, who deliberately lured sailors to their deaths, and there's the Scottish "Selkie", which lives as a seal in the water, but sheds its skin to become human when on land. In fact, uh, I think the mermaid stories haven't always been nice. The stories I remembered, like *The Little Mermaid*, were recently changed to focus only on the happy bits of the story. The original versions were much, much darker and more violent.

'And, uh, do you know that the Danes and the Japanese both had a legend about a giant sea monster with lots of tentacles? The Danes called it the Kraken, and it was big

18

enough to swallow whole ships. So, uh, what I mean is that I think we should think about these stories as being more than just stories. I think we should start treating them as fact.'

You could have heard a fish fart. The whole room was completely silent. It was properly awkward. Staring Crone had never stopped doing her thing, of staring into the distance, so it was never like she was definitely talking to us. But now it wasn't clear whether she'd stopped talking to us. Then, for no reason at all, there was a sudden release, and everyone just started to clap crazily.

'This is brilliant!' said James, excitedly beating his fist on the Jellyfish's surface. 'I can't believe it!' What the . . .'

'If she wants to just carry on staring at stuff and then coming forward every so often and saying something amazing, then that's OK with me,' said Lana. 'I'll even take her her food.'

'Bloody hell,' said James. 'This is the best thing ever!'

My cheeks hurt with grinning. I mean, the idea that those old stories might actually be true? And that this whole big killer jellyfish thing might not be new? It was amazing! Also . . . it sort of made sense, weirdly, or more sense than most of the other theories people had come up with, anyway.

'Thank you very much.' Dr Jones stood up. 'Very much indeed.' She frowned at us, her matted brown hair tied back neatly with a natty orange strip of plastic. She raised her hands and the crowd settled down slightly, but there was still an undertone of excited muttering. 'I think we probably all have a few questions. Would you be prepared to take them?'

Staring Crone moved slowly, now focusing her stare down towards her audience. Her long grey hair parted as she did so; beneath, you could see her white chapped lips and almost-glowing black eyes. 'Yes,' she said. 'Some.'

'I'll start, if that's OK?' said Dr Jones. 'Why do you think the stories should be treated as fact?'

'There are too many of them,' said Staring Crone. 'It's just uh, a pattern. Some of the stories are ancient so they will have been changed over the years as they were told in different forms. But uh, the two big problems we're facing are common to the stories. We've got creatures on land who kill humans – the kriks – and, uh, we've got giant sea monsters with multiple tentacles that sound like giant jellyfish. We humans are in a mess right now, but I don't think it's the first time it's happened.'

'Sorry?' said Dr Jones. 'You don't think this is the first time it's happened?'

Staring Crone tilted her head slowly towards Dr Jones, so that her hair fell over her face again. There was a pause before she spoke: 'Noah's Ark.'

The room immediately erupted into chaos again. This time, there was no way Dr Jones could control us. People were standing up and shouting, some people were laughing crazily, I think both Lana and James were just making random noises of amazement.

Noah's Ark? When sea levels had risen in the Bible? I

honestly think it was the cleverest thing I'd ever heard. Because that was just like us, wasn't it? Floating along after sea levels have risen and maybe most people have died. I know Noah wasn't on his ark for very long – only forty days, or something like that – but him and his friends were stuck on there with a whole load of animals, and that might actually have been more annoying than all the people here. Living with a crowd of lions and owls and badgers and everything would have been a nightmare. That would be much worse than Old Albert having food in his beard, or Stinky farting in his sleep – though, on the plus side, Noah was on an actual boat and not a crazy living jellyfish, and he could land that boat on the shore without being attacked by kriks. Yeah, maybe it was just luck Dr Jones chose Staring Crone to speak straight after Pete's 'almost-escape'. But I think not. I think some of the other people knew what she was going to say. I'm not sure Dr Jones was surprised. Staring Crone's talk was definitely the second big thing which made us rethink our chances of escape.

It took a while to get the room quiet again, and there were a lot of people who had something to say – though it was mainly to repeat what Staring Crone had already said, using different words. But eventually, Dr Jones managed it. Then she spoke to Staring Crone again. 'What do you think we can learn from those stories?' she said.

There was another long pause. Staring Crone didn't immediately look as though she had noted the question, but then there was a movement in the hair, a flicker in the matted mess in front of her mouth. 'What can we learn?

'Uh . . . we can learn that people survived. The stories are told by people who survived.'

4

Survival was the thing I most liked to spend my time thinking about. It was probably the thing we *all* most liked to think about. But after Staring Crone's talk and Pete's almost-escape, there was the possibility that what had just been thinking might now become reality, so it felt like legitimate planning rather than time-wasting, staring-into-space daydreams.

I was still unclear about the actual details, especially anything that involved getting myself off the Jellyfish, but I always liked to spend at least an hour a day picturing myself on land again, walking on ground that didn't move beneath me and wasn't covered in slime. The kriks didn't feature in my fantasies. Definitely not. It was more about me just walking around in golden sunshine (unrealistic), my long blonde hair blowing in the breeze (also unrealistic as my hair's brown) while eating buckets and buckets of fruit (possible, maybe).

So I was happily sitting on that cold jelly surface the next morning, thinking away to myself about escaping, as usual, when James interrupted – also as usual. 'Hey, hey, hey!' he shouted. 'All rise for Jellyfish Rugby!' He was standing by the Big House, and throwing the rugby ball from one hand to the other. 'If anybody wants to get changed into their gym kit, they've got two minutes to do it.'

A couple of people went into the Big House, because it's important to keep up standards. I would have gone, but I got changed before sports yesterday and I never really get that sweaty anyway. Mostly you're just standing around trying to avoid getting pushed into the sea, so there's not that much of a workout. Plus, you're just changing your own set of rags for a plastic bag with tastefully ripped head- and arm-holes. It's not like we actually have gym kit.

'Ball inspection,' said Soldier John loudly. He strode over to James and held out his hands for the ball.

'Bollocks,' said James. 'It's fine.'

'Let me check whether it's fine,' said Soldier John even more loudly. To be fair, he never speaks quietly, so he wasn't being particularly threatening.

'It is,' said James, holding to his chest the bundle of plastic bottles we hilariously call a ball. 'Don't worry about it.'

'*I'll* tell you if it's fine,' said Soldier John. 'Don't make me force you to give it to me, boy.'

'Are you really going to hit me over a rugby ball?'

'I didn't say I was going to 'it you,' said Soldier John. 'Why, do you think you deserve a slap?'

I was going to answer that one, but Lana got there first.

24

'Yes,' she called. 'He does.'

A few other people were starting to look suspicious now, and started making their way towards James in a determined fashion. There were hands on hips and furrowed brows.

'If it's that important to you, then of course you can look at the ball,' said James, throwing it at Soldier John crossly.

Soldier John didn't reply. He held the ball up, inspecting it from underneath and looking in closely at the bags that were holding it together. He squeezed it a couple of times, and then turned it over slowly. He shook it with a knowledgeable air. With a very serious expression, he turned to the other suspicious people and held it out to them. There were a few prods and squeezes, and a few glum shakes of heads. Almost nobody made eye contact with each other, which is important, because you don't want to be on the same side as somebody about being suspicious, and then find out that you're playing rugby against them the next minute. That's really awkward.

James stood angrily, his hands in his pockets, muttering to himself. 'It was my idea to play. It's not like I'd tamper with the ball.'

Jellyfish Rugby is a very important event. We do play it pretty much every day, though we spice it up sometimes by playing Jellyfish Football instead. We used to have leagues and tournaments, but it got out of control and some people are still bitter about it. I'm not going to go into the details, but let's just say it wasn't just balls that were tampered

25

with back then.

The whole crowd was quiet now, the only sound the gentle lapping of the Jellyfish's tentacles. Soldier John held the ball up in the air again for another look. There were a few indrawn breaths; the tension was mounting.

Soldier John started, 'I think—', but then he suddenly paused. Slowly he zoned in on a small patch on the underside of the ball. He gave it a scratch with his finger, peering in even further. The crowd held their breath. Then he pulled back again. 'I think it's fine,' he said.

'Yay!' cheered a few people, and there were sighs of relief from others.

'I know it's fine,' said James. 'I told you it was fine.' His face had an expression of infinite sadness, like somebody who has known the unfairness and discrimination of mankind, has fought for justice but has lost, losing both his faith in the world and in humanity. Which was unreasonable really, because last week James did try to cheat by covering the ball in a layer of slippery jellyfish slime when the other team were allowed to start instead of him. He's more than happy to sabotage his own team if it prevents the other side from winning.

During Jellyfish Rugby, those of us who are sensible stay round the edges of the pitch, where we'll make an effort sometimes to get the ball, but only if it's actually coming in our direction and then lands in our hands so that we can't really avoid it. Quite a lot of the people on the Jellyfish aren't sensible though, and they like to arrange themselves in a sort of crazed fighting mob in the middle. That's what happened this time.

The mob moved over to the left of the pitch, Staring Crone breaking away from the pack and weaving in and out of the defenders. She ran fast, the ball tucked carefully under her arm, and her tangled hair streaming out behind her. But then another defender tackled from the left, ramming into her legs. She fell to the ground, dropping the ball behind her, and lay there wobbling gently whilst the rest of the pack scrabbled around. The ball was slippery by now from all the jellyfish mucus, so it took a while for anybody to get a grip, but when they did, they were off again, the ball flying towards the other side of the pitch.

'Come on, man!' shouted Soldier John loudly.

'Yeah, we can do this!' came calls from a few of the others.

The pack moved off quickly, the ball being passed along the line at speed. James's defenders were much weaker than ours, and over on the other side of the pitch I saw Lana duck her head down and wince away as the ball started coming towards her.

They looked a fearsome mob, with lots of shouting and random grunting. It was very difficult to tell who was on which side, which is always a hazard, and I think might need to be investigated in the future as I'm fairly sure not everybody stays on the side they've started on.

We started a jellyfish wave, as usual. 'Whoop!' came the

27

shout from my left, and round the whole of the Jellyfish, a wave was passed along the defenders. Each in turn, we waved our arms and bodies in the air. If the match is dull, sometimes the movements can get complicated so that it turns into more of a dance routine. Sometimes that's part of the team tactics too, because some of the defenders (naming no names, Lana), can get more caught up with what moves they're supposed to be making than what's going on in the game.

I don't know what happened this time, actually. Somehow, it was Old Albert who ended up with the ball – unlikely as that might seem. He's never great at kicking, so I had high hopes we'd still win. But this time he twisted his whole body and gave a belter of a kick, sending the ball right past the plastic bottle goal markers. The ball went flying right over all of our heads and landed at least ten feet out into the sea.

'Oh, well.' Old Albert shrugged. 'It's a shame, but we'll just have to make another ball.' He made to head off to the Big House.

'Hang on,' said James. 'Where are you going? You've almost scored.'

'Yes, but my kicking was too good,' said Old Albert, as though this, too, was inevitable. 'I can't get the ball back now.'

There were groans and boos from the crowd. Most people started making their way to the edge to have a look at the ball. There was a good chance it might float back again. Sometimes it did.

'To score, you've got to get the ball back from the Jellyfish,' said James. 'You know the rules.'

'Well, I won't be scoring, then,' said Old Albert with another shrug. A few people were starting to argue with him now. The arguments are the main point of Jellyfish Rugby, sometimes enabling people to bear a grudge for weeks afterwards.

And then James looked up at me. He raised his eyebrows significantly, and I suddenly realized he had a plan. It was the perfect opportunity for another escape experiment: now was our chance to see whether it was possible to distract the Jellyfish so it would let people through. And the bonus was it would be Old Albert who would be involved in the tricky part of the experiment and not one of us.

'Lana! Kate!' I shouted, knowing that nobody would notice amongst the noise. I pointed to a spot on the edge, at some distance from the crowd. 'Quick. Let's go. When Albert jumps in, we need to make a distraction over there. Like when Pitiful Pete jumped in. We need to make loads of noise to see if it distracts the Jellyfish again.'

'What?' Kate looked round, flustered. 'What can we do? Quick.'

The noise from the arguments was still loud, but it sounded like they were starting to settle.

'You should jump in,' said Lana. 'And shout. That'd properly distract the Jellyfish.'

'Oh. Do I have to?' said Kate. 'I'd rather not, if that's OK.'

'Fine,' said Lana, squinting and not looking at her. 'We'll just sing loudly.'

The crowd was quietening now, and Old Albert was starting to take off his clothes. I could make out the complaining tone of his voice from here, but not the words he was saying.

'Lean right over the edge,' I said. 'Let's just scream.'

I could see James looking over at us to check we were in position. I gave him the thumbs-up, and he turned to Old Albert.

'Go!' I shouted, starting to scream. With Lana and Kate screaming too, we were making a fearsome noise. A few of the rugby players looked round in irritation, putting their hands on their ears, or gesturing to us to be quiet. We were leaning so far over, I couldn't see what was happening with Old Albert, but I saw what Lana was going to do before it happened. She reached over and, with a sudden lurch, pushed Kate in. She began to scream even louder, as Kate surfaced, spluttering.

'Kill me later,' shouted Lana, with a couple of bonus screams. 'Just don't stop screaming.'

Kate started screaming again, as she trod water. 'You're so mean!' she shouted. 'Agggggghhhhhh! I'm really cold!'

The tentacles were already gathering round her body, stroking her torso and pulsating as they oozed mucus trails across her hair. Kate grimaced as one slid over her face, pulling at her cheeks, and her screams became muffled – though perhaps more genuine – as the feelers slimed across her mouth. With a sudden slither, she was pushed back on to the surface of the Jellyfish, right at Lana's feet. The squeaking slurps of the suckers as they released her were audible even above our screams. I stood up. It had been no more than thirty seconds, but that was longer than anybody had ever managed to last in the sea. On the far side of the Jellyfish, the crowd were silent, watching the water. As we stared, a long tentacle rose, carrying both a naked Old Albert and the ball. Stretching over the heads of the crowd, it twisted, before smashing him down on to the wobbling surface. He lay there while the ripples of jelly flesh spread out across the mesoglea beneath our feet. But it was James I was looking at. Beyond Old Albert, on the edge of the Jellyfish, James stood with his arms raised in triumph.

'It worked,' he called across to us. 'Your shouting actually worked! Albert was out there for longer than normal. He could have got through.'

Still lying on the surface, Old Albert gave a little splutter, spitting up some seawater.

'And also,' added James, 'we won the rugby!'

5

'What would you do if you could get off the Jellyfish?' said Kate.

'It's not a jellyfish!' shouted Dr Jones.

'Yes, yes,' I said, but not very loudly because I didn't want to stop her being happy. Following the mermaid lecture Dr Jones was in particularly good form, as loads of people had been asking her advice about fish and sea creatures. She'd been able to spend a lovely few days starting sentences with phrases like, 'Actually, invertebrates . . .' and 'You see, gelatinous zooplankton . . . . .' All over the Jellyfish people were eagerly talking about the disadvantages of a hydrostatic skeleton, and were speculating on the possibility of finding weak spots in the mesoglea. But it was nothing that we hadn't already thought about before. A lot.

'Would you even want to get off it?' asked Kate.

'I think so,' I said.

'I think I would too,' said Kate.

'What would you do if you got off?'

'I don't know,' she said. 'It would be weird. I think I'd want to check that everybody else had got off OK too.'

'Oh. Yeah,' I said.

'Then I think I might want to find some food that isn't fish or seaweed. And maybe some new clothes?'

'Mmmm. Yeah. Can you remember what things that aren't fish taste like, though?'

'I dream about them sometimes. Lovely dreams, where I'm eating potatoes and butter and bread with jam. I don't fancy eating an animal any more, though. I feel like that was always weird.'

We both looked up at the sheep on the cliffs above the town. Kate screwed up her face. There were at least forty of them today, with their heads bowed towards the grass, but they came and went so that sometimes there were more and sometimes none. Once or twice we'd seen cows up there too, also peacefully eating and apparently unbothered by the danger of kriks.

The part of the town which was visible to us was squeezed into a gap between those cliffs, a place where the land sloped gently towards the sea. When the tide was out the rusted metal of factory roofs were exposed below the cliffs. Their tall chimneys had stood above the water at first, always over-loaded with jostling seagulls perched on their caps, but they had mostly all fallen over now, bashed away by the stormy waves of winter. Around that area sometimes the sea was still a funny colour – from the leaking chemicals, Dr Jones had told us. When that happened, the Jellyfish moved away.

Below the cliffs nearest to us were the ruined houses, their walls and chimneys covered in seaweed and only visible at low tide, but still interesting. Still empty places I liked to think about, imagining what it had been like to live in them, back when the sea had been lower and the town had been full of people. It was a strange thought, one that always seemed fake, no matter how much time I spent trying to picture it. And there were boats inside the houses now anyway. Boats which had been emptied of their passengers and which had floated aimlessly on the sea before ending up here, parked on top of somebody's old kitchen. I liked thinking about the boats too: what might be inside them, where they'd come from, where they might go, and what we could do with them if they should ever happen to drift over here. I had my favourites – we all did. I liked the sailing boats the best, because they could still move even if they were out of fuel. There were a few of these, including some which looked like they might still have proper sails.

In the middle, between the houses, the cliffs, the factories and the sheep, was a dark, tarmacked road. We called it Long Street because, you know, it was long and also a street, and we were all great with names like that. It went straight past the houses, past the factories, up the hill, between the cliffs and then away. That was the best thing about it: it led away.

Today, there was nothing moving in the town apart from the sheep and gently bobbing boats. All was quiet. Kate gave

34

a loud sigh. 'Which is your favourite house, Martha?' she asked. 'Mine is that white one.' She pointed to a house just below the cliffs. 'Can't you just imagine how lovely it would be to live in it? You could grow flowers in the front garden and you could hang your washing out on the line and sit on the sofa in the evenings.'

'Yes. And also you could shut the doors and windows if it was cold or started to rain.' I felt these were more important points, and definitely something I'd be interested in when looking for somewhere to live.

'Have you two losers finished your maths yet?' asked Lana. 'Because you're really distracting me if you haven't.'

'Yes,' I said, but quietly again so that Dr Jones didn't hear me and set me some more.

'What's that last number?'

'It's an 8, I think,' I said. But it wasn't very easy to see. One of the problems with using fish blood for ink, and plastic bags for paper, is that the ink fades quickly when it dries. That means in really stormy weather we don't have to do anything that involves reading or writing, because fish blood also gets washed away pretty easily.

'I'm going to say it's a 10,' said Lana. 'That makes the sum much easier.'

'I'm with you,' said James. 'It's definitely a 10, or it will be if at least two of us argue that it is. And I think I'd like crisps when we get off the Jellyfish. Cheese and onion! They were great.'

'I don't think things that come in packets are OK to eat any more,' said Kate. 'I think it's only things you can grow.'

'Crisps will be a priority for my new civilisation.' James sat back, arms folded across his stomach. 'When I'm king of the new world, I will find all the crisp factories and I will open them again.'

'James,' I whispered. 'Sit back and pretend to work. You'll never be king if you're that stupid.'

'What?' he said.

'Ah, James,' called Dr Jones. 'You've finished. Lovely. Let me just check your answers so that we can move on to your extension work. After that, we've got English.'

'What scintillating tasks have you got for us this morning, Dr Jones?' said James.

'Well that's a lovely adventurous adjective you've just used there.'

'Wasn't it?' James gave a smug smile at the rest of us, sitting back again with his arms folded. Lana rolled her eyes and picked up her fishbone quill again, writing deliberately. Both me and Kate also bowed our heads as though deep in thought. I kept my pen poised over the plastic in case Dr Jones looked at me.

'Oh dear, James,' said Dr Jones. 'You got a few wrong here. I'll go over them with you again.'

'I don't think I have,' said James. 'Some of your sums were difficult to see, so I might have made some mistakes because of that. This number is a 10, isn't it?'

'Ah, no,' said Dr Jones. 'It's an 8.'

'It's definitely an 8, James,' added Lana. 'I can give you some help with them, if you want?' She smiled at him generously.

When Dr Jones took James away for help with his maths, the rest of us returned to our work, making sure we really were finished. I like maths and English. One of the good things about life since the world ended, the people on the Jellyfish like to tell us, is at least educational standards have improved. I think this is probably a pretty extreme case of looking on the bright side, but it's true that class sizes are small. Then again, that is because most of the students who were our age have been eaten. So, yeah . . .

Actually, we do normally work really hard in lessons. We have good incentives, to be honest. The main one is that we're so bored it feels good to learn things. The other reason is because it gets us out of gutting fish or following Soldier John's rigorous training regime. And anything's better than that.

Behind us, I could hear Soldier John shouting. There was a large group of people who were doing what he wanted, which seemed to involve jogging back and forth across the centre of the Jellyfish, so that every couple of minutes the creature swayed slightly while it adjusted to the weight of everybody shifting around. But as usual, there were also a few people sitting around on the edges, either staring at the world, or fishing and chatting. It was business as normal on board.

'What's that on the shore?' asked Kate, pointing to a spot near the white house and the church. It took me a few minutes to work out what she was showing us. There's always movement on the coast: waving trees, curtains ballooning out of windows, packs of sidling dogs. But we were always hoping for other humans. Signs of survivors. Especially now, when it'd been so long.

'How many are there?' asked Lana.

There were shouts from Soldier John's crew now. Others had spotted them too.

'There's about ten,' said Kate. 'I think.'

I shuffled round to get a better look. It was hard to tell.

'People,' said Lana. 'They've got to be people.'

'It would be really nice if they were,' said Kate.

We sat, watching, and squinting through the patches of spray breaking between us and the coast. I didn't want to miss seeing any moment of the people, and we all scanned the town eagerly.

'There!' pointed Kate. 'That top window, in that grey house near the church.'

'They're probably human, then,' I said. 'If they've gone inside a house, then they must be.'

'That's a load of crap, for a start,' said Lana. 'How do you know kriks don't go inside?'

I didn't bother answering, but I felt she was being a bit unfair. It's good to have a theory, even if you can't prove it and don't have any evidence for it. That's called a hypothesis, and

38

scientists like to go on to research things to find out if their hypothesis is true or not. Plus, it would be very nice if kriks couldn't climb stairs, because going into houses and running upstairs was how I'd always planned to hide from them, if I ever got to land.

'There!' shouted Kate again. 'They're out.'

Emerging from behind the church, the ten figures appeared on the road, one by one. For a minute we sat, peering at them and hoping, but it was soon obvious they weren't human. They walked sideways, for a start. And it wasn't really a walk – more of a scuttle, their curved limbs bent under their shelled bodies and sliding past each other with jerky, artificial bursts of speed.

Kriks.

When they scrambled over rocks or the cliff face, they moved more like large crabs, but on the flat tarmac of the road they were ungainly, their limbs weirdly elongated so they bobbed up and down with exaggerated rhythms as they moved. Most of them still only had four limbs, but a couple – the larger ones – had four extra stumps growing out of their shells. It was their claws that always drew your attention the most: bigger and more powerful than the legs, they were mostly kept low and extended in front of the bodies, but sometimes they were raised, snapping and threatening. Seeing them was one of the few times I felt glad to be on the Jellyfish, and away from the land.

'Ugh, vile,' said Lana. 'I hate those ones with the really

wide shells. Yuck.' She picked up her pen again. 'Go on and show me what you got for number 15.'

I passed my bit of plastic over to her for her to copy.

'How are you girls getting on?' asked Dr Jones.

'Fine thanks,' I said. 'Just checking our answers against each other's now.'

Dr Jones looked over at Lana's work suspiciously.

'How old do you think those ones are?' I asked.

'The kriks? Oh, I'd say they're about two years old.' Dr Jones squinted over at them. 'Those ones with the extra limbs are possibly older.'

James came and sat back down next to us.

'Right,' said Dr Jones. 'Are we all ready for English? For today's lesson, I'd like to look at writing letters. Who can remind me of the format?' She turned back to the board, picking up her pen ready to write.

James looked at us all and sniggered. 'Dr Jones, we've just seen some flippin' kriks raiding the town. There's nobody left alive to write a letter to. And even if there is somebody out there, I don't think they'd really care if we sign it "sincerely" or "faithfully".'

Dr Jones stared at him. 'But what if they do care, James? Are you willing to take the chance? Because I can't begin to tell you how stupid you will look if you sign off a letter incorrectly.'

6

There was always something disturbing about seeing kriks on the land. I didn't like being reminded that everything might not be good out there, that life on land might not be like my pleasant daydreams, or that if we did manage to escape then things might not be much easier off the Jellyfish. I also hated seeing kriks on *our* bit of land, by those houses that felt like ours, and scuttling on that road I could so easily imagine myself walking on. I just knew their feet would make an annoying scratchy, tapping noise on that tarmac – could almost hear it, if I turned my ear towards the shore. They were so skin-crawly, the way they moved with those unpredictable, erratic, sudden movements and random direction changes so you couldn't tell where they were going to go next.

I was already feeling krik-y and tense when we were called in for that evening's lecture, but as soon as I saw Soldier John standing at the front of the Big House I knew things were about to get worse.

41

'Killing.' Soldier John gave a long pause, staring at us each in turn. 'That's what tonight's demonstration is about. Killing.' He gave an even longer pause. The people on the front row started to shuffle awkwardly.

'Well, that sounds jolly interesting, John,' interrupted Dr Jones with a bright smile. 'Is it a lecture on the history of killing?'

'A demonstration.'

A few people in the front row took the opportunity to move away.

'Right. But we normally do lectures, don't we?' said Dr Jones.

'A demonstration would be more use. Military tactics. I need volunteers. You'll do.'

'Lovely,' said Dr Jones. 'You're not going to kill me, I hope?' She gave a hearty chuckle.

'Stand here,' said Soldier John without smiling, directing her towards the centre of the lecture area. 'Tonight, ladies and gentlemen, we're gonna be learnin' about survival. We're gonna be learnin' about killing kriks.'

There was a relieved cheer and a quick burst of applause from the audience. We do love drama, and I looked forward to the chats afterwards about whether Soldier John would be prepared to kill somebody during a lecture. My view would be . . . possibly.

'I want you to imagine Dr Jones 'ere is a krik.' Soldier John waved his arm up and down the full length of her body and

Dr Jones smiled, doing jazz hands.

'This is a great idea, John,' said Dr Jones. 'Because funnily enough, we saw some kriks today.'

'I know,' said Soldier John. 'That's why we're thinking about how to kill 'em.' He picked up a sharp shard of hard plastic. 'Now, how to kill the fuggers. Your basic krik gets 'arder to kill the older it is, you see. When it's first born, its shell is softer and it's smaller, so it's just the same as killing a 'uman. You just stab 'em in their vulnerable areas. Any questions?'

We looked at each other.

James stuck up his hand. 'Erm . . . imagine that we've never killed a human before. How would you recommend best killing one?'

Soldier John looked at him as though he was a complete idiot. 'You just stab them through the 'ead, or the 'eart. You can also slit their throat, or strangle them to cut off their air supply. I'll do another lecture on killing 'umans one evening. A useful skill.'

'Thanks,' said James. 'Yes. Useful.'

'The impo'tant thing with a krik, though, is you've got a shell to get through before you can get to the vulnerable areas. So.' Soldier John gave a flourish with the large shard of plastic. Standing behind Dr Jones, he pointed it at her head. 'The best way to kill a young krik is by stabbing or cutting 'ere.' He held the shard against the top of Dr Jones's head. She gave a cheery smile. 'You'll need a lot of force, but it's still easy. If you can't kill 'em,' he glanced sideways at James, 'then at least try to wound them. Slice off one of the legs, so that they can't chase after you.

'Kriks that are older,' he continued, 'are a different matter. Very different.' He shook his head and curled his lip, giving another long, dramatic pause for effect. 'Older kriks are faster than 'umans, stronger than 'umans, and can only be killed with a knife if you've broken through their exoskeleton first. You don't stand a chance of gettin' through it without smashin' it first. I recommend metal bars, or wooden planks.'

He held up a wooden plank. I hoped it wasn't one taken from the Big House, because I found it difficult to sleep when it's really draughty. 'You want to bash your plank 'ere.' Soldier John tapped it against Dr Jones's head. 'Or 'ere.' He tapped her lower back. 'This is where there are gaps in the shell for the food to go in, and for the shit to come out. Use those gaps to lever in your weapons. Or if you can't get either of those areas, just make sure you give a good bash somewhere so that you knock the enemy over. Their shell is softer underneath. The easiest way to kill 'em, if there is more than one, is by planning. Plan to kill 'em, think about killing 'em, and practise killing 'em. There's still petrol in most of those useless cars out there.' He gestured vaguely towards land, but it was dark and we were in the Big House anyway, so we couldn't see where he was pointing. 'Get the petrol out and spray it on the fuggers, then set them alight with a match. They burn

44

well. Really well.'

James put his hand up again. 'How do we spray the petrol on them?'

''Owever you want,' said Soldier John. 'So long as you do it quickly. Any more questions?'

Kate put up her hand.

'Yes?' said Soldier John.

'Do we have to kill them? Can't we just put them all in a zoo or something?'

'No. You need to kill the fuggers, and you have to kill them hard. Next question.'

'Oh,' said Kate. 'OK.' She gave a sniff and started chewing on her thumbnail.

'Ah, John, if I can just interrupt here,' said Dr Jones, stepping forward. 'Kate, love, it's really dangerous out there. Maybe, in the future, we might be able to just treat them as tricky wild animals, like lions or something. But there are too many of them. They have killed most of the people in the world – or at least we think they have. We just don't have the facilities or knowledge to keep them as . . . pets. Think back to when we studied the food chain. In the past, we used to be at the top of that – but now, well, we're not. Kriks are on a higher trophic level than us. We have to kill them, or they will eat us.'

There was a pause while the others in the room thought about it.

'I wouldn't mind eating one of them. I'm happy to help

45

humanity,' said James. 'And if I did, wouldn't it mean that humans would be on a higher trophic level than kriks again? Ooo, and do you think they'd taste a bit like crabs?'

'Errmmm . . .' said Dr Jones.

'Dr Jones?' I stuck up my hand. 'Dr Jones, *are* they basically just giant crabs?'

'They're certainly crustaceans,' said Dr Jones.

'Their 'ands are like claws,' said Soldier John. 'They can't 'old weapons. But they don't need to, because their 'ands *are* weapons.'

'They also like to kill their food,' said Dr Jones, 'whereas crabs are scavengers, generally feeding on food which is already dead.'

'Do they mainly attack humans?' asked somebody in the audience.

'Dunno,' said Soldier John. 'I've never stayed around long enough to find out.'

'They are a significant threat to humans,' said Dr Jones. 'If you've got a convenient cow or pig around then, yes, try throwing it in their way, but to be extra safe, I'd also run.'

Soldier John gave her an incredulous look. There were a lot of hands up in the audience now. Soldier John pointed to one. 'Yes, you.'

'How do they breathe? I don't understand how they can live both underwater and on the land?

'Well, the "giant crab" theory has some merit here,' said Dr Jones, 'because crabs have always been able to cope on both land and sea – just like kriks. Marine crabs have gills at the top of their legs which enable them to breathe on land, or in the water. The gills needed to be kept moist, I seem to remember, but some crabs were able to do this with, erm, their own bodily fluids, and so could survive for long periods out of the water.'

'Does it have to be seawater?'

'If they're like marine crabs, then yes. They probably can't get very far inland. But it's worth bearing in mind that there used to be freshwater crabs too. I don't think we know too much about how kriks survive. It could be either of those options – or neither of them.'

'How long do they live for?'

Soldier John shrugged, grasping his shard with the air of a man who knew they wouldn't live long around *him*.

'There are a lot of factors there,' said Dr Jones. 'Obviously their food supply is rather a big issue – and their food supply may well have . . . erm . . . decreased recently, leaving them with less to eat.'

The Jellyfish gave a shudder beneath us – a sudden vibration as it shifted in the sea. Outside the Big House there were a few answering splashes as the larger tentacles swished around, spraying water against our walls.

'Do they prefer to eat adults or children?' said Lana.

'I think they probably prefer whichever option is larger . . .'

'So what happened to all the other children?' asked Lana. 'And the old people?'

James put his head in his hands.

'Well, they got eaten, didn't they? They were the weakest who couldn't run fast enough,' said Soldier John. 'Only the strong survive – or are worth saving.'

7

*J*elly. I remember jelly, from before.

I remember the bright colours, the tangy sweet touch melting on your tongue, the spoon sliding, cutting through. I remember that little polite, quivering wobble. And you could see through it, almost. See the spoon beneath as you held it in mid-air, balancing it carefully on the way to your mouth.

Or maybe I just remember what other people have said about it. Maybe my memories aren't real. Because some days I'm not even sure if *I'm* real (feeling pathetic alert!). Some days it would be lovely if I wasn't.

Our jelly is different. When you're up close, touching it all the time, you can feel variations. Little changes in the texture as you walk across it. Sometimes the change is so subtle you don't notice, until you do notice. Suddenly your feet are sinking into wet, slimy flesh when seconds before you'd been walking on hard, smooth floor.

In the middle, where the Big House is, and where we have

our driftwood fires, the flesh is hard so that if you bang on it you can make a noise like a drum. You always know it's not secure, though. You can always feel that beneath the armoured coating there is something muscular, ready and moving. It's like a vibration, maybe a low humming sensation. There are small pits here too, indentations which pool with fresh water that you can drink. I guess the water tastes of the Jellyfish – bland, but somehow also bitter – but I can't remember how fresh water is supposed to taste so it doesn't bother me. The pools move around as the Jellyfish shifts around, but they're always there somewhere, even when it's stormy.

At the edges of the Jellyfish the flesh gets softer, more rubbery and stretchy. Sometimes your feet seep into it like you're being absorbed. It's not slippery though; the mucus sticks to you, holding you to the surface. When you stand up, or pull your feet away, a slimy trail of translucent goo falls off you too, pulling back into the creature's skin. Interesting fact: you can eat that goo. It doesn't taste very nice, but sometimes we eat it when the fish supplies run low. I hate the feeling of that sliding, wobbling mass in my mouth, though. And it tastes the same if you vomit it back up again.

There are darker shapes inside it. The jelly flesh, under the epidermis, is called its mesoglea, and within that quivering white mass, you can see things: strange, hazy shapes. Sometimes shapes appear where there was nothing before. And sometimes the shapes disappear, so we think it might be the Jellyfish eating and digesting. We've tried cutting into the mesoglea with hard pieces of wood and even clawing with our fingernails to get at the shapes, in case they're a vital organ and mean that we can kill the Jellyfish. But now I can see those same pieces of wood beneath my feet. When we gave up they become shapes absorbed into the Jellyfish too.

We don't know what the bigger, changing shapes are. We say they're fish, because we think the Jellyfish eats fish. But sometimes the dark blobs look like they have arms and legs and heads and hair and clothes and shoes. I might be wrong. I like to think I am. But I've seen others looking in closely too, and wondering, watching as the shapes get smaller and thinner, until they disappear.

When you lie on the Jellyfish at night, inside that cramped shack, you sometimes feel like you're becoming part of it. Your breathing matches its gentle rise and fall on the waves; the vibrations go through you too so that your body quivers and starts to feel like it's made of jelly; you wonder then what others can see beneath *your* surface.

It's not like the jelly that was on your spoon. Not like the jelly from Before.

It had felt like something was going to happen, like there was going to be a change. Not that we were going to escape or anything – I wasn't an idiot, I'd never have let myself hope for that. But that there was going to be something different in our days. It had felt like Pete's almost-escape and Staring Crone's revelations and Old Albert's rugby match swim *must* be leading to change.

But now . . . nothing. We were still stuck, we could still see land so close by, and there was still *nothing* to do. Today that was almost unbearable. I felt like I was going to explode with something: energy or boredom or irritation or laziness.

'Why are we here?'

I meant that question in a lot of ways. Because it was one of those days when you felt like you needed another night's sleep, as though you could have slept right through the day and back into the night again. I would have liked to do that, but it's too cold when the others get up. I'd end up just lying on the floor of the Big House, hunched and shivering, and feeling even more sorry for myself.

'Why are we here? Ha!' Lana gave a bitter laugh.

'We're fine here,' said Kate. 'I think we're probably fine.'

'Yes,' I said. 'But why are we on here? Why hasn't it eaten us? Why won't it let us go?'

'We're its pets,' said James. 'That's why it feeds us with fish every day. Or most days, at least.'

'We're like parasites, aren't we?' I said.

'Nope,' said James. 'The Jellyfish is the parasite living under me.'

'Like the fleas on top of a dog,' said Lana, ignoring him. She dug into the surface with her fishbone pen and we watched as she carved a large 'L' for Lana. By the time she got to the bottom of the letter, the jelly was already starting to seal itself closed again at the top.

'But why do you think it feeds us?' I said. 'Do you really think a jellyfish would want to keep pets?'

'People used to keep fish as pets Before,' said Kate.

'Losers did,' said Lana. 'Why would you want to keep fish in your house? That's weird.'

'No, I suppose I don't think a jellyfish would want to keep pets,' said James. 'I think it might want to farm us though, like people used to do with sheep and cows. And didn't people also used to have fish farms in the old days too?'

'Really? Is that what you think it's doing?' I asked.

'Yes,' said James. 'I honestly think that's the only reason we're here.'

'But nobody's had a baby,' I said. 'Aren't farms about producing more animals?'

'Well, we can change that . . .' James gave me a big wink and nodded his head towards the Big House.

'No, James,' I said. 'Seriously. No.'

'Oh, come on, Martha. I'm so BORED!' he wailed.

'If it's farming us,' said Lana, 'how come nobody's been eaten, then? And who's it farming for? Is it for another creature? Or for itself? None of that makes sense.'

We all sat staring out at the coast. The same group of kriks had been patrolling back and forth for days now, scuttling in and out of the houses along the shore. There was a sort of sick *need* to watch them, to check up on where they were. You didn't want to look, but somehow your eyes always ended up on them, even if just looking at them made the shivers run down your spine. It was like picking at a scab that you knew wasn't ready: even though you knew it would just bleed again, you couldn't stop playing with it, and scratching around it, and worrying at it, until finally you gave in and ripped it off. And ignoring the kriks was just like that. Each time they went into another house, I imagined what it was they were doing, and what the house looked like inside. I pictured them scrabbling over the sofa, clawing up the stairs, searching for food in the kitchen, with that weird mechanical lurch of theirs. Were they finding any food? I couldn't see any human life out there, but if any humans were hiding from the kriks, they'd also surely be hidden from us. *Was* there anybody?

Above the houses, the cliffs rose, the birds circling over their nests and calling as they had for thousands of years. Beyond them, the sheep grazed peacefully in the overgrown scrub land which had once been fields. The road – that pathway away from the coast and into the unknown – was still clear of vegetation. It was still wet from the morning's rain, shining silver in the weak sun like a beacon. I knew it wasn't really a beacon, and that that was all just rubbish inside my head. But still . . . as the dark clouds overhead drifted slowly across the sky they cast shadows on the land below, shadows which never seemed to reach the road. As they crossed it they seemed instead to create deeper, more intense patches of brightness, like the road had a magic of its own.

'We just have to get off this thing,' I said. 'We've got to get over there.'

8

*D*eciding we needed to escape was easy; figuring out how to actually do it was another matter. Trust me, if we'd had any idea at all how to get to land we'd have been away, running through the green grass of those hills towards freedom. That didn't stop people having plans though. And there was zero chance of keeping those plans quiet on the Jellyfish. There was zero chance of keeping anything quiet. In fact, there was no quicker way to make sure everybody knew your secret, than to try and keep it a secret. Gossip spread really quickly, and we loved it. Not that there was anything particularly interesting to gossip about, mind you.

Things people might want to keep secret normally fell into three main categories:

1. You've found something really good, like a nice fish, or an interesting piece of rubbish that's drifted in from shore, and you want to hide it from everybody else so you don't have to share. This is a pointless secret. I understand why you

wouldn't want to share, but imagine, what are you going to do with your brilliant item? If it's food, you'll have to eat it at some point, which will mean revealing it, and if it's not food, what's the point of it being so brilliant if you can't flaunt its brilliance at others?

2. Gossip about somebody else. They're either annoying, or they fancy somebody. Something like that. This sort of secret would be fine if it stayed a secret, but it's when it doesn't that it's a problem. Then there's a great old riot and everybody wants to get involved with their view. And, oh yeah, we've all got loads of views.

3. You're embarrassed about something you've done, or a bodily function. Keeping this a secret is selfish, in my opinion, and in the opinion of everybody on here. This is a chance to laugh at you, which is the only thing that keeps us going here.

Going to the toilet could be a secret, and we have a shack for that. It's called the Small House, obviously, and it's right on the edge of the Jellyfish so that your business just goes over the side. But we can usually tell what somebody's been doing in there based on the time they spend crouched down. Our bowel movements are a hot topic of conversation in some groups, probably because for some people, going to the Small House is one of the best parts of the day.

So, yeah, what with all of our non-secrets, I knew something was up.

Our morning lessons were almost over and we were still

sitting towards the front of the Jellyfish, on that part near the Big House where you felt the least movement so it was easiest to write. It had been a pretty ordinary day. The birds were still circling over the cliffs as usual, the sheep were still in the scrublands as usual, the kriks were still patrolling in the coastal houses. But the other jellyfish people were not behaving as usual.

'Three, two, one, GO!' shouted Soldier John. There was a pounding of feet behind us, and the Jellyfish gave a sudden lurch to the left.

'Oh, for goodness' sake,' muttered Lana as we grabbed our plastic sacking and our fishbone pens. 'I wish they'd flippin' stand still. This wobbling's making me feel sick.'

The ripple of jelly came in little waves beneath the mesoglea as the Jellyfish adjusted to the shift in weight. Globules of flesh rose and fell under us so that for a few minutes Lana, Kate and James bobbed up and down where they were sitting. The tentacles nearest to us went wild, waggling and swooshing in the water so that clouds of spray covered our work. Then it all calmed down again, and we were able to get our pens back out. This morning we were writing a play which we were going to be allowed to perform later on in the week instead of a lecture, so we were all enjoying it. It was about a farmer who meets some aliens, and it had a complicated plot, but we still thought it would be very funny. Well, me, Kate and James did. Lana wanted it to end tragically, with most of the characters dying. I wasn't

absolutely sure the individual scenes that we'd taken respon-
sibility for were going to link together very well. Still, we were
all concentrating and creating something together, and we
were all having fun.

'Get ready!' shouted Soldier John from behind us again.

'Flip's sake,' muttered Lana.

We gripped our plastic as we continued to write. The feet
pounded behind us again, this time going in the other direction. There was a lot of noise too. Organised noise, which is
unusual, as Soldier John spends much of his time telling
people to 'shut the eff up'.

The Jellyfish lurched to the right. We grabbed our stuff
again. It was lucky we were on the sticky part of the creature
and its gloop held us in one place.

'What *is* it that they're all doing?' I asked.

'They'd better not be trying to tip the Jellyfish over,' said
Lana. 'Because that's seriously what it looks like, and I don't
want to get wet.'

'Or die,' said James.

'Hmmm,' she agreed.

'Uh oh!' said James, 'Somebody's fallen in. Oh . . . yes,
no . . . it's two people.'

'What!' Lana put down her pen, stabbing it into the Jellyfish to keep it in one place. She stood up gleefully to get a
better view.

'Yes, there's definitely two,' said James.

At the point where the Jellyfish had tilted from the

weight of all the people, there was now a big fluster of movement and fuss, and water was definitely being splashed around too.

'They've been down there a while, haven't they?' said Kate. 'I hope they're OK.'

'It's not that long yet,' said James.

On its high side, the Jellyfish started to seep back into the water, its hard surface bending back down again, and the mucus-y jelly beneath perceptibly moving almost as a liquid, reforming and adjusting. In a final lunge it righted itself, sending those jelly ripples across the surface of the mesoglea.

'Ugh,' said Lana. 'Here it comes.' Lana, Kate and James started bobbing up and down again as the waves reached us. 'This is just so stupid,' said Lana. 'Our life is ridiculous.' She said it with an air of dignity, like her natural home was a palace rather than a floating bit of crud. I had to bite my cheeks to stop from laughing, because in truth she did look really silly bobbing up and down.

Over to the right-hand side, Soldier John was now shouting commands, though it was difficult to tell what they were exactly, over all of the noise from everybody else. The crowd were waving and calling to whoever was in the water. But the first tentacle was already rising, and then, with a slap, and then another whack, two giant muscular limbs crashed down, thrusting the sodden people on to the surface near the Big House.

'I don't think you *can* tip it over, can you?' I pointed out.

'It's just oozing itself back into its normal position.'

Kate was kneeling down on to the surface, looking beneath at the jelly. There were a few of those mysterious dark shapes down there this morning. These ones were very hazy and deep – several metres in, at least.

'Hold on,' said James, nodding over to the crowd again. He grabbed his stuff in preparation.

'Ready!' Soldier John pointed at Pitiful Pete and Stinky. They nodded, crouching down to the jelly on the edge of the creature. 'Go!' The rest of the crowd set off towards the opposite side, Soldier John leading the way at a run.

'They've finally snapped, haven't they?' said Lana. 'This is it.'

'No,' said Kate, standing up. 'I think I know what they're doing.'

We watched, silently, as the Jellyfish started to tip over towards the left-hand side. As the crowd reached that side and the Jellyfish buckled under their weight, water started to lap over the edge. On the right-hand side the creature lifted, so that its tentacles were wildly swooshing in mid-air again. The two men were stranded, high up, and right on the edge. As we watched, Pitiful Pete raised his arms above his head and dived into the water. A split second later Stinky followed.

'Oh . . .' said Kate, glancing over the edge. For a minute I thought she was going to jump in too.

There were sudden bellows from Soldier John's crew. They were stomping on the mesoglea and shouting loudly. At their end there were also a couple of splashes, from other people who had jumped in, or possibly fallen. The Jellyfish was at a very strange angle.

'Hey,' I said, 'they're copying our idea of creating a distraction.' It was hard not to be cross that everybody else seemed to be in on another escape plan which they hadn't bothered to tell us about. I was happy to be treated like a child when it meant we got to write plays instead of gutting fish – but when it came to escape attempts, I felt like I had as much right to be included as anybody else. More, really, because I was younger and so would live longer than most of the adults on board. I'm not saying I felt like my life was more valuable than those of the adults – just that my survival was likely to be more useful for the human race than that of old people, because they were closer to death anyway.

'Can you see Pete?' asked James, standing on tiptoes. The Jellyfish started to correct itself, the mesoglea tilting down slowly, and the jelly rippling back underneath. Over on the right-hand side it was starting to rise again, its passengers lifting up, as spray from the churning tentacles misted over them.

We strained to see Pete, but it was another couple of long seconds before the Jellyfish was low enough again on his side. With a sudden, juddering lurch it fell and the jelly ripples started to wave out across the surface. There, about twenty metres away, two heads were visible in the open sea, powering through the water. Waves were breaking over them, and their legs were kicking wildly. Pete hadn't had time to take his clothes off, and I could see the yellow of his jumper clearly through the water as he swam with all his might.

Soldier John's distractions had worked. This was it: the furthest anybody had ever got.

Next to me, Kate gave a little sob.

They were no longer trying to remain invisible, speed was all, and they were splashing more than I'd seen anybody before. Pete was moving his arms so fast: first one, then the other. *Go, go go!*

'Those dickheads are going to make it!' said Lana. 'Oh my god! Hurry up!'

Somehow the rest of the Jellyfish people had arrived round us, and somehow I was now standing on the edge. I think some people were shouting, but it felt like more an energy, an excitement. It was going to happen! They were going to do it!

Kate's hand was in mine, Lana was grasping my shoulders. They were thirty metres away now, powering towards the cliffs, far, far away from the tentacles.

But then it came, that pink fork, rocketing through the water, with its slipstream of waves fizzing behind. It grabbed Pete, and then Stinky, ducking them under the water, before sucking them, and pulling them up into the air and back to us, with their backs arched and their arms flailing.

9

We were all cross after Pitiful Pete's latest failure. Most people had spent the afternoon sulking, but, you know, when everybody is in a bad mood together, it ends up being fun.

We'd all spent at least an hour complaining about how rubbish our lives were, and then the adults had spent several more hours enthusiastically whinging on about how glorious life used to be – before the monsters came out of the sea, that is. Lana had managed to start several arguments by reminding everybody that the sea levels rising was all the adults' fault anyway, and that if they'd taken better care of the world then the monsters would have stayed where they were and climate change wouldn't have happened in the first place. She'd had a great afternoon.

Me, Kate and James had spent that time more sensibly, by cutting a hole into the Jellyfish's surface and then stuffing it with spiky bits of rubbish. We'd had a wee in there too, in the hope that we'd poison the creature. Now we were all in the Big

House listening to the evening lecture by Old Albert. He was on classic form tonight, his eyes raised to the ceiling with an expression of extreme sorrow.

'They all died horribly, terribly and in agony. Their limbs were wrenched apart, eyeballs pulled out of their heads, faces shredded off, skin peeled away . . .'

There were sighs and a few tuts. Other people were openly chatting.

'We must be thinking on the ways they died, so we can think on our own horrible, brutal deaths. It'll be soon! You mark my words, you're all going to die soon.'

Lana rolled her eyes and gave a loud yawn. Kate tilted her head and nodded sympathetically. She also made direct eye contact with Albert, which is difficult as his eyes can be unpredictable. We've told her before never to do that, because just one person who is prepared to at least pretend they're listening is all Albert needs. Everyone else had zoned out.

'Do you want some water?' whispered James. He was holding a can of water in his hand, and had three more in front of him.

'No, you're all right,' I said.

'There'll be blood. Lots and lots of blood. The streets will run with rivers of your blood . . .'

'Sounds like Albert reckons we'll get off here at least, then,' said James. He raised his can and slurped the water loudly.

Lana yawned again. This time her mouth stretched so far

back that she exposed all her teeth. She had to shake her head afterwards, such was the power of her yawn.

'Your flesh will be ripped from your bones, your hair will be torn from your scalp and your clothes will be ripped off. You'll be naked, and bloody . . .'

'He looks pleased about that,' whispered James. It's true that Old Albert was getting quite enthusiastic about his Dire Warnings tonight. There were white flecks of spit at the corners of his mouth as he continued:

'Naked, and dragged down to the depths to be drowned slowly and eaten. Your bones picked clean, and the human race finished . . .'

Even Kate was starting to look bored. She still had her eyes pointed at Albert, but she was fiddling with a loose thread on her jeans, and I was fairly sure she was no longer listening.

'There will be no more humans, and the world will return to the fish and the animals, the way it was before Eve ruined things in the Garden of Eden. There's no time to repent your ways. You were born evil, like all humans, and now jellyfishies will kill you and return the world to nature.'

He paused and licked his lips. Quick as anything, Dr Jones leapt up. 'Thanks so much, Albert,' she said. 'Very thought-provoking . . . umm, insights.'

'We're all going to die,' Albert reminded us. 'We're going to die, killed by jellyfishies, those same ones what attacked the rest of the world. Like the one we're standing on.'

'Ah, um, Albert.' All around us there was a hush.

66

Conversations stopped, and heads twisted round. This was a controversial point, and might just make the evening interesting. You could see the internal conflict in Dr Jones. Her mouth was half open, her hand raised. You could almost see her mind ticking over as she swayed between thanking him for his lecture just to get rid of him, and starting a fight she was bound to lose. She puffed air into her cheeks, and then blew it out slowly.

'No, sorry, Albert, this almost certainly isn't a jellyfish.' She pursed her lips and you could see she was already regretting her decision. 'And, while we're on the subject, Albert, I'm not sure that your description of the . . . erm . . . attacks is quite accurate.'

'It was horrible ' Old Albert started again, this time with relish. It was unusual for him to have an interested audience. 'Jellyfishies rose up to the surface, millions of them, in the dead of night, attacking everything living on the sea. Crushing all the boats and ripping babies out of their mother's arms. There was crying and shrieking. Oh, the wails were terrible. And the oceans were red with blood.'

'The creatures to which you're referring, whilst they may be related to jellyfish, are nevertheless distinct organisms,' said Dr Jones patiently. 'They appear to be solitary animals, unlike jellyfish. There certainly weren't millions of them.'

'Everybody drowned, all the sinners. Only the pure were left, but not for much longer, because you're all going to die . . .' Albert raised his arms to the ceiling and then waved them round the room to make sure we knew that it was us he was talking about. He didn't need to do that, though, because his point was clear.

'OK.' Dr Jones was on a roll now. 'I was there, as was everybody else in this room. All of us were taken during one of those attacks, which is why we're here now. There was no blood at all, because as the creatures rose out of the sea, they just tipped us out of the boats and absorbed any humans who fell into the water. There was no ripping of flesh, no hair pulling, no eyeballs being sucked out and no limbs being pulled apart. There was also, Albert, and I feel like we've talked about this before, there was also NO nudity. Why you think a species of scyphozoa would have an interest in removing your clothes, I have no idea.'

'. . . naked as the day they were born, they returned to Hell, where the human race belongs. All the sinners . . .'

'Nope. No nudity. We've still got our clothes on now, Albert, haven't we?'

'. . . and they devoured the flesh of all the humans. They preferred the young ones, for their juicy, fresh meat . . .'

'And, again Albert, we've got no measurable evidence for any of these statements.' Most of the audience avoided eye contact at this point, but it was true, technically. We hadn't definitely seen it devouring anything. Just, you know, those slowly disappearing shapes beneath us.

'And it seems unlikely that they have a preference for age or, just in case it comes up, gender.'

'. . . they liked to rip apart the women, tearing at their breasts and pulling off their hair, a sign of women's vanity . . .'

Dr Jones gave a very loud sigh. 'Their breasts? Again, I'm unclear what evidence you're using to base your hypothesis on.'

James gave a snigger.

'Are you laughing because they said "breasts"?' I whispered.

'Absolutely!' he whispered back. He was leaning back now, gleefully watching the whole performance and openly grinning. 'Breasts!' he repeated.

On my other side, Lana had her eyes open wide, and was making an effort not to show any emotion at all, which was giving her face a weird, stretched expression. I knew this would be a conversation we'd be analysing a lot tomorrow.

'Look, Albert, what we know is very limited. The facts are few, because there simply wasn't time for detailed scientific analysis before the world . . . well . . . ah . . . went into chaos.'

'We don't need no scientific gobbledegook to tell us . . .'

Dr Jones started talking more loudly. 'Probably as a consequence of sea levels rising or climate change, creatures emerged from the deepest parts of the sea. They attacked ships in hefty numbers, though there were never "millions", Albert. Their route of travel was never predictable, but they were able to travel quickly and silently, absorbing all life within their path. Fish as well as humans. We don't think they could discriminate.'

'. . . crushing ferries, destroying the world . . .'

Lana had given up and was openly grinning now. We *never* talked about Before, or about what had happened, so it felt like this was an exciting, forbidden moment where Albert was breaking loads of rules. Dr Jones spoke even more loudly. 'They didn't destroy the world, Albert, as you can literally see on a daily basis. And they didn't even go on to land at all. The coastal erosion there is as a consequence of human failings and environmental disaster, not animals.'

'. . . and they brought their fishy friends with them to do their work, destroying and eating any of the disgusting humans left behind. Torturing them, twisting their minds, pushing their pincers into their brains . . .'

'If we're on to kriks now – and it's a little hard to tell from that description, Albert – then there is no evidence to suggest that the two are connected.'

'What?'

'Eh?'

There was general incredulity in the audience. Quite a few people were starting to interrupt now.

'Yes, yes!' Dr Jones raised her hands for quiet. 'I know that they appeared at the same time, and both probably emerged as a consequence of sea levels rising – but that doesn't mean they're connected.'

Old Albert gave a phlegmy cough. He hacked and hacked, so that you could really hear the rising bubbling mucus at the back of his throat. It was a masterful debating technique, because most of the audience were so revolted they had to grimace and flinch instead of shouting. 'Look here, Missy,' he said, waggling his finger at Dr Jones. 'We don't need your scientific whatnot here. When two different monsters come out from the depths of Hell, we know they're together and we know what it means . . .'

Dr Jones nodded, her lips pursed, and walked off, defeated.

'It means we're all damned, that's what it means. Mark my words, and think about your coming death. Do you want to be eaten by a killer jellyfish, or do you want to have your flesh gnawed by a giant crab?'

10

The sun was starting to break through, and there were beams of light shining in several spots on the sea; more beams were appearing every few minutes or so, like they were slowing ripping the clouds apart. Most of the sky was dull, though: grey, boring, slow-moving. The morning was still bitter, and there were white trails of frost in the shadows of the cliffs. We were hunching at the front of the Jellyfish, sitting on our hands until we absolutely needed to write. For me, that wasn't going to be soon, because after Old Albert's talk last night, I was finding it difficult to think about lessons. There was also a wailing noise coming from just beyond the Big House, and one of those quiet men, the muscular rugby types, had his head back and his arms outstretched. He was wailing enthusiastically, and with great emotion, whilst waving his right arm across his left arm every so often. From this distance it was a bit tuneless – though that's not to say it wouldn't have been a bit tuneless if you were close by too. I'm just mentioning the distance to point out our good fortune in being far away.

'I think Stinky is pretending to be a violin again,' said James. 'Do you remember the last time?' He started to laugh. 'God, it went on for ages . . .' His laugh was hysterical now. Dr Jones was striding off towards Stinky, so it was possible we wouldn't need to beg him to stop ourselves, but it also gave us a few minutes to chat without being asked if we needed any extra maths.

'What do you think?' I said, '*Are* the kriks and the jellyfish working together?'

Everybody sat up immediately. I knew they'd all been wondering the same, after last night.

'Really doesn't look like it. I know what Dr Jones said,' said James, 'but apart from the fact that they both come from the sea, they've got about as much in common as us and birds. Or cows, or sheep. Like, they're a whole different species.'

'But they appeared at the same time, didn't they?' I said.

'Don't know,' said James. 'Sort of the same time, I suppose.'

'I think,' said Kate, 'I think that's because Dr Jones said that there was climate change and sea levels rising. I think that would disturb a lot of things. You know, if where you'd been living for millions of years suddenly changed, you might want to change too. And you might want to move somewhere else too.'

'Yep,' said Lana. 'I really know the feeling.'

'No,' said Kate, 'I mean I understand why the jellyfish and

73

the kriks are here. If things have changed for them where they used to live because of humans, then they have the right to be angry, and they have the right to come and try to attack us. They also have the right to try and survive. And I suppose surviving, for them, means eating us.'

'Do you think that's what the Jellyfish wants?' I asked.

'I don't know if it even knows what it wants. It's just been disturbed by us – by humans, I mean – in Before. It can't live where it used to live, because we destroyed wherever that place was, down deep somewhere, so now it's come up here to try and live instead.'

'Do you think the human race will die out?' I said. I didn't much fancy the idea, to be honest.

'It might . . . be a good thing for the world if we did,' said Kate. 'I don't think we've always taken good care of things.'

'WHAT? If I flippin' die out, I'm taking something else with me. Something big.' Lana raised her voice and narrowed her eyes. 'And something that's wobbly and something that's see-through and crap. Naming no names!' She stabbed her pen into the Jellyfish's surface at that point, and gave it a little slice for effect, her hand gripping so forcefully that her knuckles were white.

'I mean . . .' I began, but I didn't know what I meant, actually, so I carried on with something else. 'Do you think the Jellyfish actually is a jellyfish? Or do you think it's some sort of sea monster? Do you think Albert's right?'

James made a spluttering noise, which I think was a laugh.

'Well, Albert can't be right, for a start!' said Lana. 'Whatever he thinks, I'd go for the opposite.'

'Well, isn't it weird that this one never goes beneath the water surface, because that's where jellyfish normally go, isn't it?' I said.

'Are you asking us because you think we're jellyfish experts?' said James. 'Because I don't know anything about jellyfish. *I've* got a life, you know?' He looked off into the distance, and shook his hair back like it wasn't manky or salt-encrusted. We all smiled at the idea that any of us might have an individual, interesting life. 'But yeah, I think this probably isn't a jellyfish,' he said. 'It's probably one of those creatures that were on the news, Before. It might not be a normal one, though, because I think I remember them being even larger than this when you saw them on television. I remember one in America, I think, and they had a drone flying above it taking the pictures, and it was the size of an island. This one is only the size of . . . a rugby pitch.'

'That must be why it's chosen you, then,' said Lana. 'Because you're not normal either.'

'Well, I'm glad I'm not if you think *you* are,' said James.

Dr Jones was still over with Stinky and, rather worryingly, Staring Crone had joined him. She was stamping her feet loudly in a regular beat on the Jellyfish's surface.

Probably the most controversial activity we do on the Jellyfish is the choirs. I think the plan was . . . well, no, I don't remember there being a plan, actually. But anyway, we do have regular choir rehearsals. Old Albert has a group that does mainly sea shanties. I don't think anybody knew any sea shanties before they started the group, so they've had to invent their own. Some of them sound good, but after the fifteenth verse, you've usually had enough of even a good thing, to be honest. And those are the short ones. When the sea shanty crew look like they're gearing up for one of their really epic songs, there's usually a drift towards the opposite side of the Jellyfish. And right now, it looked suspiciously like Old Albert's crew was forming at the far end of the Jellyfish, whilst Stinky's group was gathering in the middle. It looked like we were in for a real session this morning.

'Shall we put our things away, do you think?' said Kate.

We had mostly finished by now, but it looked like Dr Jones was thinking about joining the classical choir by the Big House. Her hands were out, and her fingers bent like she was about to start playing the air piano. She nodded her head at Crone . . . and they were off! Stinky started moving his arm back and forth, though he was wailing more quietly now. Dr Jones was making 'plink plonk' noises, that I think she once said were chords. Staring Crone started stomping more rhythmically, and a couple of others joined in with air trumpets: 'Doo, doo, doooo!'

'Oh dear,' said Kate. She spoke for us all.

Lana folded up her work with a dramatic sigh, whilst James threw his over his shoulder into the sea. He likes to do that most days, I think because it means he doesn't have to tidy up.

'What shall we do now?' said Kate. 'Shall we have a sing?' She said it more politely than excitedly, because I think she wasn't that keen herself.

'Nah, you're all right,' said Lana. 'I'd rather eat a rotting pile of raw seaweed.'

'I'm sure that can be arranged,' said James. 'Eating contest? Who's in?'

'NO!'

'No.'

'Nope.'

'But think of the diarrhoea!'

'We are, James. That's why none of us want to do it.'

'It's funny, though.'

'Nope. No, it's not.'

'Well, let's play krik races, then,' said James. 'Everybody choose your favourite krik, and see which one makes it to the end of Long Street first.'

The kriks were scuttling back and forth again. At the moment, they were in front of the church, around the houses nearest the dark, mossy cliff. There weren't so many birds' nests on this cliff face, as it didn't catch the sun, but every so often you could see little scurryings or movements on the grassy outcrops of rock, and the adults had said these were rabbits or deer.

'I call the big orange one,' said Lana immediately. And it was a good call. It had well-developed pincers and extra

77

limbs that almost reached the floor. When it sometimes decided to run, for no obvious reason, it was able to move very quickly, and very unpredictably.

'The mottled one with the big stomach,' said James. This one was currently poking its claw into the corner of a garden wall, though it was impossible to see why.

'The dark brown one's mine,' I said. Mine was carefully chosen, not because it was particularly strong-looking, or fast, but because it was the one which was already the closest to Long Street, and therefore the most likely to get there first.

'Good choice,' said James. 'I see your strategy. Cunning. Kate?'

'I think . . .' said Kate, 'I think I'd like that one . . .' She pointed to the smallest one, which looked a little starved. It was obviously male, because one of its pincers was larger, but even from this distance, he just looked a little ill.

'Whatever,' said Lana. 'He doesn't need you to be kind to him, Kate, and your kindness is literally helping him in no way at all.'

'He's my krik,' said Kate loyally.

'Go!' said James. 'Come on, GO!' For a minute his krik paused, as though he'd heard, and then he removed his claw from the wall, and scuttled back towards the cliff.

'Bollocks, you stupid thing,' said James. 'Turn around, idiot.'

'Good boy,' muttered Kate. 'Good boy.' Her krik showed no sign of moving at all, and looked as though he'd stopped now to eat from a pile of dried seaweed by the water's edge.

And I don't know if it was because we were all watching so intently, or if it was just luck, but at that point we saw some humans run across, from one side of Long Street to the other.

11

'There!' said Lana, pointing. 'Look! Humans! They definitely are!'

But we'd all seen. There were five of them, each carrying spears or crossbows. They edged down Long Street slowly, their weapons raised and ready. The funny thing was how smoothly they moved, with no jagged lunges or sudden, bobbing turns. After all that time spent watching the kriks, it was the humans who now seemed to move strangely.

There were two females and three males, dressed all in black – like a sort of uniform. The hair of the women was brightly coloured: one was a bright red, and one a bright green. They had it tied up, but you could tell even from this distance that they'd done things like wash it in clean water. And brush it.

Next to me, Lana gave a sigh. I knew it would be about the hair.

'I know,' said James. 'We've got to warn them.'

For a second I'd forgotten, but then I realized. The kriks!

'Hey!' shouted James, jumping up and down and waving his arms. 'Hey!'

'Hey!' I joined in. 'Watch out!'

'Let's do it together,' said James. 'Watch out. On the count of three. One, two, three . . .'

'Watch out!' we all screamed. 'Watch out!'

The kriks seemed to pause momentarily in their scurrying and scrabbling. We were making a fair bit of noise, what with the choirs and the shouting, but the people didn't seem to hear. They continued steadily down the centre of the street, turning to face each doorway as they passed, and keeping their weapons aimed and ready.

'Look!' said Lana again. She was pointing to the top of the cliffs, where there was another woman in black. This one had bright blue hair, hanging loose over her shoulders and blowing lightly in the breeze, in the way that I think I remember hair moving when it wasn't in dirty clumps and coated with a thick layer of salt. She looked amazing in her tight clothes and weapons belt. I couldn't remember that it was possible for humans to look so sleek and beautiful; would it even have been possible for one of us to ever look like that? She also had a pair of binoculars, and was watching the town below.

Suddenly it didn't look like it was the people who were the ones in danger. And I think we all realized it at the same time.

There was a low vibration beneath our feet, and the Jellyfish shifted, so that we had to turn to continue watching. James had stopped shouting and waving. 'What the . . . ?' he said.

'I know,' I said.

Behind us, the singing had stopped, and others were gathering beside us to watch, Soldier John squeezing in right next to me. At some point, Lana had grabbed my hand, and she was squeezing it painfully. The tentacles in front of us gave a sudden ripple, flexing up into the air in turn, before dropping down again and sucking at the water.

The five people continued silently and smoothly down Long Street, only metres away now from the clueless kriks. My krik was still picking at something on the ground, and Lana's was still scrabbling in another wall.

As the team got to the intersection the woman with green hair held up her hand in a signal to stop. The others gathered in line beside her. Above them, on the cliff, the watcher rotated her arms in a repeating pattern: a signal to those on the ground. Two of the men immediately stepped forward, rounding the corner, and ran at the closest krik: mine. Their spears raised, they both hit him fast, one in the back, and one through the head slit. The tips of their spears went right through his shell and head, emerging in a spray of blood and gore which was visible even from where we were standing. At least I think it was. Lana said I was exaggerating as usual when we talked about it later. Anyway, it all happened very fast, and the krik crumpled into a crabby, shelly pile on the floor, shaking like a piece of wet seaweed as the men pulled their spears out.

The other kriks hadn't even noticed; they continued with their scrabbling-based activities. Lana's krik was happily staring at the cliff, bobbling up and down and snapping his mighty pincers.

'Look at the way they got through that exoskeleton,' said Soldier John. 'Beautiful.'

'Like a tentacle through water.'

'Pow!' said James.

The team on the ground were running on towards Kate's krik now. One of the men was walking backwards behind the others, to guard them in case of attack from the rear.

The two women ran on ahead, their spears raised and ready. The green-haired woman reached him first, and leapt, kicking him to the ground and holding his pincers out of the way with her spear. The second woman jumped on his head slit. Then again. Then she raised her spear and struck a third time. It would definitely be dead. I couldn't see the blood, but I imagine there would have been a lot of it, and it would have been mixed in with shattered exoskeleton.

'God,' said Lana. 'They're amazing.'

And they really were. They were so slick, so brilliant. So practised. It was like watching a dance – but a dance where only half the people have bothered to rehearse.

James's mottled krik ran towards them now, and then a fourth, their pincers raised and their powerful legs moving in attack. But the two men already had their crossbows loaded, and first one krik fell, then the other. I didn't even see the arrows, they were so quick.

'Yeah!' shouted James. 'Come on!'

'Beautiful,' muttered Soldier John again. 'What training. Fabulous!'

Only Lana's krik remained visible now, and he was still some distance away at the base of the cliffs. He turned his armoured body slowly, confident in his power. The orange exoskeleton was enormous, circling and looping in a twisted shell pattern, the pincers extending beyond the reach of a mere human, the claws muscular. His eyes were a hidden shadow, a darkness sunken inside the bright shell casing of a crustacean, the mouth a gaping slit in the exoskeleton. He moved with menace, a monster disturbed from his meal by something worthless. The five humans were barely deserving of his attention.

Above him on the cliff, the blue-haired woman signalled with her arms again. Immediately the team of fighters rearranged themselves: the two women got their crossbows out and crouched down low, whilst the men unhooked their spears. They waited, ready. For a few minutes there was nothing. No movement from the shore. Above, on the cliff face, the bushes waved gently in the light breeze, and beneath us the Jellyfish shifted, rearranging its tentacles as it sometimes did. But the humans did nothing. They remained, their weapons out, and ready.

It was like we were there with them, right behind them and not just watching. I could feel it, that pretend crossbow in my hands almost itching against my fingers. I wanted to be there so much. Just doing something. Anything. Beside me, Kate let out a sigh. But the others stayed tense; I think we all held our breath.

Then the krik turned his shell, casually, like he was just out for a normal scuttle along the shore. He moved a claw forward slightly. A couple of the fighters on the shore responded by shifting their weapons higher.

And then he lunged.

Faster than I'd ever seen one of them move before, the krik pounded straight towards the humans, closing the distance between them in seconds. The first of the arrows flew, bouncing off the krik's shell and falling, useless, behind. The krik's pincers were up, massive and fibrous, each one half the size of the humans' bodies, and his claws were a haze of speed, springing towards them. And yet they stayed in position. More arrows flew, and veered off, seemingly without a scratch. Then a spear. It hit the krik in the chest and, for a beautiful couple of seconds it stayed, juddering as he ran. But then it, too, fell beneath his feet.

He was closer now, ten metres away, a blur of menace. The humans held their line. He raised his claws further, ready for the attack. Next to me, Kate covered her eyes. More of the useless arrows flew, bouncing off and scattering to the ground.

But then, as one, the three men stood and pointed their spears directly at the shell on the monster's stomach. He couldn't stop, the force of his legs propelling him directly on to their spiked ends. The men were pushed backwards in that moment, by those terrible, muscular claws. But then they pushed forward together, righting the krik, so that he lowered his claws in readiness for attack again.

But it was enough. In that split second of confusion, in that one moment of attack, the woman with the red hair stood up, directly in front of the krik, taking careful aim with her crossbow. And she shot him straight in the shell slit.

He wobbled, teetering. And then he fell backwards, with a thud we could hear even from the Jellyfish.

12

For a moment we stood, staring in amazement, but then the Jellyfish gave another one of its little judders, as though to remind us where we were, and a giant cheer broke out from everybody on board.

It was honestly the best, most exciting, most utterly glorious, incredible thing I had ever seen. Kate couldn't even speak. She was just hugging everybody and sobbing. Even Lana was smiling, and James was off doing high fives with Soldier John and the rugby crew.

The whole thing must have taken less than two minutes. In that time, we had witnessed five humans kill five well-formed kriks with what looked like very little effort on their part. Even now, as we screamed and shouted in amazement, they didn't even look as though they were celebrating. Two of the men acknowledged us casually with a wave, but the others didn't even pause as they went to pick up and readjust their weapons. The women still had their gorgeous hair, and they all, even from here, just looked so clean . . . and so fabulous.

'Get us off!'

'Get us off!'

'Help us!'

'Help!'

As the team of humans started to look as though they were getting ready to move on, the mood turned to desperation. That couldn't be it, could it? Surely? Surely these people weren't just going to leave us here, were they?

'Where are they going?' said Kate with a sob. 'Please help us!' she shouted.

'Help us!' shouted Lana. 'Help!'

'Help us!' A chant started up. 'Help us! Help us!'

There were a few splashes as several people jumped off the Jellyfish and started making for the shore. They only lasted seconds before they got pulled back, of course, but I understood it. 'What would happen if we all jumped in at the same time?' I asked. 'Some of us would probably make it, right?'

'Wrong,' said Lana. 'the Jellyfish would just grab us again. The stupid, bloody, bollocking thing.' She gave it a kick.

Up on the cliff, the blue-haired woman was scanning the town with her binoculars. She moved her arms from side to side in a deliberate signal. On the ground, the team quickly conferred, and then one of the men replied with the same motion.

'What are they doing, do you think?'

'Not rescuing us, that's what I think,' said Lana, turning

away. 'It's fine. I didn't want to live in the stupid world anyway. I'd much rather live on top of this crappy blob in the middle of the ocean. That's much better, thanks.'

Kate gave another sob, but it was proper crying this time, not happy crying. Her shoulders were shaking with the emotion. I'd never heard her sound so sad. I didn't feel like I had the energy to give her a hug. I know that might sound mean, but I knew if I did, despair would just leak into me and make me feel sad too. And right now, that wasn't what I was feeling. I'm not sure what I *was* feeling, but it might have been hope. Hope? That wasn't something I was very familiar with anyway. The thing is, seeing those fighters had shown us that defeating death – and defeating it easily – was possible. Other people were doing it, so couldn't we? I know it might seem weird that being abandoned to our cruel fate by some kick-ass fighters might be a moment when I felt like things were going to improve but, well . . . it was.

Lana stormed off, muttering loudly to herself and still kicking at the mesoglea.

'Where do you think they came from?' I asked.

'I don't know,' said James. 'It can't be that far, because they didn't come in a vehicle.'

'But then why have we never seen them before?' I asked.

'Because they're staying away from the sea? I'd want to stay away from the sea too, if I was on land.'

Behind us came the wet, flopping sound of the day's fish starting to arrive. I could hear Lana cursing it, and shouting at the tentacles delivering it. A few people wandered off to scoop it up and get it ready for eating. But most stayed, still quietly watching the shore.

'I don't get it, though,' I said. 'Did they know we were here? Because they don't seem very surprised to see us.'

'No. To be fair, though, they have been busy, what with the killer kriks and all.'

'I s'pose so,' I said. I didn't want to spread my hope to anybody else in case it was false. But it just looked like the team of fighters would have a plan. They looked like everything they did had a plan.

'Where do you think they live, then?' I asked.

'I didn't see them come along the cliffs in either direction,' said James. 'Did you see them come along the road?'

'No, I don't think so.' But we hadn't really been looking, had we? I wasn't definitely sure.

'They must have come through the town, then,' said James, confidently, as though that answered my question. But none of us knew what that meant really. We couldn't remember what was out there beyond the shore. We didn't know what it looked like. We didn't know where they could live.

Next to us, Kate had stopped sobbing. Her shoulders were still shaking, but it was with the aftermath of a big cry, when you're tired from the effort of your tears, and your body is still quivering and gasping randomly without you meaning it to. I risked reaching out to pat her on the back sympathetically.

'They're amazing, though, aren't they?' I said.

'Yeah,' said James. I waited for the smart comment, for him to say something like how they'd learnt their skills from him, or something like that. But there was nothing. He just stood there, watching them too. They were moving back up Long Street by now, the two women leading and the men behind. Their crossbows were strapped on to their backs again, but they still carried their spears. Above them, the blue-haired woman was still watching the shore below with her binoculars. Every so often she'd also scan slowly across the water and up to us. I wondered what she was looking for.

'Do you think they'll ever come back?' said Kate. She gave a sigh.

Neither me nor James answered. It was amazing just to know that they were out there, somewhere. But, yeah, I really hoped they'd come back.

They turned left, up one of the streets that were obscured from our view by houses. The crowd around us dispersed and choirs started to form again.

'There'll be a whole sea shanty saga in this, won't there?' said James, with a grimace. 'I reckon they could come up with ten verses about it. At least.'

'Oh, a hundred, I'd have thought,' I said.

'If we're lucky, they might have it ready by tonight,' said James. 'What a treat!' He started laughing. 'Oh god, if that happens, I want to sit next to Lana during the performance; she'll be full of rage. Brilliant!'

The blue-haired woman had started to gesture again. The reply of the fighting team wasn't visible, but she seemed to pause, and then repeated the movements again.

'What's going on?' I asked.

'Wait,' said James, 'it's the same sign . . .'

'As what?'

James stood up straighter, squinting out at the shore. 'The same sign as when they were fighting the kriks before . . .'

'So . . .'

James walked over to the left, frowning. 'So, yeah . . . I think there are more. There must be more kriks that we can't see.'

'So they're not leaving us?' said Kate. 'They're coming back?'

It was impossible to see what was going on. There were gaps between the houses, but they were full of trees, or overgrown bushes, or rubbish, or just stuff that blocked the view. I couldn't even work out how far along the people would be, so it was hard to tell where we should even be looking. Above, on the cliff, the watching woman was the only clue. She was standing motionless now, staring down at the street below. I tried listening instead, but it was hard to tell if the distant noises I was hearing meant anything, or if they were just the normal noises of an abandoned, decaying town.

It seemed to take longer this time, but the watching woman gave another hand signal. She waited for a couple of seconds, and then gave a different signal.

'They're still down there,' said Kate.

'Yes,' said James. 'Some of them, anyway.'

When the fighters emerged back on to Long Street, there was another cheer. They still looked gorgeous, they still looked fabulous, and they still looked ready for battle. Their spears were hooked back on to their belts again, and this time they all gave us a wave.

We all went mad then.

13

I'm not even embarrassed to admit it; we were properly leaping up and down and screaming. I think I might have even injured Kate a bit because I was hugging her so hard. It was an amazing feeling to have them waving to us, when we'd just seen them defeat the kriks so easily. Even the blue-haired woman on the cliffs gave us a giant wave with both arms.

I wanted to be them, to be like them, so badly. Not just because they were on the coast instead of on an amorphous ocean blob, but because they were brilliant, and gorgeous, and just everything I wanted to be in life. I swear the hair of the women seemed to give a little extra blow in the breeze right then, just to show how silky and clean it was.

I knew that they would be here to rescue us, to get us off. They would definitely have a plan, like a helicopter or something. Something brilliant. But at the same time I didn't want to let myself think that, because I didn't want to be disappointed when I also knew that they couldn't possibly have any solution. That led to mental confusion, I'll be honest. It meant that I ended up more doing a little dance of awkwardness, rather than a dance of triumph.

What *was* going to happen next? Well, because of my little dance of awkwardness, I stopped celebrating before everybody else, so I saw the reactions of the people on the shore.

After giving us that wave they just stood staring at us, but then I think our cheering went on a little bit too long for them. They started talking amongst themselves, and the blue-haired woman got her binoculars out again. She was definitely using them to scan the water. She went back and forth slowly, very carefully this time. And then she gave another signal to the team on the shore. Others said they saw that too, but I was fairly sure I saw her shake her head. It might have been that I was too far away to see that and, yes, I could be imagining it. But the movements of the people on the shore seemed to confirm it. It was like they were shrugging, and saying, 'Oh well. It was worth having a look at these people, but they're doomed to die on this jellyfish, so we might as well get back to our happy, free lives.'

By this time, most of the Jellyfish people had stopped cheering loudly, and were just smiling to themselves, or sobbing quietly with joy. We were all eagerly watching the shore, however, to see what these brilliant, efficient, organized people would do.

One of the women started waving more obviously to us, and pointing to the road with exaggerated gestures.

'What's she doing that for?' I asked.

'To tell us where they've come from?' said Kate. 'So that we can go there when they get us off?'

'They're not waiting for us, then?' James muttered at me. 'Not exactly planning to get us off in the next half an hour, are they?'

I nodded. Because already I was thinking that they might not have a plan, that they might just have come down here to have a look at us. They didn't seem to have that useful helicopter hidden anywhere, or a magical bridge. In fact, they didn't seem to have anything different from other people we'd seen; they were just more organized, that was all. Already I was thinking – no, knew – that they wanted to leave now without seeing us all crying.

James gave me a glum look. The blue-haired woman was still scanning the water with her binoculars, and it was just taking way too long. What was she looking for?

'I think they look annoying, actually,' I said.

Lana screwed up her face. 'You're bonkers. You've got literally no reason for saying that at all.'

I hadn't, so I didn't add anything to my point. But it was a strategic move, because it meant that if they failed to rescue us, then I could glory in having been the first to complain about it. I wasn't the only one, though. 'Don't like it,' Old Albert was muttering. 'Don't like it at all. Nothing good'll come of it, you mark my words.'

The blue-haired woman gave a hand signal. But she kept

her binoculars up. On the shore the team looked at each other, and had a quick chat. Then two of the men ran over to some of the boats which had been washed up in a high tide. They started pushing them into the water.

'That's it?' said Lana. 'Bollocks to them, then.'

Around us there were mutters of disgust and anger.

Three boats were pushed towards us before the fighting team gave us a final wave and ran back up Long Street.

'They could at least have pushed in the good boats,' said James. They'd pushed in the three closest ones, but had ignored our favourites: the yacht with what looked like an intact sail, and the red one, which we liked because, well, it was red.

Kate gave a big sigh.

'Do you think it'll be worse being stuck here knowing that they're out there?' I said. 'You know, worse than it was yesterday, when we thought there was nobody else alive?'

'I never thought we were the only ones left alive,' said Kate. 'Did you really think that? How horrible.'

'No, I suppose I didn't think that. I suppose I thought that anybody who was left alive must be having a much worse time than us, and that they must just be being killed slowly on land. Because otherwise they'd have come to rescue us, wouldn't they? Kriks must be there – inland too, not just on the coast, because they go away somewhere and then come back, don't they? So, you know, I thought everybody might as well be dead.'

'Brutal, Martha!' said James. 'That's cold.'

'Yeah? Maybe, but it looks like it *is* pretty brutal out there, so at least I'm being realistic. What are *you* spending all your time thinking about? How lovely the world is and how great it is to live here on this wind-exposed hellhole?'

'That's really unfair, Martha. I don't see much evidence of brilliant things going on in *your* head,' said James.

'Or *any* evidence,' said Lana.

'What are you joining in for?' I said, turning to her. She was scowling and still kicking at the mesoglea. 'You always have to be at the centre of everything. Especially if it involves being mean. This has got nothing to do with you, it's just me and James.'

'You wish it was just you and James.'

'Well it never is, is it? You're always here, hanging around, wherever I go,' I said.

'It's not like I've got a choice. Trust me, if there was anywhere I could go, then I would love some time away from you. All three of you.'

'Stop it!' said Kate. 'Stop it. You're all making it worse.' She started to cry. 'It's not going to help if you all get cross with each other. It's just . . . it's just . . . for a minute there, I thought . . .'

We all knew what she thought because, yeah, for a minute we'd been thinking it too. I could almost feel that hard tarmac beneath my feet, imagine that stable, unmoving earth.

'I feel sorry for the rest of the human race, actually,' said

James, 'because they don't get to experience our gorgeous sea views.'

I smiled up at him, and Kate gave a more cheerful sniffle.

'Wait, what?' Lana sat up. 'How stupid are you dickheads? Do none of you even think about it all? Do none of you think about our world? What the bloody bollocking crap *do* you think about?'

'I spend a lot of time trying *not* to think about the world, Lana,' I said, because it was true. And I think it was true about most of the people on board the Jellyfish. If we thought about it too much, our lives would be rubbish, wouldn't they? Even more rubbish than they already were, I mean. 'Go on, then. What should we all have been thinking about?'

'Well, you don't think we're the only ones stuck on one of these things, do you? That's a start. There's no way we're the only humans in the world who are being kept like flippin' animals in a zoo. There's no way this jellyfish is a complete one-off freak of nature. There've gotta be others, that didn't just destroy ships and then go back beneath the water. So, yeah, other people have got the sea-view hellhole, James.'

We sat there for a minute, completely shocked. Because, the thing is, I *had* thought we were the only ones. And even though he tried to hide it by looking fake-casual and giving a yawn, I don't think James had ever thought anything else either.

The tentacles nearest to us sank suddenly below the surface, leaving behind a smooth, glassy area of water. Only the occasional drifting bubble or dark shimmer gave a hint of the threat below.

'And those flippin' crab kriks out there are running out of food now, aren't they?' added Lana. 'We're not seeing as many humans as we used to, so they've caught all the easy ones. The only humans we've seen in the last few months have been krik killers, right?'

'Right.'

'So what are the kriks going to start doing? Are they going to start eating each other? What do you think they're living off?'

I hadn't thought about it. I didn't really want to start thinking about it now, even.

'Those animals up on the hills?' said James. 'There are loads of those still left.'

'Yes, there are,' said Lana, 'but those animals are really fast and really hairy, and we've not seen kriks eating them before, have we? Maybe that's because they can't catch them, or maybe it's because they don't eat them.

'And the thing is, crabs don't live very long, do they?'

'Don't know,' I said.

'I don't think they do. So are the kriks about to start dying?'

'That'd be nice. But I don't think so,' said James. 'There're still a lot of them and they probably breed or something. Plus they're not actually crabs, are they?'

'Yes, well, our options are that either they're about to start running out of food and dying, or we're being kept here to feed them when food supplies run low, so *we're* about to start dying.

'I think things are about to change. They're about to change soon. I don't know *how* they're going to change, but I want to be one of the ones to survive.'

We all stared out at the shore. The lumpy bodies of the dead kriks looked smaller than they had when they were alive – maybe because they were all hunched over now, or because of blood loss or something. They didn't exactly look less evil or anything – but they did look sad and not at all like the scary monsters they had been. Over each of them there was already a squabbling cover of seagulls picking at the flesh beneath. They'd pull and peck, then turn their necks upwards to chew and call noisily. Every so often, for no obvious reason, all the gulls on one of the kriks would rise upwards and fly round shouting, before swooping back down again to pull at that dead flesh once more.

Up at the top of the cliffs, six black figures emerged from behind the houses. At a steady jog they ran up the road away from us. We watched them until they were out of sight.

14

'What shall we do?' I asked.

We were sitting outside the Big House, and a few people were still inside pretending to sleep so that they didn't have to face the day. I don't really know why I asked, because there was nothing anybody could have suggested that I'd have wanted to do. I definitely didn't ask out of politeness either, because being polite to others had not been a priority that morning. There had been serious amounts of rudeness and grumpiness from pretty much everybody.

'Bog off,' said Lana.

It was the answer I'd expected. It was the one I'd have given her.

All three of the boats were still visible. Two were bobbing near us, sometimes coming closer and fooling us into hope before floating away again. The other one was back on the shore again, tapping against the walls of the submerged houses in an annoyingly audible fashion. Whenever there was a moment of silence, a drop in the wind, you could hear the tinny tapping. It was irregular too, which made it more difficult to ignore. *Ting ... ting ... ting ...*

'Morning!' James sat up. 'So, I've made a decision about today.'

Lana ignored him, and continued idly stabbing at the mesoglea beneath her feet. She was wrapped in a coat of plastic bags against the light drizzle and spray from the waves, looking like the very image of misery – which I think was the fashion statement she was going for.

'Well, come on, guys!' said James. 'Ask me about my decision.'

'Right, James. But I've got a feeling that I'll regret asking, won't I?' I said.

'How could you regret asking, Martha? This is something I've been working on for a very long time.' He looked hurt at my doubt, which confirmed my opinion that it wasn't going to be anything good.

Lana looked up, interested for a second. Surely there was no way he could have been working on something for a very long time? We'd have noticed.

I gave a loud sigh to show that I was already bored. 'Go on then, James. What is the decision you've made about today?'

'I'm glad you asked, Martha,' he said. 'I've made a big decision about . . . my bogey. Yes, that's right. My monster bogey.'

Lana slumped back into the Jellyfish again. James gave a

shrug, then carried on with his story anyway. 'Yes. I've been working on it for weeks now. Quite a few times I've needed to blow my nose, but I haven't. I've carefully sniffed the fluid bogeys back up into my nose and let them dry up there. A few times I've even had to lie back to prevent all that loose bogey sliding back out again. I first realized that it was going to be a real beauty a couple of days ago, when I scratched the side of my nose and the bogey hurt me through the side of my nostril. It was hard and pure then.

'Now, at that point, a weaker man than myself might have caved and picked his nose, or an even weaker one might have blown it. But not me, oh no. No, since then, I've been saving it and saving it. I can't even breathe properly any more, my nostril's so full. What a treat this is going to be – and a monster like this shouldn't just be blown into the sea! When I eventually pick my nose – oh the relief! Imagine the joy!'

'Right,' I said. 'So are you going to pick it by yourself, or are you going to do a grand show?'

'I'd be surprised if others didn't want to watch, actually. I have been giving updates to a few interested people.'

'Let me know how you get on, then,' I said. 'I think I might just stay and watch the boats.'

James sidled off. I think he went reluctantly, but then he'd given himself a big build-up, so he sort of had to go. Lana wrapped the plastic bags further around herself, leaving a small ventilation hole at the top, and lay down.

'Wahey!' Shouts began behind me, and the chant, 'James,

James, James, James!' It takes so little to get our interest here, especially when we're busy avoiding thinking about something important. But it was starting to become more difficult to block out thoughts of escape, and even as everybody else was cheering, I couldn't take my eyes off the slowly moving boats.

The closest boat bobbing towards us was a small, two-berth river boat. The second was a larger, but rusting, sail-less yacht. There was a mighty dent on one side, and a crack leading up to the deck. It wasn't definite that either of the boats would ever reach us. The Jellyfish didn't seem to mind letting small objects past, like the plastic bottles and bags which arrived every day, but I wondered whether it would let through large ones, like boats.

'Well, how are things over here, Martha?' James came back up behind me. 'You look just the same. Same life, same fashion sense, same friends. That's so sweet, you know? But we can't all live like that. Some of us have to try new things, gain new experiences.'

The pile of plastic bags that was Lana gave a disgusted snort.

'Did you pick your nose, then?' I asked, if only to make him shut up.

'Yes, Martha. And it was every bit as magical as you'd imagine. A glorious moment in my existence.'

'Probably was, actually.'

'Probably.'

We looked at the boats for another couple of seconds.

'I'm going to go insane,' said James. 'Absolutely insane.'

'Yeah,' I said. It was an option which a number of people on board had already taken. And I had wondered, a few times, if it was actually me who was insane, and this whole Jellyfish thing wasn't real. In dark moments, like this one, it was always quite difficult to tell.

'I think . . .' I said, and it was an exciting sentence, because I didn't know how I was going to end it until I did: I really was just thinking it as I spoke. 'I think . . . I'm going to try and escape. Today.'

15

James looked round at me. There was a rustle of plastic bags, and Lana emerged.

'Anybody want to help me escape?'

Lana gave a shrug.

'It'll pass the time, I suppose,' said James. 'What's your plan?'

It wasn't a fully developed plan at this point, but I was flattered James thought it might be. 'I want to get that boat,' I said. 'The closest one. I want to make sure that it definitely comes over here, rather than going back to shore. So I think we should make a rope by tying plastic bags together, and then throw it on the deck with the rugby ball attached. It'll hopefully get caught round the boat's railings and then we should be able to drag it over here, at least a little way.'

'No,' said James. 'No. You're not using the rugby ball.'

'It's to get us off the Jellyfish and save our lives,' I said.

'In your dreams it is,' he said. 'No way are you using my rugby ball in something risky. See, if I wake up tomorrow morning and I'm still on this flipping thing and there's no rugby ball, then there'd be problems.'

Lana was already pulling apart her plastic bags and tying them together.

'Well, what do you suggest, then?' I said. 'We need something that's heavy, but easy to throw.'

'I'll chuck one of you losers at it in a minute, if you don't help me,' said Lana.

We both grabbed some of the bags.

'How about a plastic bottle?' said James. 'With water in it and the lid on?'

I gave a nod. We set to work.

All of the best ideas we've ever had have also seemed like the most obvious ones afterwards. And the plastic-bag rope was one of those. Looking back on it now, it seems weird we hadn't thought about tying them together before, but we honestly hadn't. You get loads, hundreds maybe, of plastic bags floating around you on the sea each day. We used them for lots of things: sleeping bags (with other bags stuffed inside as padding); fashion accessories (when twisted together and looped into necklaces or colourful belts); raincoats; clothing; for sitting on when you just couldn't stand the feel of that gloopy mesoglea beneath you; or even just for burning. But a rope was something we'd never made before. The possibilities seemed endless.

'Zip wire, I think it was called?' said Kate. 'I remember it from Before; it was in a park just for children to play in. It was so much fun! You'd get on at one end, and then sort of slide along the rope to the other end really quickly. It would pull you along.'

'How would it pull you along, though?' said Lana. 'Because we've not had much success making anything mechanical out of shredded plastic bags and seaweed. If we could do that, we'd have built a flippin' aeroplane and got us off this thing ages ago.'

'It might have been called a Flying Fox?' said Kate, with a frown. 'No, it can't have been. That's a silly name. I don't know how it would pull you along. But we could attach the rope at this end, and just climb along it. We wouldn't have to slide along.'

'What would we attach the other end *to*?' said Lana. 'Where would we be sliding *to*?'

'The boat,' said Kate. 'When we get it here, we could tie the end of the rope to it and then push the boat away. Then when it got past the tentacles we could climb along the rope and swim to shore.'

'That sounds crap,' said Lana. But she said it more out of habit than conviction. We'd tried much stupider ideas before.

'I need another load of bags,' said James, calling over to the Big House. 'Oi! John, have we got any more bags coming?' John gave him a wave. Half the people on board were working on our project by now, and the Big House was full of people ripping apart the elaborate plastic-bag wallpaper inside.

'What do you think that wave means?'

'It means he's sorting it out, James,' I said. 'He's not the sort of man to wave just to say hello, is he? Look, we've all pretty much finished. Shall we join our ropes together to make one long one?'

We laid our ropes out on the surface.

'They're a bit thin, aren't they?' said Lana.

'They're great!' said Kate. 'I think we've done really well.'

'Right,' said Lana. 'But would you like to climb this one on your zip wire, out over the tentacles?'

Kate looked at the pieces of knotted plastic. She scrunched up her nose, but didn't immediately say no.

'How about we plait them together?' I asked.

'But that'll mean we've got far less rope,' said James.

'Yes, but what we've got will be stronger.'

'But what we've got here would probably be long enough to reach the boat already,' said James. The boat had moved towards the shore a little, but with a good rugby kick we'd still be able to reach it. And combined together, the four plastic-bag ropes we had between us were easily long enough to reach beyond the tentacles.

'I think . . .' I said, looking over at the activity surrounding the Big House, 'I think we should make it strong and not worry about reaching the boat for now.'

'What are you thinking, Mystery Martha?' said James.

Kate started plaiting three of the ropes together.

'I'm not sure,' I said. 'But I know we've made loads of

escape attempts before. I don't even know how many. We've never tried something with rope though. We can tie things up now, and lasso things and maybe pull things towards us. That's new.'

'And us,' said Kate.

'Us what?'

'Well, us coming up with the escape plan. That's also new.'

Dr Jones dropped a large pile of plastic bags next to us. Most were shredded, or discoloured by time spent floating in the sea. 'There are more on the way,' she said. 'Not all are as good as these, though. And it might take a few minutes.'

Up at the Big House, Soldier John was now having a loud argument with Old Albert. It was fairly obvious what it was about: Albert gets territorial about his bags, and spends a lot of time rustling about at night building a nest around himself. Normally most of the people on board would have been over, picking a side in the shouting match and loudly giving our opinions. But things had changed now, and most of us were busy. Staring Crone was still silently staring – but I think we all felt that was OK right now, now that we knew she was thinking life-shifting thoughts. There was a group training, trying out moves used by the people we'd seen on shore. And everybody else was gathering together all the plastic bags we had. The whole Jellyfish was buzzing with the human energy on board and it just felt hopeful, exciting . . . and as though something was going to happen. Something different. Beneath us even the Jellyfish seemed to sense the mood, and it had gone strangely still and stiff like it was a boat. Its surface was moving on top of the waves – lightly up and down – and not absorbing the movement as it normally did.

I started knotting the rope together more quickly. It suddenly did seem urgent, after all. The drizzle had turned into light rain, and without our normal plastic bag coverings, it was definitely cold. My hands were numb, which was making it fiddly to tie the knots, but nobody was showing any sign of wanting to sit in the Big House.

'Go and fill a bottle, would you, James?' I said. He moved, without arguing, towards the edge of the creature.

'I wonder what it would be like to sit inside one of those houses on the shore?' said Kate. 'Do you think it would be warm?'

'I think the windows would be broken and the roofs would leak,' said Lana. 'Besides, if I ever get off this thing, I'm going to run so far inland that I'll never even smell the sea. I don't want any rivers, or lakes, or even a puddle. I'm definitely not friggin' wasting time going into one of those houses.'

'I don't think the windows in my white house are broken,' said Kate. 'And its front door is still shut. I don't think anything has been inside.'

There was a little bubbling feeling of excitement with every plastic bag I knotted. I tried to squash it back down again so the disappointment wouldn't be too bad if, you know, we failed. But this time it felt like what we were trying was different – more than that: it felt like the time was right, that this was more than just *another* escape attempt. I tried not to listen to the others talking about what they'd do if we got to land – but the truth is, it *did* feel like we were closer to walking on those streets than we had been yesterday.

Soldier John held on to the end of the rope, wrapping it twice round his wrist. He gave James a nod.

James centred the bottle, rearranging the mesoglea beneath so that it would stand upright. Then he took a step back. Around him most of the Jellyfish people were now standing, silent and hopeful. Some still held soggy shreds of plastic, ready to make more rope.

James gave a giant kick, and the bottle flew, soaring into the air, arcing over the squirming tentacles and beyond, above the little wavelets lapping at the edge of the creature. It landed a couple of metres to the side of the boat, and disappeared into the darkness of the water.

Silently, John pulled the bottle back, the wet rope collecting in piles of drips at his feet as he did so.

James grabbed the bottle as it slid up out of the sea. He checked the rope attached to it, placing the bottle back into the dimple still visible on the mesoglea from last time. He took a step back again. There was the sigh of muttered prayers from the watching crowd. And he kicked.

This time the bottle seemed to spin gently in the air, looping even higher, and seemingly slower than last time. It fell, with a booming thud, on to the deck of the boat.

'Let it go, James,' said Soldier John. 'Let the rope out. Slowly.'

James released the rope inch by inch, and the bottle started to slide down the bow, back towards the sea and leaving the rope still hanging over the rail of the boat.

'Now twist the rope round the bottle,' said Soldier John.

Some of the Jellyfish people were now holding hands and praying together, their eyes shut.

James flicked the rope towards the boat again, and then again. It caught, and wrapped itself round the bottle.

James heaved. The boat slid towards us, tentacles stroking it and slowing it as it moved. As it came nearer a wave of translucent jelly seeped out of the creature and gathered around the bow, pulling it in. Soldier John and others ran forward to help secure it.

James turned and raised his arms in triumph. But beneath his cheery grin, his facial muscles still looked taut and tense, his face still pale and with a sheen of moisture on his forehead that was more than just drizzle.

16

The Big House seemed smaller, and even colder than normal. The walls, without their intricate plastic-bag coverings, were now obviously mismatched, ramshackle pieces of sea junk. The gaps between the strips of wood and warped plastic seemed to focus the force of the wind into fierce lasers of biting cold air which attacked you no matter where in the hut you sat. Most of us were now hunched, silent and dispirited. We also stank. You do get used to the smell of unwashed clothes, which is a mixture of rotting fish and something dirtier: an underlying tangy, vomitous stench. But every so often, when we're all huddled together, the smell becomes too much. Normally the smoke from the fire covers the worst of it, but today, the feeble sparks emanating from a little, bedraggled pile of sticks in the corner hardly provided even a floating feather of sooty vapour, never mind any warmth.

The room was unusually silent. What were we going to do with the boat, now that we'd got it? It was a tense . . . and frightening . . . subject. Nobody wanted to talk about it yet. But somehow, not talking about it and avoiding the issue meant that nobody seemed to have anything else to say either.

I dug my fingers into the mesoglea, squeezing it and twisting it. You can't rip chunks out of this central part of the Jellyfish, because it's too hard, but you can mould it and shape it, so it's good to play with when you're feeling stressed or nervous.

'Good evening everybody!' Dr Jones came forward and stood at the front, in the space we'd left for speakers. 'We are lucky enough to have two lectures tonight . . .'

'Oh. My. God,' muttered Lana. She looked murderous. Normally her rage would have been the guarantee of a good night, and me and James would have enjoyed playing with her emotions, prodding her during the more boring parts of the talks. But tonight I understood where she was coming from. I looked over at James; his face was resting on his knees. On the other side of me, Kate was also fiddling with the mesoglea.

'The first lecture will be from Carol and it will be on keeping bees? Is that right?'

Carol nodded, giving a brave smile.

'Lovely,' said Dr Jones. She didn't sound as if it would be lovely at all.

'And our second lecture tonight will be from Albert. I'm unclear about the title, but it's a general warning about the future. Is that right, Albert?'

'Arr,' said Albert.

'Oh. My. God,' muttered Lana again. 'He is turning into a cartoon pirate in front of our eyes, and nobody is doing anything about it.' She made as though to stand up in disgust, and she has walked out several times before, but then she sat down again with a dramatic groan instead. Walking out would mean sitting outside in the dark drizzle by herself. There really wasn't anywhere to go.

Carol came forward slowly and reluctantly, stepping over the people in front of her. She normally wears stripes of plastic bags on her chest, woven in and out of her top. But without those, all that was left was a ragged brown T-shirt which contained more holes than material. She had retained one blue plastic bag to cover her breasts, but still, her clothing was now barely decent.

With a sigh, she started. 'Bees are little flying creatures which have black and white stripes on them.' She gave another sigh and paused, looking at Dr Jones.

Dr Jones gave an encouraging nod. I'm not sure she would have been so keen for Carol to speak if Old Albert wasn't scheduled to go next.

'They make a noise which sounds like *buzzzzzzzzz*, and they make a nice thing called honey. The thing about honey is that it lasts for ever. When the tombs of the pharaohs were opened in Egypt last century, the honey stored with them a thousand years earlier was found to be completely edible.

117

We'll probably never see a bee while we're living on the Jelly-fish, though.'

'Oh, for goodness' sake!' Lana stood up. 'Aren't we going to talk about it? Aren't we going to do anything about it? What are we going to do about the boat?'

There were murmurs of approval from all over the room. Carol immediately sat down. Nobody stood up to take her place.

'Well?' shouted Lana. 'We've got the boat here, we know that there are other people out there, on land. We know we just have to get to them. What are we going to do? How are we going to do it?'

Cautiously, Dr Jones stepped forward. She raised her hands for quiet.

'We have two very generous offers of evening lectures tonight. I think we should just listen to those first before we discuss escape plans,' she said.

I thought Lana was going to explode. She made an inco-herent roaring noise which, luckily for her, was drowned out by the rage noises coming from the rest of the people in the room.

'OK, OK!' Dr Jones raised her hands for quiet again. It took a little bit longer this time, because nobody wanted to risk having to listen to Old Albert, and a few other people stood up to make exactly that point. But eventually there was hush again. 'OK, why don't those of you who want to listen to the lectures go to the back of the hut, and those of you who want to discuss escape plans come to the front.'

Nobody moved, including Carol and Old Albert.

'OK, then,' said Dr Jones, with an air of solemnity, and possibly also tiredness. 'We've managed to get a boat here, which was kindly pushed out to us by some people on the shore.' There were a few hisses at this point.

'They pushed another two out to us as well. One of the other boats might eventually make its way here, but it might also just head back to shore. Given that we know the Jellyfish wouldn't let us escape on any of the many, many rafts we've made, what are we going to do with a boat that's different?'

There was an immediate surge of suggestions. In fact, there were so many suggestions it was really difficult to hear any of them. Lana sat down. Her face was calmer.

'A boat is different from a raft, though, isn't it?' whispered Kate. 'It's got a roof and sides. And it's much more professional.'

'Yes,' I said. 'But I've been on a professionally built boat before. In Before. I seem to remember that's how I ended up stuck here.'

Lana, Kate and James smiled.

'It's not different from a raft at all,' said James. 'A roof and sides wouldn't stop tentacles getting inside it.'

'Yeah, well, it was abandoned and floating on the shore,' said Lana. 'It's not like its owners had time to park it neatly in a boat house somewhere.'

'I'm sure they got away though,' said Kate. 'It might just

have floated out of where they parked it.'

James sniggered. 'Yeah Kate. That's absolutely what happened. In no way were they dragged out of it and pulled down to the ocean bed.'

'The tentacles aren't even as annoying as you three,' said Lana. 'At least with a boat here I can go and sit somewhere and get away from you.'

Around us, the room was quietening down again.

'So we've got a list of things to try which are different,' said Dr Jones. 'Ideas which we haven't tried before.'

There were nods and smiles.

'Before we settle tonight, let's have a vote on which plan to go for first.' She waved her hands to quieten some of the dissenters. 'I'm sure we'll succeed this time,' she added. But she said it out of habit, like it was one of those phrases you use all the time without thinking about what it really means; she didn't even try to smile to make it look like she was hopeful. I wondered how long ago it was that she'd given up.

We stayed up late that night talking and planning. Long after I'd lain down I could hear the murmuring of voices and the rustling of plastic bags from others who couldn't sleep. But the Jellyfish was still: unmoving, unusually stiff, unusually calm.

17

We had all been awake since before dawn. It would have been a good night for sleeping, I imagine, because there was far less snoring and sleep-talking in the Big House than normal. But by the time light was breaking, we had all got bored with pretending to sleep. We still lay there, though, because at the same time, I don't think anybody wanted to start the day. There's this glorious bit of excitement that you can have before you try anything big. It's mixed in with nervousness about the fact that you'll probably fail, of course, but because the two emotions are mixed in together, it's really hard to tell the difference. There's maybe a bit of hope thrown in there as well, but, like I said before, that's not really a feeling I'm very familiar with, so I can't be sure. I think we all wanted to savour that glorious mix of emotions, before . . . well, you know. . .

The weather had settled, so we could clearly see the coast-line, even the far edges of the bay. The sea had calmed too, and we could even make out some of the concealed wrecks of the houses normally covered by the waves. That would be useful, if we made it close to the shore.

It was a 'raw fish breakfast' day, which is my least favourite start to the day, but we were low on firewood. So anyway, all of that meant that we were ready far too quickly. If we failed, we'd know about it before people would have even got out of their beds in the old days – back when people used to sleep in beds, that is.

James had his arm round me and was leaning his head on my shoulder. He'd been like that since we woke up (well, pretended to wake up, anyway). Quiet, and clingy, and un-usually sweet. I would have been worried about him, or stopped to tease him, but there wasn't time today.

'Morning all,' said Soldier John.

There were polite murmurs in reply. But mostly, people just gathered around John in silence, grim-faced and tense.

'It's a good day for a mission. Clear weather, clear coast. Can I have confirmation that the Jellyfish is behaving as normal?'

'As normal, sir,' called one of the men.

'As normal,' called another.

The Jellyfish gave another low vibration beneath us; a tiny, almost unnoticeable ripple ran across the whole of the creature like it had just woken up and was starting the day with us.

'And any active movement spotted on the shore?' said Soldier John.

'None definite,' said Staring Crone. 'Though there might be something in the treeline at the top of the cliffs.'

'Noted,' said Soldier John. 'Keep an eye on that for us, please.' He turned to the crowd, a serious expression on his face. 'There is to be no maverick behaviour here. It's important, if this plan is to be successful, that we all work together. Is that clear?'

There were more murmurs and nods. I wasn't sure what he was asking, but it was clear there had been some sort of disagreement last night that we hadn't been aware of.

'So most of you are creatin' a distraction. You're bein' loud, and you're movin' around a lot. Got it?'

We nodded.

'Pete is goin' in the boat, and you lot are 'oldin' the tentacles out of the way so 'e can get through. OK?'

He pointed to the people with the important tasks.

'Does everyone know what they're doin'?' he asked.

Again, everyone nodded. I couldn't see that he was talking to any one person in particular, but there was an edge to the question which made it look as though he was.

'Can the boat volunteer step forward, then?'

Pitiful Pete gave a wave as he walked off towards the boat. We gave him a round of applause, but by this stage you could really feel the excitement, so it was a quick clap, and nobody really looked at him.

'I'm nervous,' whispered Kate. She held out her shaking hands to show us.

I gave her a reassuring smile, but I felt strangely distant from it all, like I was looking down at it happening to somebody else. Like I could see a load of people, little specks on a piece of wobbling phlegm, buzzing around pointlessly on a tiny, insignificant corner of the sea.

'Can I have the tentacle teams up?'

Four others stepped forward. They grabbed the plastic-bag ropes and went off towards the boat.

'The rest of you. Get to your positions. And good luck to us all.'

'Good luck.'

'Good luck.' We all nodded at each other, and walked slowly towards the centre of the Jellyfish. James still had his arm around my waist, just casually, as though he'd forgotten where he'd left it. Today, right now, I didn't want to remind him. And I didn't care if the others made fun of me afterwards. It felt good to be close to somebody.

'Get ready,' said Soldier John, looking over towards the boat. He put his hand up in the air. For a moment, all was silent, apart from the wind. We kept our eyes fixed on him.

Then he shouted. 'Choir, go!'

We started to sing, loudly, and tunelessly.

'More!' he shouted again.

We started to scream, and shout. No longer words, just utterances. Lana was red in the face with the effort, and several people were shaking their heads as though it would make the noise come out more loudly. The Jellyfish seemed to stiffen beneath us, as though it was listening to what we were doing.

Then Soldier John dropped his hand.

Immediately, we started walking towards the far side of the Jellyfish, the boat and the shoreline at our backs. We pounded and stamped and jumped towards the other side, as far away from the boat as possible. We screamed and shouted and roared. We waved and spun and swore. Wilder and crazier and louder.

'Come on!' shouted Soldier John, his voice somehow booming above everything else.

The water was already starting to pool around my feet, the jelly already starting to tilt.

'Don't stop!' shouted Soldier John.

Louder and louder, we pounded forward, wailing. Slowly, the jelly began to rise behind us, then more rapidly. I could feel the mucus forming around the back of my ankles, the angle of our world starting to change.

'Keep going!'

We were right on the edge now and shouting louder. The Jellyfish tilted right up behind and then, with a juddering lunge, it suddenly jumped twenty degrees further. All that was holding us on now was the sticky mesoglea, but I could feel even that shifting and liquefying beneath my feet. Three people jumped in, then four more. They started swimming away from the creature.

'Don't stop the noise! We need more time!' shouted

Soldier John.

We started screaming again. Next to me, James jumped in, and then Lana, both of them shouting and bellowing with all their might. I jumped in too.

Beneath me in the sudden coldness of the water, I could feel the short tentacles squirming around; so many, like a mass of twisted seaweed or fur. Sometimes they'd catch on my skin and clothes, a moment of stickiness before continuing to move. Moist, smooth flesh forming and adjusting itself around me.

The last of the people jumped in, or fell in, so we were now all in the water. Some of us stayed next to the creature, but others swam wildly out into the open ocean. We all carried on shouting, but our energy was dipping.

Up above us I could no longer see the boat, only the gap in the jelly where it had been. And on either side, four men were hanging off the plastic-bag rope, which they had tied around the tentacles. They were gripping firmly, and the long tentacles were still restrained, their muscles pulling against the rope, the thinner tendrils at the top careening wildly in mid-air.

Kate grabbed my arm and gave me a grin. Her loud song was about 'being happy' and 'this is great' and 'we're doing it!'

But then suddenly there was a shift. With a great groaning roll the jelly mesoglea started to seep backwards, in oozing waves of mucus. The men disappeared from sight as the Jellyfish levelled itself, and Soldier John clambered back up.

Behind us, the tentacles started collecting and throwing upwards those people at our end who had swum the furthest away. There was a change in the movements in the shorter, stroking tentacles. More menace, more stickiness, more a sense that you were being pushed back in towards the creature again.

'Climb back on!' shouted Soldier John. 'Climb back on!' There was a note of desperation in his voice which I'd never heard before, not ever, during any of the other escape attempts. 'Now!' he shouted again, his voice cracking in his urgency. He leant over and started pulling people up. Over our heads there was the flying buzz of the large tentacles whipping somebody out of the water.

I swam quickly, reaching up for the hands that pulled me in. And then I looked over, saw what they saw. There, on the other side, was the smashed mess of the shattered, shredded boat; there was the fragmented remains of the plastic-bag rope; there were the angry, waving tentacles. But there were no people.

Of the people who had been holding the ropes in the escape attempt, there was now no sign.

18

Everything felt emptier and bigger and quieter. Right from the minute we stood up and walked slowly towards the remains of the boat, it felt like there was more space on board. It also felt like everything that we knew for certain had changed.

There was a sudden wave of cold, dank pain pouring into my stomach, so intense that I could barely move, and my whole body clenched with the wrongness of it. It felt like I had been slapped with shards of sadness too sharp to bear. What could we do now? What was going to happen? Why had this happened?

'Do you think they did it? That they made it?' said Kate, with a choke. She was staring only at the fragmented pieces of wood still lying by the edge of the Jellyfish. There were three large pieces, big enough to still build a raft from or to re-roof the Big House; and there were smaller, splintered pieces scattered in a ring around those. In the water there was other debris now drifting away, or caught in the tangle of the tentacles. But of the larger parts of the boat, of the metal railings, of the roof, of the hull, there was nothing.

'Well, do you see them?' said Lana. She didn't say it angrily, or sarcastically, like she normally would, and it was hard for me to tell what she was thinking because her face didn't seem to have any expression left on it. And right then I just wanted to know what everybody else was feeling, so that I knew what I should think too. So that I could have some way of telling what it was all about.

Kate lifted her head up reluctantly and we scanned the water silently for a few minutes. I don't think I looked properly, because I'm pretty sure I already knew, but there was lots of driftwood, lots of debris. Lots of things that could have been something. But nothing that was waving to us, or shouting cheerily about having escaped.

'Maybe over there,' said Kate, pointing towards a large, black lump floating near the shore. It could have been somebody, because the tentacles can punch people really far. But if it was, whatever it was, it wasn't moving.

By the Big House, most of the remaining people were slumped on the surface whispering to each other, or crying gently. Soldier John was sitting by himself with his head in his hands. Staring Crone had found her way back, to her normal position, staring at the coastline. But even she seemed to be closer to the house right now, as though she was gaining comfort just from being vaguely near to everybody else.

'Pete has finally managed to get off this thing then,'

129

muttered James. 'Oh, I've got to go.' He bowed his head and walked away towards the creature's muscle ring. I went to grab his arm, but he shook me off.

'Let me know if . . .' I called after him, but then I stopped because I didn't really know how to finish the sentence.

'Where have they gone?' said Lana. 'If they're not here, then where have they gone?' She was still expressionless. 'What has the Jellyfish done with them? What?'

'I don't know,' I said.

'What shall we do, then?' said Kate. Then her face creased up into sobs.

I caught Lana's eye, and that's when I realized I was crying too. For a time we stood there, clutching each other, the three of us, while we wept. Gut-wrenching, stomach-crunching sobs of pain and sadness.

When we had stopped, exhausted, we sat with the people in the centre of the Jellyfish, dejected and sad.

'What are we crying for?' I said. 'Them? Their deaths? Or us?' I paused, both because it was a big frickin' statement, and because I was fairly sure it was the meaning of life. I think I may have even raised my head up slightly, and stared off mysteriously into the distance.

'Bog off, will you, Martha,' said Lana. 'I am so not in the mood for your over-the-top bullshit self-pity today.'

It was a fair point. But I think sometimes you need somebody to tell you you're being a wanker, before you know for definite.

130

'What are we going to do then?' I said.

'What do you think, Martha?' said Kate, looking up at me.

'Well . . . get off here, I suppose. And quickly. We don't have time to think about . . . what's happened.'

James came back at this point, and I think it's probably a good thing that he did. He was pale, and his eyes were red with crying, but he looked determined, and like he wanted to do something. It made me say some stuff which I hadn't even been realizing I was thinking myself.

'The thing is,' I said, 'I don't know how it knows. How can the Jellyfish tell when we leave?'

'It can see us?' said Kate.

James frowned. 'Where, though? Where are its eyes? They're not on the muscle ring. Are they on the front?'

'Well, where is the front?' said James.

'Does it have eyes in the same way we have eyes?' said Kate.

'Maybe it has feelers?' said Lana.

We all thought about it for a minute. Maybe that was right. Maybe it felt us when we moved around, or when we were jumping up and down.

'Is it maybe that it can hear us, or smell us?' said Kate.

'It's one of those, though, isn't it?' I said. 'The five senses.'

'You know when the Jellyfish moves, can we tell anything from that?' James asked.

'Yes, of course,' I said.

'Yes. You can tell when it's grumpy and happy,' said Kate.

Lana raised her eyebrows. '*You* can. I can't. I definitely don't speak jellyfish language.'

'But you *do* know when it's really cross and the tentacles get dangerous,' said Kate. 'Or when it's happy and the tentacles are just waving.'

Lana looked at her, eyebrows still raised.

'I don't know if I can tell anything more than that,' said Kate. 'It was cross before it . . . killed. But I don't know if that tells us anything.'

'So,' I said, 'it probably can't see us, because it doesn't seem to have any eyes.'

'Unless they're on the ends of the tentacles?' said Kate.

'Yes, that could be an issue,' I conceded.

'But the others died before they'd gone past the ends of the tentacles,' said James.

'OK, then,' I said. 'Hearing's probably out, because we were shouting so loudly.'

'But then why are we shouting at all?' said Lana. 'It definitely works a bit; it definitely distracts the Jellyfish.'

'Yes,' I said. 'OK, we'll say there's some proof of that hypothesis having been tested.'

'And found convincing . . .' said Lana.

'Yes. What about smell? Can it smell us?' We avoided eye contact at that point, but I heard James snigger. 'Yes, probably,' I said. 'It probably can smell us.'

'And so could anybody within a mile,' said James.

'Yes, yes, fine. Can we rule out taste?' I said.

'Yes,' said Kate. 'Most of us walk around barefoot now, whereas we used to have plastic bags on our feet, so I don't think it can tell the difference.'

'What about touch, then? What about that sense?'

We stood there silently for a minute. That did seem to be all that was left.

Kate opened her mouth for a second, and then closed it. She left her tongue partially out, though.

'What is it?' I said.

'Oh no, it's nothing,' she said.

'Is it?'

'Well . . . maybe it's weight,' she said. 'I've just always thought it could tell if we were on here or not by the changes in the feeling. Like if a fly lands on you, you know? You know he's there if he moves or tickles, but he's so light that when he flies off you can't really tell. But if a fish lands on you you know straight away, don't you? Not because it's moving, or because it smells, or because it's making a noise, or because you're tasting it . . . but because it's heavier than a fly.'

'Let us pray,' said Carol.

We put our hands together, and some people bowed their heads.

'Let us pray for the five brave, unfortunate souls who died today. Let them rest, Lord. Let them truly find rest, as sailors on the sea did in the past. We remember them today, and always, for their bravery, and their spirit.'

133

We stood there, with the wind sighing above us and the gentle slap of the waves all around. Nobody was crying now. I think we had all exhausted our tears. Instead, our sadness was turning to anger, and to thoughts of revenge.

'And let us pray for us all,' added Soldier John. 'Let us pray for an end.'

And even as we stood there remembering, beneath us there were new, darker shapes in the jelly. Deep down, so that you couldn't be sure, and so that you couldn't clearly see. But if you walked back, and then forth again, and squinted, and let your eyes refocus, then there were what could have been limbs. And what could have been heads, and empty, lifeless faces.

19

James stood throwing the rugby ball up and down, and up and down, in the space between the Big House and our cooking fire. Around him, those people who weren't inside dejectedly trying to sleep, were sitting down, dejectedly trying to get through another day. He'd been throwing the ball for several minutes now, and every time he missed and it dropped on the mesoglea, a few people jumped. The padding of that bouncing plastic was the only noise other than the wind against the water and the gently splashing tentacles.

James's face was still pale and his lips were squeezed tightly together in a thin line beneath his beard. He had been staring straight ahead towards the opposite side of the Jellyfish, but then he suddenly seemed to come out of his daydream, and turned towards the people clustered around the Big House. I saw him give a weak smile to himself.

'Whoop whoop!' he shouted, the sudden noise making a few people jump again. 'It's time for Jellyfish Rugby!

'Come on. It's time for a game! he shouted again. 'Jellyfish Rugby!'

'It's time for nothing. It's time to smash in your ugly tentacle face,' said Lana. A few people hunched over even more.

'Harsh, Lana,' he said. 'But fine, you can be on the other team, if you want.'

'Bog off. I'm not going to be on any flippin' Jellyfish Rugby team. I'm not doing anything that involves . . . doing anything.' She gave a grimace to make it absolutely clear how disgusted she was at the prospect.

'Well what do you plan to do today, then?' he said.

'I want to have a sulk, I want to sit here quietly, and I want to avoid dying for a little bit longer, thanks.'

'Wise move,' said James. 'But I think the best thing to do to avoid dying is to behave in the way we normally do. Until yesterday, nobody had died. Yesterday was when we did something different. So I also don't want to die. So I'm going to play rugby. Now, who's in? Anybody who doesn't want to die can be on my team.'

He stood there grinning, looking deliberately smug and annoying. Nobody else smiled exactly, but a few people looked like they were starting to shift out of their misery.

'Those who fear death come to my team. Those who don't, well . . . you can sit around and we'll throw the ball at your heads.'

'What the hell, James?' said Lana. 'You are being so irritating right now.'

136

'Excellent. Rugby rage. Just psyching out the opponents,' said James.

'James is right,' said Soldier John, coming out of the Big House. He looked tired, and there were more lines around his eyes than normal. 'Everybody stand up, and let's get started. Today we're gonna play rugby – though no scoring. Then we're gonna fish for a while, and then we're gonna 'ave choir practice. We'll reassess the situation and discuss it again tonight.'

'Oh,' said Kate. 'Excuse me, sir. But if we're doing everything as normal, shouldn't me, Lana, James and Martha have school this morning?'

'Ah, yes,' said Dr Jones, standing up whilst Lana narrowed her eyes at Kate. 'I think we'll cancel school for this morning, love. You can have an extra session tomorrow instead.'

'So you're telling us that we have to play rugby, or we'll probably die?' said Lana.

'Umm . . . yes,' said James.

'Well that's a pretty flippin' convenient theory, considering you love rugby and you always want to play it,' said Lana.

James shrugged in a *well, what can I do?* sort of way, but almost all of us remaining people were now standing around by the Big House, and, although reluctant, everybody looked like they were getting ready to play.

'Fine,' said Lana. 'But it's going to be more like a rubbish game of catch rather than rugby, isn't it? If we can't actually score. I want Martha and Kate on my team.'

'Well that sounds like you're planning to do a lot of standing around and chatting rather than playing rugby,' said James.

'No. We can take your side on, whoever's on it, and defeat them,' said Lana. 'If we want.'

'And we can do dancing too,' said Kate. 'We might be better than your side at dancing.'

'No!' said James. 'Rugby is not, not, not about dancing. We need to get started right now. Immediately.'

'Do you remember that dance we made . . . you do the three spins and then you waggle your arms?' said Kate. She demonstrated superbly.

'Oh, the Tentacle Twist!' I reminded her.

'Yes, yes! The Tentacle Twist. Who's going to join me?' A few other people started to join in with her arm movements, and there was some laughter. There's nothing funnier, when you're facing impending death, and standing metres above the putrefying bodies of your old friends, than waving your hands in the air in the pretence of being a jellyfish.

'No. That is absolutely not what I meant,' said James. 'No.'

'Oh, come on, James,' said Kate. 'the Jellyfish can't tell what we're doing. Can't we play rugby *and* do a dance? That way everybody will be happy.'

'No, everybody won't be happy,' said James. 'If you're dancing, then you're not playing rugby properly.'

There were a couple of people who both muttered that neither rugby nor dancing would be enough to make them

138

happy. But then that made lots of other people smile, because they'd both complained about their rubbish existence, something we enjoy doing, and they'd done it at exactly the same time.

We started to scatter across the Jellyfish into the positions we're normally in for rugby. Most of us hadn't been assigned a team yet, so it was obvious that most people didn't really care, but in the centre, by the Big House, James was talking loudly, and gesticulating, still trying to get people enthusiastic and organize them.

Kate did a little dance by herself, spinning around and leaping a few times. She was humming a tune I couldn't quite hear, swaying her head to and fro in time to the music. 'Hey Martha,' she said, 'do you think the Jellyfish can tell whether it's rugby or dancing that we're doing?'

'Martha's doing that not-talking thing she does sometimes,' said Lana. 'She probably won't answer you.' She got herself into position, as though she was now suddenly waiting to catch the ball, and not deliberately being mean.

'Ooo, yeah,' said Kate. 'I suppose she has been quiet. Are you doing OK, Martha?'

'I'm fine thanks, Kate. Don't talk about me as though I'm not here, Lana,' I said.

'Well you need to join in, then, and actually behave like you're here. Because sometimes you're more like a walking tentacle,' said Lana.

I thought that was unfair, but it's hard to complain about

something that doesn't even make sense. I just screwed up my face in her direction, as though I was really confused about what she meant (which I was, to be honest). 'What, are you calling me fast and sticky?' I asked.

'No. Silent and wet.' She looked right at me as she said it, her eyes narrowed, then turned back to look at the ball again. I knew she wasn't interested in the rugby.

I was honestly hurt, not because she was comparing me to a tentacle, which I know is ridiculous, but because she was deliberately trying to offend me. Does that make sense? Even though I knew she was just taking her rage out on me, which is something she does a lot, actually, it was still really hurtful that she did. And I know that makes me a bad person, because I find it funny when she takes her rage out on other people. But it's rubbish when it's me.

'I just don't want to say something when I don't have anything important or useful to say,' I said. I don't know why I go quiet sometimes. It's not on purpose. It's more just that sometimes I don't feel any need to talk.

'Well, if we all stuck to that rule, then nobody would speak at all,' said Lana. 'You're boring when you don't speak, Martha.'

I opened my mouth to reply . . . but then I didn't have anything really good to reply with. So I thought now would be one of those good times to say nothing. And, yeah, I get the irony of that. So I walked off towards the muscle ring.

'Oh, Martha, don't go,' said Kate. 'Lana will say sorry.'

'No, I won't,' Lana said, 'because it's true.' But she said it quietly, because she normally does say sorry eventually.

I gave Kate a quick happy wave to show that I was fine, but I didn't turn round, because I wasn't happy and I did think I was probably going to cry.

As I walked away, my head down, I kept seeing those dark patches beneath the surface of the Jellyfish, and they seemed already smaller; there were parts of them already being digested. We'd been avoiding looking in that direction, and nobody else was standing over at that end. I felt that rush of sadness again, but also fear. And then just loads of tiredness.

I couldn't be properly angry at Lana. Not just because she was right, I suppose: I can be boring a lot of the time. But also because there's something about staring out across the heaving, wide, endless ocean, that makes any argument feel ridiculous and pointless, like you're so insignificant in the world that your petty squabbles don't matter.

20

In the murky light of early evening two people were lying on top of each other grunting and groaning, just twenty metres away from the Big House. Because – like most of us – they both had such matted dirty brown hair, it was impossible to tell who they were, or even if they were male or female. It was impossible to tell what way up they were, or even to tell for definite what they were doing. Inside the Big House, there was only the light from the pitiful fire, so it was also difficult to see who was missing. There're a lot of dark corners in here at night-time and I've never thought about dodgy stuff going on in them, but maybe that's because I've been young. Or stupid.

It's not that we've never had a 'no sex' rule explicitly – or maybe if there has been one, nobody's talked about it in front of us. It's just that nobody . . . well, you know. You wouldn't want to get pregnant. And you wouldn't want everybody to see you having sex, would you?

'Right,' said Soldier John loudly, 'I think we need to start looking at other strategies for tomorrow.'

There were murmurs of agreement from the rest of the room. The murmurs were also loud. Most people had moved so that they had their backs to the door, but even still, you could see them quickly stealing a glance now and again.

James gave a snigger next to me. Kate had covered her mouth with her hand and was looking determinedly ahead.

'I think we should spend at least a couple of hours practising the attack moves that we saw being used on the shore.' Loud murmurs of approval again. 'We'll repair the rope and make a raft out of the remaining pieces of the boat.'

'Yes, yes . . .' People were also talking deliberately quickly to avoid hearing the grunts.

'And then at least we'll be doing something useful, rather than some people I could mention,' said Dr Jones. She made her voice go really loud on the 'some people' bit.

There were a lot of tuts and the vigorous nodding of heads.

'It's the breakdown of society, that's what it is,' she said. 'Everything's going bad.'

'Yes. If everybody can just focus, though,' said Soldier John. He still looked tired, and in the firelight he looked thinner, and less powerful than I remembered. Probably because he was now missing his plastic-bag coat.

'I don't get it,' whispered Lana. 'How did they decide to do it? How do you talk about that?'

'You just ask the person you fancy, I guess,' I whispered back.

'No, I mean, how do you go from not being couply and kissing and stuff, to just suddenly having sex in the open? I feel like they've missed out some stages. Did any of you notice anybody kissing or being couply today?'

We shook our heads. It was a proper mystery. There were a few sort-of couples on board, but they didn't go round humping each other and grunting instead of coming to the evening meetings. I'd never noticed them doing anything except being extra nice to each other.

'Listen to what fun they're having, Martha,' whispered James. He gave me a grin.

'Uggh,' I said.

He laughed. 'They sound like two cows mooing. And what about all that hair? Do you think they're accidently getting each other's hair clumps caught in their mouths?'

'James!'

'Mwh, mwh, mwh.' He pretended to kiss his hand and then lolled his tongue around.

'James!' I said again. Kate and Lana were laughing hysterically, so much so that Kate was struggling to breathe.

'And maybe bits of beard are getting stuck in their teeth. Dirty beard hairs, with old fish scales attached. Yum. Salty. Just imagine, Martha, their hands creeping up underneath their rags . . .'

'Uggggh, stop!' I said.

James was laughing now as well. 'And his tentacle . . . in the muscle ring . . .' He wiped a tear of laughter away.

'No,' I said. 'Please, no! I feel sick.'

'Are you sure you don't fancy joining them? We could find a spot a few metres away. Maybe over by the Small House?' he said. 'Go on, Martha.'

I did a being-sick face.

'Yeah, no, don't worry about it,' said James. 'Seeing that has set me back about ten years. I'm happy to die a virgin now.'

'Really? Are you happy to die?' I said.

He gave a sigh. 'No. Don't remind me. I forgot for a minute there. Not really.'

'Then what are we going to do?' I said. 'We have to try something else to get off this thing.'

Lana and Kate had stopped laughing so much now, though Kate was still hiccoughing. Reminding them about our future deaths was a bit of a mood kill, and we sat for a few minutes thinking, or at least pretending to think. In the centre of the Big House, Soldier John and some of the others had now moved on to talking loudly about combat techniques for killing kriks.

'I think we should say something to Soldier John. There's no point in learning to kill kriks if we're never getting off here,' said Kate.

'There aren't even any on the shore at the moment,' said Lana.

Suddenly there was a particularly loud grunt. A few of the people in front of us flinched, and immediately we four started laughing again.

'Uh, uh!' said James, doing an impression and putting his arms out as though he was going to grab Lana. She slid backwards to try and get away from him, whilst the four of us laughed even harder. I had to hold on to Kate just to keep myself upright. There were tears rolling down our cheeks, it was so funny.

'Children!' shouted Soldier John suddenly. We all jumped. I took a quick gasp of breath. The funniness went immediately. John's shout makes the walls feel like they're shaking, and makes you feel your blood pulsing so hotly round your skin that it blurs the edges of your vision. The room rustled as everyone turned to stare at us.

'We're not children,' said James.

'You're certainly behaving like children. And you *are* a child, my boy. You are the youngest four on board, and in the old days you'd have just been worrying about exams at your age, and playing computer games. Or doing flute practice.' James frowned and opened his mouth to argue. I nudged him and he shut it again. 'I'm sorry that this has happened to you. But you are here, and you're not dead. You need to be thinking about how to save yourselves . . .'

Soldier John paused for a second. Were we supposed to reply to this, or say something? There was an expectant silence in the room that was uncomfortable, and not just for us. Other people were shuffling awkwardly too. Soldier John never spoke like this.

For a minute, I wasn't sure that he knew how to finish what he was saying, or whether he'd maybe even forgotten that he was speaking. He was no longer really looking at us, but more at the darkness of the walls behind us.

But then he seemed to shake himself out of it. Fiercely, he glanced round the room. 'And there's no reason for behavin' like idiots,' he said. It was exactly the sort of thing he normally said, several times a day, and there was a sigh of relief from all around the room. It wasn't clear if he was still talking to us, to the rest of the people in the room, to the people outside, or whether it was just general life advice. We all looked at each other, but seriously this time, covering up our smiles.

There was another pause in the room, because most people didn't want to risk saying anything. Or maybe because there wasn't much to say. That was the advantage of Dr Jones's evening lectures. They gave you something to do when you couldn't be trying to escape.

And it was into that silence that Old Albert came rushing.

'You'll all want to know this,' he said, as he entered the doorway.

There were quite a few things we wanted to know. You could see that the entire room was shocked. We should have realized it was Old Albert who was missing, because the evening's discussion had been strangely rational. Next to me,

Lana started shaking with silent laughter, so much that there was a ring of wibbling mesoglea all around her. Which was making Kate giggle even more.

'The dirty dog,' whispered James with exaggerated disgust.

'You'll all want to know this,' said Albert again. 'That other boat is here. The yacht.'

21

'**P**ull!' shouted Soldier John. 'Steady now . . . ease her in . . .'

The yacht edged slowly forward, its bow turning to one side.

'Gently, gently . . .'

The boat crept through the mass of tangling tentacles feeling and stroking it.

'Now . . . wait for it . . . wait . . .' Soldier John held his arm up until the bow was just inches from the edge of the creature. 'Now . . . cut!'

With a jagged piece of wood, Dr Jones started to quickly saw through the edge of the mesoglea, leaving a mooring space for the boat. As it came right up, a sudden mass of jelly bubbled out of the creature, gathering round the bow of the boat and pulling it in.

'Get it through that,' said Soldier John. 'Into the cut.'

Both teams pulled hard, guiding the hull through the sticky fluid.

'Now 'old 'er there – 'old. We need a few minutes to make sure it's secure.'

Already the jelly around the bow was starting to change from a viscous, colourless liquid to a translucent solid.

The yacht was around fifteen metres long and it was very damaged, in a much worse state than it had looked from a distance. Along the full length of the deck there ran a mighty crack, and the mast now tilted at a dangerous angle. Right in the centre of the deck was a metre-wide area that was smashed completely, where something had obviously hit it once before.

'OK,' said Soldier John. 'Do I 'ave a volunteer?'

He looked around the crowd and it was one of those 'wobble in time' moments, where a split second seems to last an hour, and an hour seems to last five minutes. I think we all probably felt that excitement and tension and fear and worry. Just climbing on board felt like the possibility of death. But then . . . so did staying put.

'Yes.' Kate stepped forward. 'I'd like to go.'

'Right,' said Soldier John. 'Somebody who's not a child.'

'Oh,' said Kate. 'I can still—'

'If there are no other volunteers then I'll go,' added Soldier John. Kate stepped back again.

Half the people on board put their hands up immediately.

'You,' said Soldier John, pointing to Old Albert. His hand hadn't been up, but I think we all felt it was a good choice.

'What do you want me to do? Up there?' he asked.

'Tell us exactly what's in there, and don't do anything else. Leave everything exactly as it is and don't touch anything.'

Old Albert nodded, though his eyes went all squinty. He put his hands on the bow rail and pulled himself up, heading straight for the hold. He peered in for a few minutes. 'There are dead in here. Two girlies and three men.'

'By "girlies", do you mean they're children? Or are they women?'

Old Albert squinted. 'Women.'

'Thanks,' Soldier John remained expressionless. 'Can you give us more info'mation?'

'They're in a room that's all benches nailed down. But there is a brown carpet and cushions which we could take off.'

'Thanks. Now go into the 'old.'

There were relieved smiles from the crowd now, and a few people raised their eyebrows at the exciting news about the cushions.

'He didn't say if they were wearing clothes. But Old Albert would have mentioned it if they weren't, wouldn't he?' said Lana. 'I want a jumper. I want whatever one of those women is wearing on their tops.'

'I'd love a pair of socks. Do you think there are socks?' said Kate.

'Socks? What about shoes?'

'I like feeling what mood the Jellyfish is in, though,' said Kate. 'I like to feel its vibrations under my feet.'

'I like to be friggin' warm, you idiot,' said Lana.

Old Albert's head appeared back out of the hatch. He was chewing on something.

'What the hell?' muttered James. 'Kate should have gone. You'd never have helped yourself to snacks, would you?'

Kate smiled.

'Yeah, then we'd have had half a bite each of whatever gone-off thing it was,' said Lana. 'Great.'

''Ave you finished?' said Soldier John.

'Yes,' said Old Albert. 'Shall I just chuck the bodies over the side?'

'NO!' shouted everybody.

'What else is there?' said Soldier John.

'There's more cushions and carpet. There's five lifejackets, some empty bottles and cans, some toilet roll—' He was interrupted by loud whoops from the crowd. 'Some string, some books . . .'

There was a sigh from a number of the people on board. Staring Crone clasped her hands to her chest in joy.

'Which books?' shouted somebody.

Old Albert gave a shrug. 'Books. And six spoons, a bottle opener, a tin opener, six forks and six knives.'

'Knives?' Soldier John interrupted. ''ow sharp?'

'Just the normal eating sort. Not for slicing things.'

'What else?'

'Ar . . . that's it.'

Lana rolled her eyes. 'He is so repellent.'

'Mwa, mwa, mwa!' James put his arms out as though he was going to kiss her.

'James, stop. It's not funny,' said Lana.

'It is. Imagine his tongue in your mouth. And seriously, who was it who was actually having real sex with him?' We all recoiled in horror while James laughed.

Old Albert was starting to unload the boat now, and people were surging forward to help. I suspected the cushion covers would be the main attraction, as the jelly surface of the creature was already soft enough for sitting on. But new cloth? For clothes? That'd be something we didn't have.

'What're the bodies like, Albert?' said Soldier John.

'Dead.'

'But 'ow decayed? Right down to the bones?'

'. . . no . . .' Albert's reply was delayed. He didn't look happy about going back to examine the bodies more closely. Especially now that most of the people on board were dividing up the materials, and were no longer watching him. 'The meat is all shrivelled up and dried out. It's still on the bones.'

'The flesh?'

'Aye.'

'If we take off their clothes, will the bodies fall apart?'

'Maybe. Maybe not.'

'Do not remove their clothes, then.'

It didn't take long to divide up the objects that had been in the hold. Anything sharp would be kept in the Big House, probably for gutting fish, and the people who needed a new addition to their wardrobe were obvious. Some were already wearing their 'cushion cover jumpers', or were busy ripping seams apart to create head and arm holes.

'Throw one of the bodies over the side,' said Soldier John. 'As far past the tentacles as you can, but where we can watch what happens.'

Old Albert disappeared for a minute, and then re-emerged, staggering, and carrying one of the women. Her hair still hung in a tight, neat ponytail, and it brushed loosely against the side of Old Albert's leg as he clambered up to the rail of the boat. Her shrunken, wasted legs and arms were unnaturally yellow, whether from the effects of the sun, or some kind of dye in the carpet. Her limbs protruded awkwardly, stuck now in the angle in which she'd been lying. She did still look human, but it was more like the impression of being human, like a scarecrow, or a cardboard cut-out of a woman.

She was almost past the stage of being repulsive, and more into the stage where it would be OK to put her in a museum like they did sometimes in the olden days. And I think people would have been interested because I know I found it difficult to stop myself from staring at her. I did feel sad, and wondered what sort of person she'd been. But I sort of had to force myself to feel that, because she just didn't look like a real person any more.

'Wait!' Carol shouted. 'A prayer!'

She muttered a few quiet words while Old Albert rested the

body on the railings. Even he looked unusually respectful, and not too obviously impatient.

But when it was over, he tipped the body straight into the sea towards the stern of the boat. She bobbed immediately upwards, resting on the swarming, writhing short tentacles. They seethed below her, stroking and feeling in blubbering waves. Then with a hiss, they seemed to relax, releasing her, and disappearing again, far below the surface.

We watched, breathless, as she slowly floated out away from the Jellyfish. One of the longer tentacles emerged, slowly stroking and touching her. It stuck to her for a few seconds, lifting her by her torso, but then it, too, let go and disappeared back beneath the surface.

'What do you think?' said James.

'I think it can tell that she's human,' I said. 'But I think she's too dead. I don't think it likes her very much.'

Beneath her now, the tentacles had cleared and parted, leaving a channel for her to travel through. They rippled gently behind her, creating small waves which pushed her through, away from the Jellyfish, and out towards the shore.

22

The sun was high overhead, and the wind had stilled so that the sea was mostly calm. Only short, occasional gusts blew across the water, sending gleaming trails of shivering waves towards the shore. It was one of those days where you could see for miles across the endless water between us, and whatever was out there. Apart from the bobbing white of resting seagulls, there was nothing behind us until the blurred line of the horizon.

And the corpse raft was going well.

The large pieces of decking left over from the last smashed boat were making it easy to assemble. Those were being used for the main part, with loads of plastic bottles beneath for buoyancy. Too many people were already involved in trying to build the raft for it to be sensible. Most of them were doing more standing around poking and commenting than actual building, and there were a lot of raised voices – not of arguing, more of everybody trying to make sure that their voice was heard. Definitely one or two people alone could have done it more quickly – but there was a lot of nervous energy on board, and I think people needed to feel that they were involved in doing something.

Over at the Big House another, smaller group was repairing the plastic-bag rope. Another big pile of sea rubbish had been found towards the edge of the muscle ring this morning, so the rope was now almost as long as it had been . . . a few days ago. All the knots were just methodically being checked to ensure that it was as sturdy as possible.

'What shall we do?' I asked.

'I have no clue,' said James. 'I might go and dig a hole and wee in it. Want to help?'

I shrugged. It was better than nothing.

Dr Jones strode towards us purposefully.

'Uh oh,' said James. 'Don't make eye contact. It looks like she's about to give us some maths to do.' He picked up a piece of plastic and started fiddling with it urgently, a frown on his face as though he was deep in concentration and doing something of vital importance.

'You four can have one between you.' Dr Jones held out a plain knife, with a smooth metal handle and a serrated blade.

'Oh . . .' said Kate, taking it. 'Thanks very much.' She clasped it uncertainly by the very tip of the handle. 'What shall we do with this?' she said, turning to us.

James grinned at me, dropping the plastic again.

'I've got a few ideas,' said Lana.

Kate slowly moved the knife round behind her back, keeping her eyes on Lana as she did so.

'No! I'm not going to stab you with it. Why would you think that?'

'I didn't think that,' said Kate. 'I'd just like to hear your ideas before I give it to you.' She smiled at Lana.

James sniggered. 'This is going to be brilliant,' he whispered to me.

'We should cut our hair – all the salty, knotted bits that hurt and scratch when you lie down on them. There's no way we'll get a brush through them when we get on shore, so I think we should cut them off now. Plus, they might smell a bit,' said Lana.

'They do smell. And not just a bit,' said James.

'The knife's too blunt for that,' said Kate.

'I'm going to give it a go anyway,' said Lana, grabbing the knife from her. 'But I'm going to try it on you first. OK?' She reached out for Kate's hair without waiting for a reply. 'Sit down.'

'Oh . . . OK,' said Kate, kneeling down on the mesoglea.

Lana grabbed one of Kate's matted clumps of hair and started sawing and sawing on those strands near Kate's scalp that were still loose. First one strand and then the others were released, until Kate was left wincing, and with one short fuzzy patch near her forehead. Lana held up a stiff lock in triumph. 'Look! Now you do me. All of my hair.'

'But you said . . . ?'

158

'Just do it, Kate. Stand up and stop whinging.'

They swapped places, with Kate taking the knife.

'This is going to be amazing,' I said to James. 'I mean, it's going to take a while, but it'll be great to sleep without the lumpy bits in my hair. It'll maybe be cold in the winter, though.'

'We need to be gone before the winter,' said James. 'You know that.'

I shrugged again in reply, but I didn't look at him. It was still best not to talk about it. It gave me a sore, tight feeling in my throat every time I thought about what was going to . . . you know . . . happen . . .

'Do you think you could try my beard?' he said. 'I imagine I'll be really good looking with sexy stubble, right?' He stroked the wispy strands on his face. They did make him look older, like one of the men. But they also hid what he really looked like, and it would be nice to see his face again.

'Aren't you worried I might miss, and accidently slice part of your cheek off?' I said.

'If you do, it'll make me look wizened and dangerous, like a pirate. People will call me Scarface, and I'll start rumours about the battles that I've been in. It's a win-win situation.'

'Come on, Fuzzyface,' I said. 'Those two are definitely going to start bickering, so let's go help with the raft.' Already Lana was muttering something to herself, and Kate had a

159

hard-done-by expression on her face that was ominous.

'Their fighting might be more interesting now they've got a knife,' said James, but he was already edging away from them, so I knew he couldn't be bothered either.

'Shall we strap the corpses on to the sides, or underneath?' This was a design feature of a raft which hadn't been considered before.

Most people were still standing on the edge of the Jellyfish near the boat, but a couple of men were on the deck itself, assembling the raft. 'I think you'll need to put them on the sides,' somebody called up. 'Otherwise it might make the bottom of the raft too uneven. Keep the most crumbly corpse to put over yourself. You don't want to risk bits of the flesh or one of the limbs falling off into the sea.'

Lana gave a grimace. 'Crumbly corpse,' she said. 'Sounds like you.' We took it as a general insult. It wasn't directed at anyone in particular.

With their new, shorn heads, both Kate and Lana looked younger and prettier, but also more vulnerable. Beneath their uniform dirty brown locks, it turned out Lana had soft white-blonde hair which was now almost invisible in the patches where Kate had cut very close to the scalp – particularly in those rare moments when the sun broke brightly through the clouds. Her scalp shone pinkly through her hair stubble, and sores were visible where the dirt and salt had rubbed against her skin.

Kate's hair actually *was* brown. Who knew? It was a deep brown colour, with lighter, golden highlights. And either Lana was better at cutting hair with a blunt table knife, or Kate's hair was thicker. It covered her scalp completely and seemed impossibly glossy and sleek. Her new haircut suited her, emphasising her jawline and dimples – but then, on Kate, the matted dirty hair we'd had for ages had looked good too.

'Attention!' shouted Soldier John, gathering people in. 'To your positions!'

There were four people on board the boat now, with the rest of us scattered along the edge of the creature. Two men cautiously lowered the raft over the side of the boat. Stinky followed, climbing tentatively on top. He had a plastic-bag rope attached round his waist, and he tugged on it several times, checking its strength. 'All good,' he said, giving a double thumbs-up sign and a nervous smile.

'Lie down, Stinky,' said Soldier John. Already the shorter tentacles were swarming around the bottom of the raft. 'Drop the body.'

The largest of the dead bodies was lowered on top of Stinky. He evened it up over himself, ensuring that its arms covered his arms, and its legs were on his legs. He turned his face to one side so that he wasn't looking the corpse in the empty eye sockets, but even still, some of the corpse's hair was spilling on to his face.

'When you're ready, Stinky,' said Soldier John. 'Good

luck, man!'

'Good luck, everybody,' called Stinky, though it was muffled, because of the corpse.

''old the rope,' Soldier John said, more quietly.

At least ten people were holding the rope, which was probably unnecessary, but they all tensed, tightened their grip, and fixed their eyes on Stinky.

'Go!'

Stinky kicked away from the side of the boat. The raft started moving slowly out, over the seething, searching tentacles. The little feelers wriggled beneath the corpses on each side, touching them over and over again, searching and fondling that dry, yellow, dead skin. And the raft kept moving. Outwards and away from us it spun round, with the tentacles bubbling beneath. They started to clear. A pathway opened in front, a way through to the shore.

Then the larger tentacle slipped up and into the air. It was pinkly wet, and the sea water fell off it reluctantly, in thick globules of mucus. My stomach clenched as it reached down and gently stroked the corpse lying on top of Stinky. It slowly caressed the body, feeling up and down the full length of the legs, the torso, the arms, the face. It seemed to pause momentarily on the hair, hovering and pulsating in mid-air above, but then it slid back into the water again.

The raft kept moving outwards. It was through the shorter tentacles now. Nobody spoke. We were all focused on Stinky and the raft. Soldier John signalled for more rope to be released. It eased out. Inch by inch. Carefully, breathlessly, through trembling fingers.

The raft spun again, nothing touching it now, and that little ripple of tentacles behind it started to wave, as though urging it towards the shore. But it came in a sort of groan first, a shift in the mesoglea beneath us, maybe. It felt as though there was a vibration, a gentle buzzing; a stirring, surging, sighing under our feet. Nothing important; nothing to worry about.

And then the larger tentacle rose back up again.

'Get ready,' said Soldier John.

It floundered for a second, as though . . . perhaps not? But then the tentacle muscles tensed.

'Pull him back,' shouted Soldier John. 'Now.'

The team pulled sharply, heaving Stinky back just before the tentacle made impact with the raft.

'Pull!'

There was a mighty smash as the tentacle splintered the raft. The corpse collapsed under the weight, dividing and separating into parts.

White mucus started leaking out from the edge of the Jellyfish, seeping towards the raft, and the corpses.

'Pull! Everybody! Pull!'

We ran to help, heaving Stinky in. His face was desperate with fear as the mesoglea reformed itself around him.

'Quick. Pull! Pull!'

We pulled him through the mass of viscous liquid which

hauled at him, battling against the creature.

It sucked at him, dragging at his body and arms.

But the rope held, and he emerged, gasping and pale, on to the surface next to us.

23

'*I*t's smell. It can tell because it can smell us.'

'It felt him, though, it was definitely touching Stinky to check if he was there. I think it can tell the difference between the dead bodies and live bodies. Stinky's softer. So it's feel.'

'It's definitely feel.'

'So if we disguise ourselves more with the corpses and put them over us completely, that should do the trick?'

'No, I don't think so,' said Kate quietly. But I don't mean she said it quietly so that everyone would listen. I mean, she said it so quietly that only we could hear. There was a general ruckus on board, with loads of shouting and sobbing and helpful suggestions. Nobody was listening. Kate would never join in with all that shouting.

'What, Kate?' I whispered.

'It's weight. It's not the senses at all. It can tell because the weight changes.'

'Why do you think that?' I whispered back. 'Are you sure?'

'It can feel us, though,' said James. 'It definitely can.'

'Yes,' I said, 'but is it us it's feeling, or just the weight of us? I mean, it can feel us when we all go to one side and tip it over with our weight, but can it feel us moving around and stuff? I don't know if it can.'

We were silent for a bit, while everybody continued talking around us. Near the edge of the Jellyfish, Stinky was still sitting where the tentacle had dropped him. His shoulders were shaking like he was sobbing, but his eyes were wide open and tearless, his face expressionless.

'I don't care,' said Lana suddenly. 'I really don't friggin' care. Does it matter if it's weight or feel or if it's got eyes or whatever? Does it matter if it's even friggin' just tracking our movements by secretly licking our feet every time we walk around? If we don't keep trying to escape, then it's going to eat us anyway.'

'Do you think it would eat the corpses instead of us, if we pull them on board?' I asked.

Right now, the corpses were still attached to the disintegrated raft, and were bobbing up and down in the wake of the still-agitated tentacles. The Jellyfish didn't seem to be paying particular attention to them, other than to push them from side to side occasionally.

'What, delay it from starting on us?' said James. 'How long do you think those . . . bodies . . . would keep it going for, exactly?'

'I don't know if it would even eat them,' I said. 'I mean,

166

they don't look great.' They looked pretty disgusting, actually, particularly the corpse which was now floating around head-less, and with a missing arm, having been smashed by the giant tentacle. 'It's just . . . well, we eat dried fish, don't we?'

'Oh my god . . .' said Lana. She blew air into her cheeks, then puffed it out slowly.

I went on. 'So I don't see why the Jellyfish wouldn't eat dried humans?'

'A stronger flavour and a meatier texture?' said James, with an exaggerated lick of his lips.

'James, NO!' I said. 'Those bodies were people once. Bit of respect.'

'Yummmm . . . chewy,' he said.

The shouting had settled. Some people were still having a little cry, but quietly, not wanting attention. Others were talk-ing about how well we'd done in getting Stinky away in time.

'I think we should swap the bodies,' said Kate. And she said it quietly again, like she didn't really want even us to hear.

'Swap the bodies?' I said.

'Swap them for us,' she said.

Having just seen Stinky almost get battered to death, trying anything involving those corpses, or even getting close to them, seemed like a very bad idea. 'Explain,' I said.

Kate's cheeks and neck were flushed and blotchy red, and her voice wobbled with the struggle of what she was trying to say. 'Well, if it can tell where we are because of our weight, then the Jellyfish hasn't weighed them yet, because they haven't been on board, so it doesn't really know they're here, I don't think? So if we can get them on board at the same time as we get four people off, then it might not realize those four people have gone.'

'Wait,'said Lana. 'No . . . that's literally the first intelligent thing you've said in your entire time here. Because that would also work if it's tasting us, smelling us and touching us too, wouldn't it? Because we'd be still swapping humans for humans.' Her eyes went wide with excitement. 'So everything that everybody's arguing about now is completely pointless bollocks, because we've got a solution.'

'Well, we've got to get them, then,' said James, standing up quickly. The bodies hadn't moved much, but they were slightly further away from us than they'd been five minutes ago. They were slowly drifting towards the shore. 'Come on. Quick!'

He ran to Stinky and started untying the rope from around his waist. Stinky looked round in confusion for a minute, but then lifted up his arms to let James remove the taut plastic.

'Hey,' Lana stood up, and waved her arms around to show everybody she wanted them to listen. She didn't really need to do that, because most people were quiet now anyway, and everybody'd turned to her the minute she'd spoken, but I think she was really excited.

'Hey! We're going to swap those rotting dead bodies, for four of us. It's Kate's idea. Kate, you say it.'

'I might be wrong, though,' said Kate.

'You might also be right,' said Soldier John. 'So tell us this plan.'

Kate paused uncertainly, silenced again by all the expectant faces. Beneath us, there was another little rippling vibration. It was the sort we'd have ignored before, but now I could feel that tightening dryness in my throat again. James was already pulling at the rope and dragging the raft closer, the corpses underneath it undulating delicately on the short tentacles flickering in the water. Suddenly the need to get off the Jellyfish was overwhelming. My whole body trembled with the desire to just jump into the water and swim.

'We need to get those bodies up on to the boat,' I said. 'And then we need to swap them for four of us, so that there are four corpses here, on the Jellyfish surface, and four people on the boat. Then the boat can sail away to shore, and the four people can save everybody else by doing really good things when they get there.'

My plan was a little vague on the details, but nobody questioned me on those. The beginning part was clear.

'Those bodies don't weigh as much as four people,' said Soldier John. 'They've lost their moisture. They're much lighter. I think three people at the most. Stinky?'

Stinky nodded in agreement.

'But they'd weigh the same as four smaller people, maybe,' I said.

'Small people, like children,' added James. He sort of

169

scrunched his head into his shoulders as he said that, and hunched over to make himself look shorter. I had to look away then because it was making me laugh; James is as tall and strong as most of the men now, and would never normally call himself a child.

'Three adults,' said Soldier John. 'Not children.'

Two people were already on the boat, pulling up the raft. Somebody else was poking a piece of driftwood at the dismembered torso still bobbing around in the water.

'Who's goin'?' said Soldier John. 'Volunteers?'

Kate put up her hand and so did James. Then so did everyone else.

'No children,' said Soldier John again. 'You, Dr Jones; you, Stinky; and I'll go too.'

'But it was my idea,' said Kate. Her face and neck had gone all blotchy again, and I could see the tears already starting in her eyes. 'Please can I go? Please?'

'No,' said Soldier John. 'Not 'til we know it's safe.'

'But it was my idea,' said Kate. She bit her lip to stop herself crying, but I could see the tears leaking out anyway.

'You can't go, John,' said Old Albert. 'We need you on here. I'll go instead.'

'Good offer, Albert. You can be in charge 'ere on the Jellyfish. We need a man of your calibre . . .'

A few people winced at the idea, and looked at each other in disgust, while Soldier John turned away to give some last-minute commands. Stinky and Dr Jones climbed on board the boat. The first two of the corpses were heaved on to the mesoglea, landing with a wet thump and skidding towards the Big House.

'I'm going,' said Soldier John, turning back to us, 'because this is dangerous. And, because if it works, we'll need somebody who's prepared to return again after reaching the shore.'

Another corpse landed nearby, its head lolling.

'And I will return. If we make it to the shore, I will come back for you.'

24

To survive here you can't think too much about reality. And maybe that's OK, because for the past few years, reality hasn't thought too much about us either. Maybe you can go on for a time ignoring life, and the world, and how things really are. But at some point reality does hit you, with its many tentacled, dripping, mucus-y, monstrous arms, whether you're paying attention to it or not.

There was too much reality now. Too much.

Next to us, on the mesoglea, there was that pile of bodies. They looked even worse now, dripping and wrinkled with saturated water where they'd been submerged, but wizened and leathery in the parts that had stayed dry. You could see where the crispy flaps of dried flesh were starting to peel away from the bone in that way that they do, particularly on the scalp. The knowledge that we were now sharing our living space with them was not a pleasant thought.

Even so, it was hard not to notice that the corpses were better dressed than us, and had much nicer hair. The Jellyfish people looked dirty, cold, ragged, sore and . . . just hopeless. They looked small too. I get that I've grown bigger since I've been stuck on here, I do know that. But when you have to think about the world out there, and then you compare it with the world on board this floating bogey . . . well, you know.

Everything out there's just a lot bigger than us.

From the deck of the boat Soldier John held up his hand. 'I'll come back,' he said again. 'If this works, I'll come back for you all. If it doesn't work, then . . . keep trying. Something's going to work. Somehow you're going to get off this thing. Good luck to you all.'

He looked at Old Albert and gave him a nod. Old Albert and a few of the others started to push the boat away. Beneath them, James cut away at the jelly which was clasping the bow to its mooring. With a final glooping suck, the mesoglea released and the boat was free. Giving it a hard shove, Old Albert and his team moved away from the edge of the Jellyfish, and returned to sit with us, near the Big House.

The force of the shove propelled the boat steadily outwards towards the shore for a couple of minutes, giving it momentum until it was about halfway through the tentacles, but then it slowed quickly to a mere bobbing drift. On the deck Soldier John, Stinky and Dr Jones crouched, motionless, each staring nervously at the water below them.

We couldn't see what they could see, but to us the tentacles seemed barely interested in the boat. The shorter fronds

173

stroked it half-heartedly as it passed over them, like they do with driftwood and other debris, and the longer tentacles almost ignored it completely, pausing only to give it a passing feel as they flailed back and forth in their ordinary fashion.

I moved my feet slowly, sinking them into the mesoglea and trying to feel if there was anything different, if the Jellyfish could tell. But there was nothing. There was that gentle, calm, humming motion within the jelly, and the soft, occasional surges as bigger waves hit.

Next to me, Kate gave a couple of sniffs, then wiped her nose on her arm. She pulled her knees up and rested her forehead on them.

'Should we do something? Something distracting?' I said it loud enough for everybody to hear, but also not that loud, because I didn't know whether it was best to be quiet, or whether we should be making noise.

None of the adults moved or responded. Some people were watching the boat intently, but others were just staring into the distance or, like Kate, had their eyes shut altogether.

'We've still got this knife,' said James. 'Shall I cut your hair?'

'I suppose so.'

The boat was already at the stage now where we wouldn't be able to save its passengers if the tentacles decided to hit it. If the Jellyfish chose to just lift Soldier John and the others out, whipping them back on board with us, then that would be fine of course. But I didn't think that was the way the creature was working any more. I didn't think it would just

174

kindly prevent them leaving, in its old, annoying way; I was fairly sure it would do something else, something that meant more dark shapes beneath us in that jelly.

For a minute I wondered why there were no kriks visible, and exactly where they went when they left the shore. The thought made my stomach clench, which added to the tightness in my throat and the tense beating in my forehead.

'What sort of style would you like?' said James.

'What sort of thing can you do?'

'Beautiful ringlets, carefully blow-dried and shampooed in a scented shop with soft music playing and a cup of tea. I could also dye it, perhaps with little strips of different colours and then some ribbons and stuff in it. And maybe glitter?'

The first of the locks fell on the mesoglea next to me. It was plaited at the bottom, from a long-ago attempt by Dr Jones to try and keep us looking neat. But the different strands in the plait had become so encrusted with salt and dirt that they had almost solidified, into something hard and spikey and impossible to separate.

'Just shut up and cut,' I said.

'That sounds vile, anyway,' said Lana. 'You've never been into a women's hair salon, have you?'

'Nope. And sadly now, because of the apocalypse, I'll never be able to.' James gave a loud, fake-sad sigh, while another of my crusty pieces of hair fell.

'I like my hair,' he said. 'I imagine it's cool and good-looking.'

175

Me and Lana gave a loud laugh. I thought Kate gave a snort too, but it could also have been a cry-laugh.

'You can imagine that if you want, but it isn't what you look like,' said Lana.

'*You* do look good,' I said. Lana raised her eyebrows at me. 'I'm just being nice, Lana,' I said to her, 'but I think you might feel better if you cut them off, James.'

Another matted clump of hair fell. The air felt weirdly cool already against part of my head.

On the boat, nothing had changed. Soldier John, Stinky and Dr Jones still knelt, staring anxiously at the water. They were moving their arms and heads now, but their legs remained fixed rigidly. There was a muttering from the Jelly-fish people.

Beneath us, there came a low, rumbling vibration. James paused in his hair-sawing, and Kate looked up. I think we all tensed, and I'm not sure I remembered to breathe. The tentacles were still swishing and waggling back and forth, to and fro, gently.

'It must just be settling,' I said.

'Yeah,' said Lana.

'It's checking we're still here,' said Kate. 'That's why it does that. That ripple, every so often.' She kept her eyes fixed on the boat, which was still drifting slowly away. It was nearing the edge of the shorter tentacles now, to that calm patch of water above where the longer tentacles hide.

'If that's what it's doing,' I said, 'then we've passed,

haven't we?'

'Yes,' said Kate. 'They're going to do it. They're going to get to shore.'

'Bollocks are they,' said Lana.

Kate shrugged.

The boat was floating painfully slowly now, and seemed to be barely making any progress at all. In the relative calm of the breeze, it was bobbing gently up and down on the little, flickering waves. It was only the darker mass of the shorter tentacles near us which gave any gauge of the boat's movement at all. The colour of the water there was different from the rest of the sea: a deeper green. You could see that the boat was first one metre, and then two metres away from that terrible darkness.

The three on board the boat didn't seem to share Kate's optimism. Even from this distance I could tell that their faces looked white and sick with fear. The lines round Soldier John's eyes and mouth seemed to stand out more sharply than they did normally, giving his face a tragic, worried expression that he didn't have when you were close up. The low-level chatting from the Jellyfish people had also mostly stopped now; people had run out of things to say. They were all now staring straight ahead at the boat, some holding hands in silent prayer, and all with pursed, anxious lips or tensed, hunched shoulders.

For a few minutes, nobody spoke. None of us at all. James's hands continued to move slowly over my head, and he was, perhaps, the only one not focusing just on the boat. But even he wasn't saying anything.

And then it happened. Slowly, Soldier John stood up. He looked over the side for a couple of minutes, before reaching to the middle of the deck and grabbing a plank. Tentatively, he slid the plank into the water, leaving it there to trail in the water, as though just another piece of driftwood. And then he pulled on the plank, using it as an oar.

Nothing.

He pulled again. On the other side of the deck Dr Jones picked up her plank.

'They really have done it,' said Lana. 'They've really done it!'

Beneath us, there came the rippling vibration.

The two started to pull, in unison, propelling the boat forward.

There was another vibration. Two of the longer tentacles lifted out of the water, their muscles tight and ready, but they merely swung around in the air for a couple of seconds, barely even agitated, before slithering back smoothly into the water.

The boat was nearing the submerged houses at the edge of the sea now, and the three passengers were guiding it in, using their planks to pull themselves in between the chimneys and roofs to either side. They were looking down carefully at the water, but we could no longer see whether there was anything to worry about down there.

They pulled to a stop, and Soldier John leapt out on to the shore. He turned towards us, and then all three raised their arms in triumph. They'd done it. We'd done it!

25

Sometimes, when really Big Things happen in your life, you go right the way through all of the emotions – fear, excitement, amazement, happiness, anger, jealousy, nerves – and then completely out the other side so that everything's almost normal. I mean, you're still sitting on a giant killer jellyfish – but apart from that.

'So . . .' I said, and I was the only one saying anything that was a real word, rather than a strange, spluttering, amazed sort of noise. A few people were hugging each other, others were standing with their arms stretched out in awe, and a couple were just rocking. Next to me Kate had her head back on her knees again, hyperventilating, and Lana was making weird wheezing noïses. 'So how long do you think it'll take before they can come and fetch us?'

Actually, no, it wasn't normal. At that point my vision went funny, and things went a bit swimmy for a few minutes. They'd done it. We'd done it! We were going to get off!

The thing that really got me focused again was James

tugging on my hair.

'Sit up, Martha. Stop moving your head around,' he said.

'Yeah,' said Lana, 'You'll look like a complete idiot with your hair half done on one side like that. I will not want to be seen with you.'

'I don't know if I'm ready,' said Kate. 'I can't remember what it's really like out there. Can you?'

'I can remember a lot of the food,' I said. 'But I suppose that doesn't count any more.'

'What do you want to know?' said James.

'What it's like. Anything,' said Kate. 'I just don't think I know any more.'

'You don't,' said Lana. 'But who cares what it's like? It's better than being stuck on this creature.'

'I'm just really scared right now,' said Kate. She started to cry again. Proper, snotty crying.

'Do you know what, Kate?' I said. 'Five minutes ago you were crying because you weren't in that boat getting off, and now you're crying because you might be getting off? I feel like you should make a decision one way or the other.'

She started to laugh, but it was a laugh all mixed up with bubbling snot, so she wiped her nose with her arm again.

'Stop moving, Martha,' said James. 'I swear if you don't have time to do my hair too before that boat comes back for us, then I'm just not going. You'll have to leave me here, on the Jellyfish, wobbling and hairy, while you go off and eat crisps and honey and wear nice clothes on the land. Or whatever.'

181

'OK.'

Dr Jones, Stinky and Soldier John weren't visible on the shore now, but they'd stood talking for a few minutes after they'd arrived, and had then run off in different directions. It didn't look like they were leaving us here. It looked like they had a plan.

On the Jellyfish, people were walking around while Old Albert shouted at them randomly. Staring Crone was staring at the shore, but her presence seemed reassuring now, something normal, and maybe she would say something brilliant again soon. Some people were doing fitness training – though it seemed now like it might be a little late to get fit for fighting kriks on the land. Others were just walking round, restlessly.

'Does anybody need a wee?' said James. 'I'd like to at least try and poison the Jellyfish before we leave.'

'I don't know if that's ever worked much, James,' I said.

'Lana, you'll help me, won't you?'

Lana stood up to go with him.

The surface was quivering with the human energy. But suddenly I felt like Kate. Or, at least, not quite like her, but not excited to be leaving anyway. Suddenly I felt quivery myself, in a different way.

'No, sit down,' I said. 'Come back here.'

James pulled a face, but Lana sat back down immediately. Cutting holes in the Jellyfish and weeing in them is only something she does when there is nothing better to do, or when she's really angry.

'What?'

'Just come in closer, would you?'

They shuffled closer.

'No, I mean, don't make it look like we're plotting.'

'But *are* we plotting, Martha?' said James.

Lana immediately edged forward more, her face gleeful with scandal.

'No. Well . . . yes. What I want to know is, what happens when the boat comes? There are no boats on the shore that can fit us all on properly at the same time . . .'

We all turned and looked at the shore, which was pointless, because we all knew exactly what was out there anyway, and it also made it obvious what we were talking about.

'And they're not going to be able to bring anything on those boats that weighs the same amount as all of us.'

'If we don't get on the first boat, we could just wait until another boat comes back?' said Kate. But even she said it without meaning it. I knew she was just saying the nice words she thought we expected her to say.

Lana screwed her face up immediately. 'They'll let us be first on the boat anyway,' she said. 'You know they will.'

'But what if they don't? What will we do?'

'I don't know, Martha. What would you suggest?' said James.

'I don't know.' I did know, but I didn't want to say it out loud. For a few seconds I went through the scenes in my head, of me stabbing Staring Crone, and Old Albert, and Dr Jones, and everybody, with that blunt knife, before leaping on to a boat and heading for the coast, leaving another pile of fresh bodies behind me on the mesoglea. But it was always an unreal scene, because I couldn't remember what I looked like and, you know, if you're watching yourself doing something in your imagination then it's like you're telling a story about somebody else, and watching the action from a distance. Maybe a better version of yourself? In my head-movie I had tight black trousers and long, flowing, curly blonde hair and a beautiful face. I had no clue what my face really looked like, obviously, but I did know that my hair and rags weren't like that at all.

'Do you think we should wrestle the others to the ground, so we can climb on board?' said James. He looked at me in a more intense way than he normally does, and I couldn't tell what he was thinking: whether he was making fun of me, or whether he was really suggesting it.

'No . . .' I said, making sure I sounded shocked. 'But we can try, if you think it's a good idea?'

'I don't think it's a good idea,' he said.

'I do,' said Lana. 'I think they'll let us anyway. But I'll friggin' stab anybody in the eye who tries to stop me from leaving first.'

'It's coming!' Staring Crone gave a sudden shout.

'What?'

'Do my hair!' said James. 'Quick!' I grabbed the knife and

184

started sawing. A crowd had gathered by Staring Crone.

'Can we do this while we're watching, James?' I said.

'I don't mind not watching,' he said. 'But yes.'

I led him, by the hair, to stand next to the others. Soldier John had chosen one of the best boats, the one we'd always said we'd try, when we'd talked about what we'd do on shore. It was small, but still looked in almost perfect condition, and had a sail which its owners had tied up before leaving it. The sail was, as we'd always hoped, in perfect working order.

Soldier John was making rapid progress towards us, whilst the other two stayed watching on the shore. He arrived just a couple of minutes later, skimming easily over the top of those tentacles. He let down the sail, gliding the last few metres in. 'Don't dock me,' he said, throwing the mooring rope at us. 'Turn the boat round first, so that I'm facing away. I may need to leave quickly.'

We started to push the boat around, as both James and Soldier John held on to the rope. We all wanted to leave quickly too. As the back of the boat touched the side of the creature, and that jelly started to seep out, Soldier John passed down two large, bulky black plastic bags. 'Take these,' he said. 'They've got buckets and some empty bottles inside. We're going to swap them for people by filling them with water to make them heavier.'

There were gasps of amazement. If we'd known this would work, we could have done it ages ago. There had never been any shortage of bottles in the rubbish that got washed up.

'Careful now. You'll have to make sure you do this on my command, so that we can do it at exactly the same time. We think we can take five people this time. We'll take the children, of course, and you.'

He pointed at Staring Crone.

26

Climbing on to that boat is one of the scariest things I've ever done – and I've done a lot of things that sound much braver than that. It just didn't feel like it could be that easy. We'd spent so, so much time thinking about leaving and escaping, surely it couldn't be real now?

There was no way it could be different now.

Soldier John raised his hand, and five people bent over to fill their bottles. Carefully, steadily, they held the full bottles out over the water. 'Martha, are you ready?' he said.

I nodded.

'Now!' he said.

As I stepped on to the boat the bottles were hurriedly brought on board and stacked up in a pile near the Big House. A pile of plastic and water which was supposed to be me. Would the Jellyfish really not be able to tell?

Under my feet the boat felt hard and clumpy, but then also stupidly flimsy. It wasn't moving in the right way; it was on the sea, not part of the sea. It was too inflexible and it felt too vulnerable up there, on top of the waves. Plus, there was a patch of water between the Jellyfish and the boat, and as I had lifted my foot over it, I had seen something slithering beneath. It was uncomfortable knowing that we were now on top of those squirming, snaky pieces of flesh.

'Come up, right into the centre,' said Soldier John in a hushed voice. 'Get under the tarpaulin. Cover yourselves well.'

I squeezed between Lana and James, but Kate was also squeezed in front of us, so that her head was by mine. She was breathing very fast, almost as though she was gulping the air. She had her eyes pressed tightly shut; I thought she might be praying. Lana grabbed my hand, and I reached out for James on my other side. He grabbed my hand too. His hands felt rough, and dry, and warm. The callouses where the skin was peeling off were scratchy – but in a good way, in a way that you wanted to press into your own hand.

The surface of the boat was cold and wet against my fore-head – really hard, again, and too solid. It felt wrong. I took a deep breath, holding the air in my cheeks for a minute before blowing it all out. The hot air bounced back in my face unpleasantly.

'Are you tucked in on your side?' James whispered.

'Yes,' said Lana.

'Enough so that if the tentacles come out . . . the tarpaulin cover won't be pulled off?'

'Yes,' said Lana.

Kate's breathing was slowing.

'I wish they'd flippin' hurry up,' said Lana.

'Yeah,' said James. 'If we're going to die, I'd rather get that out of the way quickly. All this waiting around is really annoying.'

We all started to laugh, which made it funnier than it was, because we could all feel each other's shoulders shaking. And then it was funnier because we were all trying to keep quiet.

'Kate, if you snot in my face, I'll tip you overboard,' said Lana. 'Stop laughing.'

'We could put her on top of the tarpaulin to weigh it down,' I suggested.

'I feel like I might fart.'

'James!' I said.

'OK, quiet in there, please,' said Soldier John. 'We're about to go. Complete silence.'

Both Lana and James squeezed my hand.

'If you fart, you die,' muttered Lana.

'Not if the Jellyfish gets me first!'

We all started to shake with silent laughter again. I definitely heard Kate bubbling with snot.

'Good luck, kids!'

'Good luck!'

'We love you!'

There were a few last shouts from the Jellyfish people and then, with a jolting push, the boat started to move. Beneath us, everything suddenly felt smoother – I think that's the way to describe it. We were no longer rocking to and fro on those little, irritating waves; instead, it was like we were gliding. There was a harsh swishing sound, like the wind just before a storm.

Then there was a juddering, and we seemed to change direction. A spray of water showered on to the tarpaulin, and also under it, so that little trickles ran down to my forehead and hair. Kate gave a whimper, and we started to slide to one side, the boat tilting.

'It's OK,' whispered James, 'It's OK.' I liked hearing him saying it, though even at the time I knew he didn't know if it was OK or not. How long had it been? Two minutes? Ten? Or only two seconds? Lana squeezed my hand even harder, her nails digging into me.

That juddering came again, and we changed direction once more.

'OK, kids,' said Soldier John loudly. 'You can get up now.'

James whipped the tarpaulin off and knelt up quickly. Me and Lana were slower, unfurling ourselves uncertainly from the protection of the deck and still holding hands. There, behind us, was the Jellyfish. The people on board were waving madly to us, but the noise of the wind in the sails and the water against the hull meant we couldn't hear them shouting. I looked for a sign of those deathly, angry tentacles, but there was nothing. They were still waggling back and forth peacefully in the sea. It couldn't be this easy. Could it?

Kate reached out her hand and I clasped hers too, each

of us kneeling silently as we came closer, and closer, to the shore.

The tarmac in front of the row of houses was covered with crispy seaweed and dried debris from the sea. We'd been able to see the shifting sand which covered it in patches, until the wind blew it away, but we hadn't been able to see that it was cracked, warped, and bending slowly towards the sea. Some of the cracks were larger, and filled with water from the high tides. Even from here I could see that they were like the rock pools I remembered from the old days, full of the gently swaying fronds of red and green seaweed. I wondered if they also had the small, darting fish and the scuttling crabs.

The row of houses behind stood silently with their decaying exteriors, peeling paint, and dark windows. Although they looked much as I had imagined them, closer up it was hard to avoid the feeling of life, of being watched, and the ghostly remnants of a mysterious society. The windows stared, gaping tears in the face of the grey pebbledash house fronts. The glass was broken in most of them now, jagged splinters slowly eating and shredding the few tattered pieces of curtain which still hung limply from the window frames. There was nothing moving up there, but I didn't like the feeling there could be hidden things behind those walls. Where had those kriks gone?

'We're gonna 'ave to let down the sail now,' said Soldier John. ''Elp me, James.'

Beneath us were dark shapes patterned in straight,

organized lines in the water.

'Were those houses too?' said Kate.

'Yes,' said Soldier John. 'Grab an oar each and get ready to push us away from them if we get too close.'

'How far out do the underwater houses go?' Kate asked.

'And could we still go into them?' said James. 'Would we find countless treasures in there that have been concealed from mankind for decades?'

'Only a couple of streets were covered, I think. Push away there.'

There was a shove from James and Soldier John's side of the boat, which angled our side towards the houses. We put our oars out, ready to push away from their walls.

'And I wouldn't 'ave thought there'd be any treasure. Just a load of old junk. Sea levels didn't rise suddenly, remember. People 'ad time to get the good stuff out.'

'But could we go round them if we wanted to? When the tide is out further?' asked James.

I didn't like the look of them at all. I didn't like the idea that people had once lived in these hidden, empty places. Nothing good was down there now. From the few exposed walls and chimneys, the houses looked like resting places for crabs, and seaweed, and mussels. They had been taken back by the sea.

'More carefully on that side,' said Soldier John. 'Lever the oars against the walls to push us forward. An' you can go round those 'ouses if you want, James, but you'll be doin' it by yourself.'

'Hullo!' called Dr Jones from the shore. 'Throw me the rope.'

Lana threw, and the rope landed wetly in the water in front of us.

'Again.'

There was a shoal of fish in the house we were passing now, following each other in one of those twisting, arcing fish dances. For a minute I thought that they must have got trapped in there during the highest point of the tide and I almost said something beautiful and profound about them being like the reverse of us: sea creatures trapped by mankind. But then I remembered that houses have doors and windows which the fish could swim in and out of if they wanted to, so it was good that I didn't mention it.

Dr Jones and Stinky pulled on the rope, and we guided ourselves in with the oars.

'That's it,' said Dr Jones. 'That's as far as we can get you. You'll have to walk along the walls.'

She tied the rope loosely round a lamppost.

'Climb down, kids,' said Soldier John. ''Ave you got enough? Any more?'

Stinky held up two black plastic bags. They were even bulkier than last time. It looked like more people would be escaping on Soldier John's next trip.

'Come on,' said James. 'Let's do it!'

We stepped down uncertainly. If the boat surface had felt strange, this was worse. The seaweed on top of the submerged houses was both furry and slippery, but underneath was an uncomfortable hardness. With every step I felt like my foot was stopping too soon, like it should be sinking further into the surface of the wall.

By the time I'd got used to the strangeness of walking on cement and brick instead of mesoglea, I was on the pavement and the others were all standing there in front of me staring at the ground.

'Have . . . we . . . ?' I said.

'Yes!' said Kate. 'We've done it. We've really done it!'

27

or a second the four of us stood, looking at each other, and the ground, and the big world, and where the sea finished – finished! And then we ended up in a giant hug, jumping on the strange, hard floor.

'We're here! We're here!'

I think we'd have carried on jumping and hugging for longer, but James is tall and Lana is short, so we were all jumping at different heights and speeds, and Lana almost jumped into my chin and bashed me. Then we just spent a couple of minutes hugging and laughing breathlessly. One of us would manage to stop laughing, but then that was funny, so we'd be laughing at each other not laughing.

'What shall we do first?' said Lana, pulling away, but still with a giant smile on her face.

'That white house by the cliff,' said Kate. 'I want to go and see what's in there.'

'I want to get some gorgeous clothes,' said Lana. 'And have a bath. Oh, no! Guys! We have to find hair dye like those women.' She looked around at the empty street in front of us, a panicked expression on her face. 'I can't remember what hair dye even looks like. Where would I find some?'

'I'd like a mirror. And some scissors,' said James, raising his eyebrows at me. 'To finish cutting my hair. Since somebody else didn't finish it.'

'A mirror!' said Lana, with a sigh. I wasn't sure I wanted one that badly. Like I said, I'm not always a fan of reality and I wanted to keep on picturing myself with that long, flowing blonde princess hair for a bit longer – and not the scraggy, uneven spikes I probably had instead.

'Food,' said Kate.

'Food!' we all shouted at the same time. This was going to be amazing.

'Children!' called Soldier John. 'You need to start by waving at your friends . . .'

We turned, guiltily, and looked back towards the Jellyfish. As we raised our hands to wave, there was a distant cheer from the people on board, who were further away and smaller now than I had realized.

'. . . and then you need to find as many containers that could carry water as possible. You need to bring 'em 'ere, in a bag, and be ready to give 'em to me when I get back with the next load of people.'

'We've done all of the closest houses,' said Stinky. 'You'll need to try the streets behind this one.'

'If you see any movements from the 'ouses, then run back

here quickly,' added John.

'And do what?' I said. 'Movements from what?'

But already Dr Jones was pushing the boat back away from us, and Soldier John was pulling the sail up. On the deck, those two bulky black bags were sitting, ready for the Jellyfish people to fill them.

'Movements from what?' I said again.

'You know what,' said James. 'But we haven't seen anything here for . . . a while. It's fine.'

Stinky set off at a run up Long Street. Dr Jones quickly followed, but Staring Crone turned, slowly, to face the Jellyfish.

'Come on,' said James. 'Worry about it later, Martha. There's nothing here now.'

We set off. It was strange, at first, to run on the hard tarmac on the ground, but do you know, because your feet don't sink into it you can run further and faster than normal, so it's also easier too? I'd forgotten the smell of land. The air when you breathe is warmer and drier, so it feels full of dust at first. But there are more smells, too; every few metres the air changes so you might get the tang of crisp seaweed in one place, then the warm petrol-y sharpness of the tarmac, then the clean sweetness of leaves. All within seconds! There were trees, and grass, and I wanted to stop and touch them to remind myself what they felt like, but Stinky was urging us on, so I knew it would have to wait.

We veered round the corner. We hadn't been able to see

this road from the Jellyfish, and it arced upwards, towards the cliff, before curving round again behind another row of houses higher up. Through there, up in the gaps between the houses, you could see row upon row upon row of other houses, and buildings and churches and just . . . loads of things. From the Jellyfish, we'd only been able to see the cliffs on either side, and the row of streets between them. The size of the town had been concealed from us and, although I'd known it was bigger than just what we could see, I couldn't possibly have imagined what was before me now. Some of the buildings were so big . . .well, what were they for? Where did it all end?

'Come on, Martha,' called James. 'Hurry up. You can look later.'

He ran into a house with an open red front door and empty glassless windows. The shredded brown remains of curtains swayed loosely from the window frames, but otherwise there was no movement.

'Here.' Stinky came running out of another house, clutching a black plastic bag already bulging with lumps. He put it into the middle of the road. 'Put your containers in here.' He ran back into the house next door.

Dr Jones appeared from the grey building opposite, pausing to put some bottles into the bag before running across the street and in through the open windows of another house.

A bucket and a couple of squashed plastic bottles lay in a

front garden. I picked them up and put them in the bag. Going into any of the buildings felt really scary. Why did they all have broken windows? And why were their doors all open? I didn't like the idea of being stuck in any of them. They all felt too closed in, like the idea of all those walls encircling you suddenly made them feel too small, like they would crush you. I could feel that tight feeling in my throat coming back again at the thought of going inside.

I looked along the street. There was nothing moving at either end, but there were loads of places where things could be hiding, where killers could be waiting. The ground beneath me seemed to give a wobble, as though the pavement was shifting and settling on the ocean waves. I stamped my feet and looked down, but it was still solid, and I was still on dry land.

James came running out of a red door. He threw an armful of bottles into the bag. 'You OK, Martha?'

I shook my head. 'I don't want to go in,' I whispered. 'I don't think I can.'

'Why? What's the problem?'

He peered at me, and I could feel tears starting to come.

'Come on,' he said, grabbing my hand. 'You can freak out later. There's no time now. There's definitely nothing hiding in this house. But there are more bottles, and you can help me get them. We've got to save the others!'

Lana came running out, wearing a red leather jacket, and clutching an armful of bottles. She threw them into the bag, before turning and running back inside again.

'Come on,' said James. 'Let's do this.'

He pulled me through the front gate and in the door. Inside, the floor was softer, with an old, sodden carpet underfoot, and light shone in from windows at the back. I didn't feel trapped, but it didn't feel pleasant either. There were long scratches on the walls, and I wondered what had caused them. Maybe just cracks in the plaster? Or maybe something heavy had been dragged through the house. Maybe that's all it was. And not the claws of kriks.

'It reminds me of the dead people,' I said. 'It's all too empty. Where did everybody go?'

'Under the sea. Now stop mooning and hold out your hands,' he called, coming in from a room at the back. 'Put these in the bag.' He thrust some plastic boxes in my hand, and sped back again to gather more.

Back on the street the first bag was full and another two had appeared. Dr Jones came running out of a building halfway up the street.

'They're coming back,' shouted Stinky. 'Hurry up!'

Dr Jones sprinted into another house, while others ran out of theirs.

'Come on. Take one,' said Stinky, grabbing the largest of the bags. We ran down towards the sea again.

The tide was suddenly much further out now, the walls of the drowned houses exposed and treacherous. This time, Soldier John didn't attempt to guide the boat in at all, instead jamming an oar into the shallow sea bed beneath him and holding the boat there as an anchor. His passengers had to jump down into waist-high water before clambering up on to slippery walls and edging along them to the shore. The water around the boat was laced with bobbing seaweed, and Soldier John eyed it uneasily. There were dark objects visible here and there, which could be stones, or rubbish, or nothing. But they could also be something else.

'I don't think you should go back,' said Dr Jones. 'I think you should leave it until there's more light, and until the tide is higher.'

'No, I can get there and back before dark,' he said.

'But then you'd be leaving just one boatload of people on the Jellyfish for the rest of the night,' she pointed out.

'I'll get them back in the dark,' he said. 'Find me some torches this time.'

Dr Jones nodded.

'You can't go back.' A gravelly voice spoke loudly, and with finality, from behind us on the shore. Staring Crone was gazing out towards the Jellyfish. 'You can't go back,' she repeated. 'The Jellyfish won't let you.'

We followed her eyes out to the creature in the sea. The Jellyfish was now perceptibly closer than it had been a few minutes ago, and its tentacles were waving wildly. You could see the ripples in the mesoglea, and the violence with which the creature was shaking the people still on board. They were a hunched group in the centre, and they were being prodded

201

and stroked by the flailing tentacles with an urgency that couldn't go on much longer. One of the larger tentacles – a great, snaking limb, taller than a tree – lifted lazily out of the water. It paused momentarily in the air, before effortlessly dropping down on to the roof of the Big House with a force that sent the people on board running. The wood from the Big House crumpled like sodden cardboard, as though the years of being exposed to water had left it soft and thin. Or as though nothing built by humans was a match for the monstrous Jellyfish.

Going back now would be suicide. But if we didn't, Old Albert and the people on board would die.

28

We stared out to sea in horror. The Jellyfish was definitely moving closer to shore, but slowly, and it was sitting lower down in the sea than normal.

'What are we going to do?' said Dr Jones.

'We can't leave them there,' said Stinky.

A few of the people who'd just arrived looked at each other then, and I thought maybe they did think we could leave them there. I don't think anybody fancied going to get them.

Soldier John threw the rope to Dr Jones.

'Tie it up,' he said, climbing down into the water. 'I'll never make it through those tentacles right now. We need to plan this.'

'Has anybody got any suggestions?' said Stinky.

'We could push a yacht out to them,' said James. 'Like those other people did to us. A yacht with the containers and bottles already on it though. And we could be in another boat too, further out, not on shore, so that they might actually get the yacht today.'

'Fine,' said Soldier John. 'But nothing is getting past those tentacles without being smashed at the moment.'

The sea around the Jellyfish was a ring of white foaming spray from the seething and swirling limbs. From here we couldn't feel that exuding menace it seemed to pulse with when it was angry, but we could still see the power of the creature. It was still easy to imagine the terror of the people on board.

'Are we safe here?' I asked. For a minute there was no reply, which showed me that the answer was no. 'I mean, not from the kriks. I know we're not safe from them on land. I mean from the Jellyfish. If it could get us when we were on a boat, could it not come on land and get us too? Maybe tonight?'

There was no answer again.

'I want to go into that white house tonight,' said Kate quietly. 'Because it's still got its windows, and its doors. I think it must be a lucky house.'

Kate's white house was right underneath the cliff. It did still look nearly perfect. The paint seemed fresher than on the other houses, and the glass in the windows made it seem less obviously abandoned. Its garden gate was still neatly shut, like its owners might return at any time.

Dr Jones cleared her throat. 'I don't know if the Jellyfish can come out of the sea or not, but I know we haven't seen it leave the sea while we've been on board. I think that means it won't come and get us tonight.'

I could see that my question had unsettled everybody. The thing was, the Jellyfish did look like it was going to do something very soon. It definitely looked angry and powerful.

'Maybe we could go far away from the sea?' said Kate. 'Then I think the Jellyfish definitely couldn't get us.'

'We don't have time,' said James. 'The sun will have set by the time we could get much further inland, and we don't know what it's like out there.'

'We could go to the top of the cliffs and sleep there?' I said.

'There's loads of houses down here,' said Lana. 'With beds.'

'Yes, but there's no way the Jellyfish could get us if we're up on the cliff. The tentacles couldn't reach.'

'But kriks could.'

'There're loads of sheep on the top of the cliffs,' I said. 'Any kriks will get the sheep first, not us.'

'But there aren't any beds up there.'

'There might be.'

'There's definitely beds down here.'

Lana narrowed her eyes at me and put her hands on her hips. Most of the other jellyfish people were standing, looking at the town in awe, or feeling the strangeness of their feet on the hard ground. A few others were staring anxiously at the Jellyfish. Soldier John and Dr Jones clambered noisily over the rocks towards us, their feet crunching on the shells and stones embedded in the seaweed.

'You just don't want to stay down here,' said Lana. 'You're

scared of going into those houses.'

'Yeah, well, do you know what?' I said, 'We've spent the past few years watching kriks crawling in and out of those houses, looking for humans to kill. We've just annoyed the flippin' Jellyfish or kraken or sea monster or whatever it is we've been living on, and I'm worried it might come on shore and kill us. So, yeah, I don't want to sleep in one of those houses.'

'You are such a friggin' drama queen.'

'You basically just want some nice clothes and some hair dye.'

'Yeah, I do.' She continued staring at me angrily.

'I don't know if you've won that argument, Lana,' said James.

Lana shrugged. 'If I can have a pillow, some blankets, some nice clothes and a book, then I'll sleep on top of the stupid cliffs.' She scowled in James's direction too.

'And some food,' added Kate.

'And some food,' agreed Lana.

Already the remaining chunks of glass in the windows nearest us were glinting redly in the setting sun. We wouldn't have long to get up there on to the cliffs, and we wouldn't have long to get in and out of the houses before they became dark and full of corners where mysterious, dangerous things could hide.

'We're going up on the cliffs tonight to sleep,' I said loudly to everybody. 'We can make a plan up there for how we're going to rescue the others.'

Soldier John looked at me strangely as I spoke, but he didn't try to stop me from taking charge. So I continued: 'Everybody get some knives. And other things you could use as weapons. And get some clothes and food, then meet back here in five minutes.'

Everybody scattered into the nearest houses. Lana grabbed Kate's hand and ran for a house with a gaping, door-less entrance. You could see right through this one to the empty windows on its other side. The rooms were light, clear, and empty, but the garden at the back was overgrown with large, shaggy plants and mounds of rubbish. The sea must have made it up through there during storms and left its mark inside.

'Don't copy me, Martha,' said Lana. 'Don't come into my house.'

'Eh . . . what?' I said.

'Just leave her. Come into this one with me,' said James. 'The one we went into before. There's some cans which were full of something, so I didn't take them, but I'm thinking it might be petrol. And there's a whole load of garden tools in the back. Giant forks with spikes on them. Want to come?'

29

It took me a few beautiful seconds to work out where I was the next morning. We were all sleeping close up next to each other as normal, so that wasn't what was different. We were all cold, and the wind was blowing uncomfortably over our heads as normal, so it wasn't that either. It was just the smells, and the sounds, and the stability of the earth that was different . . . and that lingering feeling of being happy. Trust me, that was the main thing. I knew from the second I woke up that I was excited and happy; and I don't remember a time when I'd felt like that before.

There was still a fresh tang of salt on the air, but the wet grass smelt sweet and clean beneath us. It was soft, yes, but you could still feel that unmoving ground through it, solid and still. I could hear the wind catching on leaves and plants as it blew through them, with a crispy rustling and a soft sighing. Plants! There were different birds too. Little ones, brown ones, singing joyously.

It did all feel familiar, like Before, but also brand new and exciting and special. Just being there on that grass was making me think differently, remember more. Things, pictures in my head, half-memories, distant dreams, were starting to become real; twisting and sliding and locking into place, images shifting and ordering themselves into patterns. I knew that if we stayed there for longer, if I let myself think, then I'd remember more about what it was like. Before. And it was a nice feeling, if I allowed it; if I felt safe. I knew the others were thinking it too, because when I sat up, Kate pulled our blanket over her hair like she wanted to go back to sleep, but I could see she was smiling.

Soldier John was already up, and was sitting near the edge of the cliff staring out to sea. When you looked at it from this side, with all of that empty water behind it, the Jellyfish was nothing really. It was a blob of whitish stuff, hardly that different from the grey of the sea and the foamy tips of the waves. It was strange to believe we'd spent so long on it and that it had been our whole world, when there was all that vastness out there.

On board, there was no sign of movement, or of any human life. There was debris, and darker objects laid out on the mesoglea which could be people. But they could also be wet chunks of wood, or clumpy seaweed, or just a shadow. The Jellyfish was calm again now, at least. Its tentacles were barely visible above the water, and the lighter water surrounding its body was the only clue that something lay underneath. The sea was quiet, and the early morning sun glistening off the waves gave a hint of a nice day to come.

'Hey,' I said softly. 'Are they still alive?'

Soldier John turned to me as though startled, but I think he probably knew I was there and just didn't want to talk to me. Soldier John isn't the kind of person you can sneak up on without him knowing. If you sneak up on him, it's because he's letting you.

'Can't be sure,' he said.

'How long have you been watching?' I asked.

'I took over the watch just before dawn.'

'How come it's calm now?'

'Don't know.'

'When did it change?'

'Don't know. It was like this when I took over.'

'Do you think . . . does that make it safe to go out again now?'

Soldier John paused before replying, more softly. 'Don't know.'

'Was there anything out in the town last night?'

'No.' He turned to face the sea again.

Other people had risen as well, and there were another couple of groups sitting, hunched in blankets and quietly talking. A few people had new clothes on and they looked startlingly bright. I'd forgotten about colours on the Jellyfish. I knew them, obviously, and remembered them, but I think they'd got paler and more washed-out in my mind, alongside the memories. When you're used to just seeing greys, whites

210

and browns, you do forget, and the perfection and amaze-ment of a colour like orange, or red, is difficult to describe. You can't just imagine it from just me telling you about it, you have to see it. I just wanted to stare and stare, and I think I could have done that all day, if only I'd felt safer.

The top of the cliff was different from how I'd imagined it when we were looking from the Jellyfish. The picture in my mind was a big grassy hill that maybe led down to a forest, and then endless nature with running deer and foxes and whatever. There was grass, and some sheep, and a few trees, but there was a paved pathway down to the town below, where we could now see the houses and streets more clearly. From here I could see where the town finished – there was more grass and hills on the other side – so I could see that it didn't go on for ever; but it was still a really long way to the other side.

On our hillside, the sheep grazed contentedly, staying well away from us, but also not running off into the town below. Their furry bodies were dirty clouds of clumpy wool, with shaggy wretched bits hanging even over their eyes. On some of them it was definitely hard to tell which end was which. They'd looked much whiter and more attractive from the Jellyfish, but I'd still have loved to go and touch one. When-ever I managed to get close, though, they just sidled casually away down the hill. A few people had muttered bravely last night about catching one and roasting it, but in the end we'd just eaten a few tins of cat food instead. We'd all complained

211

and winced exaggeratedly as we'd taken those first few mouthfuls, but in truth, it was glorious. Delicious meaty pieces which just seemed to fall apart in your mouth, with barely a need to chew. I'd tried to savour each spoonful, but somehow they'd each just slipped down my throat before I felt that I'd tasted them enough. Nobody had complained or winced for long; and most people had scooped out their tins with their fingers afterwards, to make sure they'd got every last speck.

'Get up. Get up!' Soldier John called everybody to attention. 'We need to rescue the others this morning.'

Dr Jones started to pass round some more delicious cat food.

'Are they still alive?' whispered James. He was leaning on a garden fork and clutching a spade in his other hand. Both would make good weapons, but I think it's more that he was proud of his ingenuity in having thought of it first. Other people had got small kitchen knives or cricket bats – nothing that would be useful against kriks really.

'Don't know,' I whispered back. 'Nothing was moving while I was watching.'

I tapped one of our petrol cans gently with my foot. Disappointingly, we weren't the only ones to have got some – and others had remembered matches too. Still, we did have three cans, and that would get a lot of kriks. If we should need to. I looked down at the town again. There was definitely nothing moving down there, but was that suspicious? Was that strange? Should there not be more wildlife than just a few sheep?

'We need to get to safety ourselves too,' said Stinky. 'Where are we going? We can't stay here another night.'

'Leave, then,' said Soldier John.

'No, I didn't mean now. Just . . . we can't stay here.'

'So go.'

'Well, we can leave it a while,' said Stinky. 'But what do you plan to do this morning?'

'I'm going to go out and save them the same way we did yesterday. We've got at least twelve hours of light.'

People looked at each other uncertainly then. It was fairly obvious that going out wasn't a good idea. The Jellyfish might be calm now – but did we really want to make it cross again?

'So you're going to go out,' said Dr Jones. 'Shall we have another group to gather food and water and something to carry it in?'

'You organize that,' said Soldier John. 'And you, you and you,' he pointed at some of the rugby men, 'you go and find a map. Figure out where we can go tonight. We want some-where we can fortify that is inland.'

The men nodded, more confidently than I'd have done if I were them. But then I didn't remember where to get maps from. Maybe that was an easier task than it sounded?

'Shall me and Kate get some clothes, and some shoes for everybody to wear?' said Lana. She tilted her head to one side and frowned to make it look as though this was an important

213

task. She ruined it, though, by grinning at us with excitement.

'Yes, yes,' said Soldier John.

'Sir,' said Kate. 'I don't think you can do the same thing as yesterday.'

He looked at her fiercely, and if it was me, I probably wouldn't have carried on saying anything. Normally Kate wouldn't have continued either – but everything was feeling different now. Everybody was feeling different.

'The way it was yesterday, the Jellyfish knows what you're doing. It won't let you. It'll just smash you up, and them too.'

There was silence then. Because we all knew she was right. Even Soldier John knew she was right.

'I'm prepared to listen to alternative battle plans,' he said. 'What would anybody else suggest?'

Again, there was silence. We'd used up all of our ideas when we were trying to escape from it ourselves. There had been wise talk about helicopters and warships and submarines when we were back on board. Actually, people had spent a lot of time talking about that sort of thing. But now that we were on land, there didn't seem to be any obvious helicopters lying around after all.

The sheep started to walk past in a line from one side of the hill to the other, and most of us turned to watch them as they bleated casually past.

'There's movement,' called somebody excitedly. 'There are still people out there.'

We smiled at each other then, some people in delight and

relief, but others in resignation that we were now going to have to mount a rescue attempt.

'I've got an idea,' I said, and even as I said it I thought it was probably stupid. 'What about the sheep?'

30

*C*atching sheep is harder than you'd think.

'Bloody bollocking crap,' shouted Lana, stomping back up the hill. 'Bog off, then, you stupid fluffballs!'

James rolled his eyes, giving the impression that he could easily have caught them all if it wasn't for everybody else's incompetence. Five sheep went careening down the hillside, chased by Stinky. They were a long way ahead, untroubled by the steep gradient that was slowing him down, and the distance between them widened. They stopped near the bottom for a little nibble at the grass and a relaxed saunter round to the other side.

On the opposite side of the hill, Soldier John was shouting and making a lot of noise. At least one person in his crew seemed to be actually growling, though it might also have been a strange sheep noise. Others were muttering curses at the animals, but everywhere I looked, groups of unconcerned sheep were pausing to eat grass. We hadn't been as successful at herding them as we'd thought we would be. It wasn't clear that anybody had managed to catch one at all. And also, there was a lack of enthusiasm about the whole process which made it seem unlikely we'd ever be successful. A lot of people were waving their arms around while bending over and shouting, but nobody looked exactly like they were planning to hold on to one of them.

'Kate, lie down in that grass,' Lana said, 'and I'll send one in your direction, and then you catch it.'

'Oh,' said Kate. 'I don't know that . . .'

'Shut up and lie down.'

Kate lay down, and Lana ran towards a group of three sheep. As she gained on them one turned its head lazily to look at her. It kept chewing and staring until she was about four metres away when, suddenly, all three sheep turned and ran in Kate's direction. For a second it looked like it might work, but then at the last moment they all swerved towards the road. Once there they slowed, and again started to chew at the weeds spurting from the cracks in the tarmac. One old ewe gave a particularly cheeky bleat in our direction as she strolled past.

'Right. This is rubbish,' said James. 'I'm going to sort this out.' He cracked his knuckles. 'Everybody get back up here,' he called. 'We need a proper plan. This is like rugby, people.'

Soldier John glared at him, but he didn't argue. There were fourteen of us on the hillside, I counted. We had Staring Crone amongst us, so that cut our numbers down to thirteen really, because we couldn't expect any help from her. There were several others who, given the chance, I thought would probably have gone off by now . . . if they'd had any idea where to go. They certainly weren't going to be reliable sheep catchers, anyway.

'Right, right,' said James.

A couple of sheep looked over with mild interest. Their third friend ignored the bother altogether, focusing on the particularly juicy patch of grass on which he was standing, continuing to munch with relish.

'We've got to think about our long-term goal here.'

'Our long-term goal is to get the crap out of here, and find somewhere to live,' said Lana. 'And I swear to bollocks if you even start to give us one of your inspirational speeches, then I'll stab you in the eye with that fork.'

James eyed the large garden fork he was holding. 'And avoiding that will be one of my many long-term goals, Lana,' he said. But I could see he was going to speak more quickly now, and he had lost his noble speech-making face that he sometimes makes. 'I just meant . . . our short-term goal is to catch the sheep, but our long-term goal is to get them on to a boat. Down on the shore. We need to see ourselves as more in those two teams. I'm thinking a pincer movement, and maybe somebody could go get some rope? So we could tie them up.' He said that last bit with assurance, but it didn't stop most of the people listening from either sighing in irritation, or looking at each other in resignation.

'Found a handy rope location, 'ave you?' said Soldier

John. 'Know where large quantities of it are kept, do you? And what are you plannin' to do? Weave a giant net?'

'Well, see now, John, you sound like that's not a serious plan, but honestly, if you just put three people on each piece of rope, and then get them to run towards the sheep . . .'

'Oh, so it's pieces of rope now, is it? We're cuttin' it? So you want us to find scissors? Or is it cuttin' with our teeth we're doin'?'

'That bit shouldn't be too hard. But you're sounding angry, John. What's your plan?'

'Well . . .' Soldier John started waving his hands around a lot, and talking loudly. Some people nodded wisely. Others stared around anxiously, or looked out to sea. I could see James setting up to argue it out. But the sheep were still wandering around unconcernedly, we still hadn't rescued anybody, and we still hadn't even had a nice breakfast.

I turned to Kate and Lana. 'This hillside's got two cliff faces, right? And the sheep won't run away down those?'

'Oh yeah,' said Kate, comprehendingly. 'Shall we just . . .'

'Yeah.' I pointed at the far side of the hillside and waved.

'Just there, down to there?' said Lana.

I nodded.

Dr Jones and some of the others had been following our hand movements. They moved closer.

'And if two more people go down and shut the gates on the houses . . .' I said.

'Then stand on Long Street,' said Kate, finishing.

219

I nodded, Kate nodded, Lana nodded and Dr Jones smiled.

'We're off,' said Dr Jones, grabbing another one of the women. Together they ran down the hill, the few sheep in their way scattering.

'Yes, if we could shear them, that would make a lot of sense,' Stinky was saying knowledgably. Soldier John had his head tilted to one side, and James was now leaning on his fork, which was firmly embedded into the ground. 'It shouldn't be too hard, I'd imagine.'

'No,' said James. 'We just need some scissors. And then we could use the wool for making jumpers afterwards.'

'Shall we go now?' I whispered to Kate and Lana.

'Yeah,' said Lana. 'Definitely. The sooner we can get this animal bullshit out of the way, the sooner I can have a bath.'

'You chase the sheep down, Martha,' said Kate, 'and me and Lana will stand in the way.'

They set off down the hill, grabbing several others, who looked like they had about as much interest in listening to hypothetical sheep-shearing conversations as we did. Down at the bottom of the hill, Dr Jones was shutting all of the garden gates which she passed. I eyed the sheep around me carefully. Most of the herd were over towards the far side of the hill, directly above the cliff face and the houses in the bay below. Four of them seemed to have decided that now was the time to look at me while having a grass snack. They stared in my direction with their blank, unblinking, featureless eyes.

'See, if we flank them on the left,' James was saying, 'then move into formation as we come down the hill . . .'

'Hmmm,' agreed Stinky. 'Should be easy enough to scoop them up . . .'

Down at the bottom of the hill, Lana and the others were now in their places. Lana gave me a wave, and I ran at the largest group of sheep. As usual they continued staring and eating until I was only metres away and then, with a sudden spurt, they bolted down the hill. Other, scattered sheep joined them, in a panicked run towards the bumpy tar-macked path. Shoaling and turning in perfect formation, the herd flowed smoothly over the bumps and dips in the grass, twisting towards Lana and Kate. But as the two girls waved and shouted at them, the sheep turned and ran towards the road instead. They ran down past the houses, stopping at an occasional piece of overhanging vegetation for a nibble, but unable to get into any of the gardens. Kate and Lana followed behind, urging them on to a run. A river of white now, they edged down towards Long Street, where Dr Jones and others were now blocking the top half of the road. The only place for the sheep to go was down towards the sea. They turned the corner and on to the seaweed and sand of the shore. Lana and Kate raised their arms in a silent cheer.

'So, Plan A . . .' Soldier John's voice was booming and clear, as usual. 'But Plans B and C as back-up . . . With one of those, we'll definitely get those sheep.'

31

Sheep wrestling is much easier than you'd think. Particularly if you refuse to have anything to do with it and go off to have breakfast instead.

From the inside of Kate's white house we could still hear the occasional angry shout or burst of swear words from the shore, but I was confident James, Soldier John and Stinky were just putting on a show to let us know they were working really hard.

'All of these,' said Lana, adding another two tin cans to the line we'd got laid out on the table. 'I'm going to eat all of these.'

On the front of each tin there were pictures of what was inside, and they were so beautiful, so colourful, offering such a fantasy of taste. There were these magical little picture details, like a tiny drop of water on a piece of sweetcorn to make it look really fresh, and hazy steam rising up off a plate so that you could think about what the food inside would be like when it was hot. There were also things I don't remember having noticed before, and would have liked to know more about, like why there were other pictures on the cans – there was a lion on one, and a small green man on another. What were those supposed to show?

Lana kept arranging and rearranging the cans, making sure that they were all exactly straight, so I could tell she just wanted to keep on touching them too.

'They're all past their use-by date,' said Dr Jones doubtfully. 'I can try opening them anyway.'

'Yes,' Kate said immediately. 'Yes.'

'I'll not open the dented ones. Or the ones that are rusty. Why don't you start opening the others and smell if they're off?' said Dr Jones.

We looked at each other. Well, me and Lana did. Kate pulled apart a packet of biscuits in the cupboard. The biscuits only half filled the packet, so it looked like they had shrivelled a lot, but Kate bit into one anyway.

'I don't know what "off" smells like,' I said. 'I can't remember.'

Dr Jones snapped back a ring, and pulled the lid off a tin of sweetcorn. We all watched her closely as she did it. I don't think I've ever seen Kate or Lana concentrating so hard on anything before. Lana was frowning, she was thinking so hard.

Outside there was another shout, and Kate peered out of the window. 'They've got five sheep on to the boat now,' she said. 'What are these biscuits supposed to taste like? This one's OK. It's sticky on your tongue. But it's nice.'

She passed us all one.

A loud string of curses came from James just outside the window.

'These are called oatcakes,' said Kate, examining the packet. 'Oh, not a biscuit, then.'

'Yes, still a biscuit, but you put cheese on top of it. This sweetcorn smells fine. Get yourselves a spoon.'

Me and Lana had them already out and in our hands. I'd put one in my pocket, too, for later. I never intended to be parted from a spoon again.

It was glorious, amazing, perfection. The little nuggets of sweetcorn were smooth pockets of joy on my tongue, each one sitting there oozing out a teasing dribble of juicy pleasure that mingled with saliva, before bursting out their mushy sweet centres as I bit into them. I just wanted to chew and chew for ever. But then it was gone. Kate's eyes were wide with shock.

Dr Jones silently handed us a tin each.

So I think I'll just mention now that we were all really anxious about the people left on board the Jellyfish. That is probably true, it's just that I don't remember the feeling exactly, because I remember the amazing food more. Just sitting in that kitchen, when it had been so long since I'd sat in a chair in front of an actual table. Using plates and cutlery. And going upstairs. And touching our feet on carpets and tiles. It was more magical even than I'd remembered, and I felt like I'd like to go for a little lie down – not just because it would be in a bed, with sheets, but because it was all too much. I'd have liked some quiet, away from the others. Just time to think.

'There's a tin of peaches here,' said Dr Jones, 'and this one's got rice pudding in. They both smell fine. Want to try?'

We leant in with our spoons.

Although I could have eaten more tinned things, we managed to make it out of the house and on to the shore with everybody else in time for Soldier John's return with the last of the jellyfish people. I made my face look serious and worried, as though I'd been thinking about getting the rest of the people to safety and away from the mortal peril they'd faced all night. I *had* been thinking about that, so I wasn't making my face into a lie, it's just that the food had been lovely, so it wasn't *all* I'd been thinking about.

Old Albert was sitting right at the front of the boat, and had an oar firmly grasped in his hand ready to steer the boat off any obstacles; it looked like he'd also happily use it as a weapon, with very little provocation. His eyes were particularly starey this morning, and the white flecks of foamy spittle at the corners of his mouth were visible even over his beard. Soldier John was professionally steering the boat in, for this last time, and everybody else was crouching on the deck, dishevelled and shocked. It was obvious why, of course: there weren't as many passengers as we'd been expecting. Some were missing. As they came in closer to shore Soldier John shook his head grimly in response to our questioning looks. Behind them all, the Jellyfish was glinting whitely in the sun, serene and silent. On board, the sheep passengers were huddled to one side, from this distance not obviously disturbed by their adventures.

The cheers were subdued as the boat docked; it still felt like it was all a dream, and that we'd wake up huddled on the floor of the Big House, trying desperately to get warm again, our faces sticky with surface jellyfish slime, and facing a breakfast of raw fish. I don't think anybody wanted to linger here.

'I'm going to go and get some shoes,' said Lana. 'And warm things. Come on, Kate. Meet you back here in a minute.' She nodded at me and James.

Most of the new arrivals were staring at the floor and stamping up and down as we'd all done, but those who'd slept on the hill with us last night seemed suddenly to be running in and out of the closest houses. From all around us people wearing new clothes and shoes were emerging.

'We need to get matches,' I remembered. 'And a bag to put the petrol in, maybe?' It was already getting annoying trying to carry three large cans at the same time.

'Oh, I know where!' James ran into a house two doors away.

Dr Jones was standing next to me, maybe also reluctant to go into the houses, but also maybe just wanting to leave the shore. Wearing proper clothes now, a blue shirt and a pair of white jeans, she looked just like how I remembered people being from Before. Apart from the orange plastic bag still tying back her hair, she didn't look like somebody who'd spent ages stranded in the middle of the sea. She looked beautiful, and younger than I'd always thought, but also more normal.

'Where are we going?' I asked. 'Are we going to find those fighter people?'

'We don't know where they are. They can't be far from here – but I think for now we'll just try and get away from the coast and find somewhere we can fortify.'

'So we'll all stay together?'

'For the time being. I think that would be sensible until we know what we're doing.'

I hadn't thought realistically about what it would be like on land, apart from me dancing around and looking like a film star in the sunshine, that is. It would be strange not living in the same room as all of these people, and not being able to see all of them at all times. Privacy was a weird thought – but would all of them *want* to leave? To separate away from us and maybe live somewhere else? That might not be completely a terrible idea with some people – but it would take some getting used to.

A few others came to join us, everyone gathering as they left the houses. Most of them looked smarter, and healthier, and more attractive just by wearing these new, unfamiliar clothes. It was amazing the difference it made. Stinky, in particular, looked . . . great. His ratty beard was gone and, well, he didn't look clean exactly, but people were happily standing within a metre of him now.

James came striding out, waving a box of matches at me and grinning. He put them in his pocket. Everybody was here now, though Soldier John started pointing at people and counting them.

'Shall we just quickly blow up the Jellyfish before we go?' said James, with a laugh. He pointed his fingers at it in a gun shape. 'Pow, pow!'

We laughed. A few people laughed more than the joke was worth, really snorting for breath and clutching each other to stop themselves falling over, it was so funny. I think they were hysterical really.

'Bollocks,' said Lana, which I think expressed it best. No way were any of us going back out there again.

We turned, as a still-grinning group, and headed towards Long Street. We were going to be safe! And warm! And fed! And live happily ever after in a castle and be beautiful and have it easy and never have to worry again!

But it was then that we saw them. A shadow, moving strangely at the bottom of the road.

'Oh,' said Dr Jones, 'I think . . .'

'NO!' said Soldier John. 'RUN!'

32

'**R**UN!'

Where? We were trapped by the cliffs. I grabbed James's hand and ran towards the white house. Behind us, there was chaos. Shouts, splashes, sounds of panic.

'Kate! Lana!' I screamed. I pulled at Kate's hand as I passed, half-dragging her at first, desperately. But then she ran.

We sped in through the door, pulling it shut behind us.

'The curtains, quick,' I said. 'Quick. Pull them across. Then upstairs.'

I could feel my panic, the cold and warm trickles of terror inside my stomach. Next to me, Kate and Lana were panting and pale, their backs pressed firmly against the door. James peered round the doorway into the front room. He ran to the windows.

'Do the other rooms,' he called, sliding the curtains across, 'nothing's out there yet.'

Lana and Kate were frozen in their fear. The edges of my

eyes were blurred and foggy. I wanted to run, to move, to get away. But there was nowhere to go. And *they* would be faster than us.

I ran into the other room, and pulled the curtains across. Behind me, I could hear the swoosh of the curtains being drawn in the kitchen. There was comfort in the darkness now; we were less exposed, less visible. Hidden.

I scrambled up the stairs, to the top where the others were crouching.

Outside, we could still hear the shouting, the frantic calls. But no screams of pain. And nothing coming closer.

'What shall we do?' I whispered.

'We need to block these stairs off,' said James.

'The beds,' said Lana. 'And the . . . big furniture.'

There was a sudden loud scream outside – closer, a word-less battle cry. Kate winced and grabbed my hand.

'We're trapped,' she said.

'They don't know we're here,' I said. 'We're safe.'

Lana and James started to move a bed, dragging it from a back room into the hallway. They tilted it on one side and pushed it across the top of the stairs, blocking anything that might come up. The scratching of the heavy wood on the carpet was painfully loud to my ears, artificial and squeaky in the silence of the house.

There was no noise from outside now. We all hunched down behind the bed, waiting for a signal, for something from outside. The house felt suddenly oppressive and weighty. I dragged my arm up and bit on it, to mask the sound of my breathing and the dull thud of the blood pumping in my ears. Next to me, I could feel Kate trembling.

'We need to see what's going on,' I whispered, my voice disconnecting from my mind. I hadn't known I was going to speak. I hadn't known I *could*.

'No! They'll see you,' whispered Kate, holding my hand tighter. Her eyes were wide and terrified.

'We need to see. We can't just wait. I'll stay behind the curtain.'

I pulled away and crawled into the front bedroom, with its still-made beds and its dusty musky smell. Here, too, the curtains were drawn, leaving a twilight of false safety. Between the curtains there was a squeezed sliver of light. I could see only ten metres or so through this gap, but I didn't want to risk moving it further. There was the empty front garden, with its weeds poking through the cracks in the paving; and there was the quiet street in front, with its waves of drifting sand, but through the thinned material at the curtain's edge, I could make out blurry movements in the water.

I pulled back from the curtains, so they wouldn't sway when I breathed. 'There's nothing outside us. They don't know we're here.' And I hoped for that moment that maybe it was true. Maybe they hadn't known how many of us there were? Maybe they hadn't seen us running? Maybe we'd been too quick for them?

231

But then there was a jerky movement to the side of the curtain, and I knew that wasn't true.

I hadn't seen one close-up. Even though I knew it wasn't going to be good, I still wanted to see. I eased the curtain an inch to one side, taking a deep breath and holding it while I looked.

The shell of the krik was rough and fibrous, glistening from the water. It was patterned, and not just one colour as it had looked from a distance; whorls of interlocking spirals in orange and white ran up the whole of the exoskeleton, decorating it with intricate markings that had a strange beauty. But the shell looped round and around its body, protecting that hidden flesh inside. Every so often there were tiny gaps, mysterious shadows, where the darkness of the body could maybe be seen if you could get close, but from here they just seemed to offer hints of danger: strange, concealed openings.

The legs and pincers moved constantly, independently of each other, searching and scratching at the tarmac, the garden walls, the air. Looking for something to grab. Almost too perfect in their sharp, smooth covering – just hardness and armour – they were ready to spike, maim, rip, hurt.

I turned away to take a breath and then looked back at the water. A boat with eight people on it came into view. It was the sailing boat we'd used in our escape from the Jellyfish. The passengers were battling to get the sail up, whilst Stinky and one other were using rough planks of wood as oars. They were not going fast, and there were three large kriks in their wake. Stinky was pausing in his rowing to bat at the kriks when they got too close.

'There's three kriks, at least,' I said. 'Eight people are safe.'

'Are they going to come and help us?' said Kate.

'No. I don't think so.'

Before the boat reached the other side of my curtain gap, they'd got the sail up, and were out of range of the kriks. It looked like they were aiming to travel round to the other side of the cliffs. There had been boats there too, I remembered. And the river. They'd probably be somewhere nice in time for lunch. A lovely lunch, without us.

I pulled back again and took another breath. There were others still left on the shore somewhere. Hopefully somewhere.

At the edge of that curtain gap there was movement again, this time accompanied by shouts. Another, slower boat was edging its way past. This one didn't have a sail, and was lower in the water. Soldier John and Old Albert were launching themselves along by pushing poles into the sea bed, and someone else was frantically trying to propel them faster by scooping at the water with what looked like a plastic box.

Soldier John was shouting something frantically. He was shouting it in our direction, but I couldn't hear what it was. He held up six fingers.

'I think there are six kriks,' I whispered to the others. Behind me, I could now hear the slow dragging of more furniture being moved by James and Lana. Kate came and crept in beside me, kneeling down so that she could stare through the curtain too.

'Why didn't we think of escaping into the water?' I asked.

'I'd never have got back into the water,' whispered Kate. 'I'd rather have been eaten.'

'Some people are missing,' I said.

Kate didn't reply. Because, I suppose, we were missing too.

The kriks in the water had now turned away from Stinky's boat towards Soldier John's, and were heading for it fast. The men were pushing the boat away with all their might, and you could see them really straining with every push, but for each burst forward, the waves pulled the boat backwards, against the rocks, and against the walls of the old submerged houses.

The kriks, unaffected by the heaving water, moved steadily forward, four of them, converging on the boat from two different sides. There were two dark orange, smaller kriks, maybe females? One of the kriks was larger, more clawed, its eyes concealed in shadow within the shelled exoskeleton. We couldn't see properly from this angle, but they were big. So much bigger and more powerful than the humans, their muscular exoskeletons pronounced and armoured.

They moved easily through the water, almost gliding over the rocks concealed amongst the sea weed, their pincers raised in attack. Soldier John was shouting desperately, and he and Old Albert pushed forward, through the breaking waves. They made one final lunge, and then turned to face their attackers.

One of the orange ones reached them first, its claws bared and ready to grab. Old Albert smashed it clean in the face, and it fell backwards, disappearing for a minute beneath the water before emerging again, to attack once more. Old Albert smashed at it again, and this time chunks of the shell encasing it went flying to either side of the water. It fell this time, seeping red into the water around them.

Underneath me, Kate flinched, and I feel like maybe I did too. But she said nothing, and we kept watching.

The men gave another mighty push against the sea bed, and the boat went further out, away from the kriks and suddenly deeper, so that the monsters were now having to reach up higher to attack.

Soldier John smashed the darker, larger one straight in the face. It paused in its attack, but didn't fall backwards. It reached up and placed its claws on the deck. Soldier John smashed at it again, and again, and then once more. It fell backwards, and sunk beneath the waves. The two remaining kriks watched, still, as the men rowed the boat away. Then, slowly, and simultaneously, they turned towards us.

I took a deep breath and faced Lana and James. 'What have we got?'

'We've got the barricade here,' said Lana, pointing to the stairs. It was securely blocked now, with a second bed in the

235

way, and a wardrobe too. Anything trying to climb over that pile would take a while, and would be vulnerable.

'We've got James's garden fork,' she added.

'We could have the curtain poles too,' said Kate. 'If we need them.'

'And we've got the petrol,' said James, pointing to me.

I set the cans down on the carpet. He reached into his pocket and pulled out the matches. He put the box on top of the petrol.

We faced each other, grimly, just as the first heavy thump of a krik hit the door.

33

We crouched behind the bed barricade, frozen and silent. The exposed wood on the bottom of the beds was scratched and rubbed. What were those marks? Was it Lana and James who'd made the marks when they moved the beds? Or was it the kriks themselves who'd shredded the back with their constant, constant scrabbling, their need to attack and kill and destroy? Or was it the people who had lived here, who'd been pulled away screaming and struggling to their painful deaths?

I could feel the fear pulsing through my veins in bursts of angry energy. But there was nowhere to go. We were trapped. I focused on the beds and tried to calm my breathing.

'Owwwwwllllllll' came a sudden scream from outside. We all jumped.

'What the hell is that?' whispered James. There was sweat on his forehead, and he was jiggling his leg up and down. When we were on the Jellyfish we'd have slapped him for that, but here you couldn't feel the vibrations of his leg through the carpet.

'Owwwwwlllllllll' It came again. It was like nothing I'd ever heard before. Like no animal voice or emotion I'd imagined: twisted, haunting, pained. A cold, ugly noise. Chilling.

We stared at each other in horror.

The wailing calls came again, but quieter, unearthly and more sinister. They were like the wind against the Big House in winter, with that same undertone of danger and power; a storm was coming, somewhere. And there was the slow dragging of something heavy bumping against the windows; they were walking round the side.

'They're talking to each other,' I said.

'Do you think they're calling more of them to come?' said James.

'I don't know. Are they loud enough to do that?' I said.

'I don't know. We didn't hear that noise from the Jellyfish,' he said.

'But if there are others in this town they'll hear, won't they?'

'Owwwwwlllllll!'

'I want to make it stop,' said Lana. She was pale again, and was wincing every time there came another call. I felt it too. The noises were like the threat of our deaths. They were like the sound of killing and maiming and pain. Each call pumped another jolt of fear into my veins.

'But if we stay here, the others'll probably send help,' said James. 'We just need to sit quietly and then the others'll come and save us.'

'What if they don't?' said Lana.

'Then we'll be more rested than the kriks, because they've been walking round loads,' he said. He didn't look at us as he said it though. He looked at the scratches on the beds. I don't think any of us felt like we were resting, crouching there tense and ready.

There was a sudden crash round the back of the house. Lana gave a little whimper. Her lips were turned down now, in a parody of crying. 'What can we do?' she said. 'We've got the fork. Shall I get the curtain poles?'

'No!' said Kate. 'Then they'll know we're here.'

I started to laugh. I couldn't help myself. It was just so ridiculous. And then James started to laugh too. Even Kate's mouth twitched, as she looked at us with her shocked, scared face. 'OK. I know they know we're here,' she said. 'But if we go and stand at the window, it'll make it *really* obvious and it'll make them go mad.'

'We just have to survive and keep quiet, and sit here for another four hours,' said James. 'Then I reckon it'll be fine.'

'What?' Lana looked at him, angrily. 'Don't friggin' make up obvious lies. Why are you even saying that? You literally have no way of knowing that we'll be fine. Probably nobody's going to bother rescuing us, are they? Those fighter people ran off and left us before, and now everybody else has left us too. They're not coming. Four hours? Bollocks.'

'Not everybody got away though, did they? Others are out

239

here too, aren't they? They'll come and rescue us.'

'No, they won't. They'll be running. Or hiding . . . or dead.'

'Let's just sit here for a while, though. The kriks don't know for definite we're here. They might go away.'

I took a deep breath, holding it in my cheeks and then blowing it out slowly. Something was still dragging round the house, sometimes bumping against things, and sometimes stopping. But mainly, just circling round and round and round. What was it doing when it went quiet?

'What's that up there?' said Kate, pointing upwards. There was a rectangle of ceiling that was wooden and indented. 'Is it . . . ?'

'I don't know,' said James. 'Shall I lift you up?'

'It's . . . a loft,' said Lana. 'An attic.'

We looked at her, hopefully.

'There might be space for us.' Her face brightened. 'They wouldn't be able to get us up there.'

'Lift her up,' I said.

She climbed on to James's back before he'd even stood properly, but he pushed her up, balancing her on his shoulders. She pushed open the hatch and pulled herself in, so that she was standing on James's shoulders.

'It's a large space,' she said. 'There's a sloping roof and it's dark. There are no windows. There's stuff up here in boxes too. It looks really nice and cosy.'

'There's a chair,' I said, pointing to the front bedroom. 'If we put that chair underneath the hatch, then we can climb up more easily . . . if we need to.' I didn't like the idea of going up there at all, though. We really would be trapped if we were up there, with no windows, no way of getting out. The thought of a cosy sloping roof made my throat clench almost as much as the noise of the kriks outside. Lana and James clambered down.

'We're going to try and kill them first,' I said, deciding. 'Before we go up there.'

The others turned to me resignedly. With the promise of somewhere to hide, their fear was more focused now. They were more interested in fighting.

'We're going to go get the curtain poles, and we'll call the kriks over to the window. The one furthest away from the front door. Then we'll break the windows, pour that petrol on them, and set them on fire,' I said.

'That might mean we're setting the house on fire, though,' said James, screwing up his face. But I could tell he was faking his confusion. I knew he'd do it really. I knew he'd fight.

'Yeah, it might,' I said. 'But I reckon that if the house is on fire, then it still means they are, too. So we'll be killing them *and* we can escape.'

There was another crash round at the back, and then another silence. What were they doing?

'How do we work the matches?' said Lana, peering at the packet.

Kate went over to the chair, and started carrying it into the hallway. From outside, from the far kitchen wall, there was a gentle scratching noise. They'd stopped calling to each other; this faint scratching was almost worse. We knew what was coming. We'd known it as soon as we'd seen that shadow on the beach, really.

'I'll stand here, with the fork,' said James. 'I'll let you know if you need to get up in the roof. Quickly.'

We nodded. Lana scratched one of the matches along the side of the packet. Nothing. She did it again, and there was a sudden fuzzing flame, startling in the poor light. It lit up her face, casting strange shadows on her cheeks as she smiled triumphantly.

'We'll have to get both the curtain poles down at the same time, Kate,' I said. 'And then if we both break the windows with those poles. They'll come then, won't they?'

'The kriks'll come round to see what the noise is,' agreed Lana.

'One can of petrol each?' I said.

Kate and Lana nodded. The scratching was louder now, more insistent.

'I love you guys,' I said.

'Don't be such a sap,' said Lana. She reached down and grabbed a can of the petrol, then walked off to position herself by the window. 'Come on, losers. Let's get this over with so that I can get some nice clothes and get out of here.'

'I love you all too,' said Kate. She grabbed both me and James by the hand, and gave us both a squeeze.

'I love you,' said James. He gave me a sudden, awkward

hug, and then turned away quickly to his watch at the top of the stairs.

'Are we ready?' I said.

'Yes.'

'Yes.'

'Yes.'

I reached up for the curtain pole, and Kate echoed my movements above her window. Behind her, Lana stood silently, clutching her can of petrol in one hand and her matches in the other.

'Then GO!'

34

mash!

The curtain poles went through the glass easily, and there was a little tinkling splatter of glass shards on the pavement below. That was the worst bit, really. We didn't have time for thinking after that.

'Ooowwwwwlllll!'

Immediately, the kriks ran round from the back of the house to attack, their claws raised and their bodies crouched and scuttling.

I smashed out all the remaining glass in my window, sending it down on to the monsters beneath. The curtain was still attached at one end, on my pole, and it flapped in their faces so that they jabbed at it, cutting and shredding.

Lana poured the petrol down while two of them were still covered by the curtain. Then she dropped a lit match. For a split second, there was nothing. Then a short, sighing *Whumph* and an answering fizz.

Then the curtain, and the kriks, went up in flames.

For a couple of seconds we stood, watching them, as they jerked and wrenched their bodies in agony. It was hard to remind yourself that they were monsters and killers. They looked, in that moment, not harmless exactly, but like animals you'd like to save. Creatures you *should* save.

'Pour more petrol on them,' I shouted.

'We can't reach,' cried Kate.

'Throw it.'

Lana was already stretching out of the window. She threw another splutter of petrol over the helpless creatures below. 'Bollocks,' she muttered. 'It's empty.'

I handed my petrol can to Lana. Pulling her arm back, and carefully taking aim, she lobbed it at the monster, hitting it centrally in the chest. There was a split second in which that beautiful, purple-coloured effervescent petrol spilled out across its body. But then it was the fire that covered it, the flames crackling and spitting across the animal, its legs wearing a coat of ornate red and orange twists. Even from our windows we could hear the wet burning sounds; the steam bubbling and squeaking as it left the monster, and that solid thwack as the creature finally hit the floor.

The last of the monsters ran, scuttling in staggered jerks towards the sea. In the final moment, it looked like it would fail, its shorter limbs flailing and its body tipping forward, everywhere covered in that dying blue flame. But it ran on, and on. It launched itself forward into the waves, and then emerged, immediately, enraged, and free from the flames. It stood there glistening wet, smoke steaming off it, and it turned towards the house with slow menace.

'Into the loft!' I shouted. 'Into the loft!'

We ran, as it ran. Kate and Lana scrambled for the chair, stumbling as they both went to push it beneath the hatch at the same time.

'James,' I screamed. 'We need to get in the loft!'

Kate launched herself up, and Lana shoved her in higher. The hatch opened with a clattering thud and Kate scrambled in.

'Quick!' I shouted.

Lana reached up, and there was a smashing crashing sound from downstairs. She pulled herself in urgently.

'The glass. It's coming through the window,' said James. He was still standing at the top of the stairs, his garden fork raised and ready to strike.

'Come on, come on!' I said. I could feel the terror running through my body again, bringing weakness in waves. *Thump, drag.* The krik had reached the stairs.

'You get up there first,' said James. 'Go!'

It felt like my arms were no longer mine to control.

'Please,' I said.

'Hurry!' screamed Lana from above. 'Hurry!'

'Come on, come on,' I muttered desperately as I reached up with my trembling useless fingers, pulling myself upwards towards the safety of the darkness. *Thump, drag. Thump, drag.* I steadied myself on the back of the chair, jamming it against the floor with the edge of my feet to stop it from toppling.

Beneath me, there was a sudden shove, as James pushed me upwards.

'Kick the chair. Kick the chair!' urged Kate.

And with one final push, James hauled himself in through the hatch too, the chair falling away beneath with a smash. He crawled in, panting and exhausted.

'Owwwwwllllll!' That chilling call again. It seemed to immediately fill the entirety of the corridor and the safety of the attic, covering all else, sending a coldness waterfalling down my spine, and forcing my shoulders to stiffen again in terror. Kate whimpered softly.

Then the slow, dreadful shuffling began. I raised my hands to my head, jamming my fingers into my ears to make it stop. *Breathe. It can't get you here.*

But even with my eyes squeezed shut and my fingers in my ears, I could feel the krik moving round in the corridor beneath us, could sense its scuttling, dragging footsteps vibrating through the walls. The diseased nausea of its sea stench came floating in warm patches of poisoned air so thick I could almost taste them each time I breathed.

I edged closer to the hatch, my jeans catching softly against the roughness of the floorboards beneath me. I peered down from the darkness of the loft, holding my breath to stop myself gagging.

The krik slowly turned its head upwards, out of its shell

slit, so that the white balls of the extended eyes seemed to stare directly at me, thick and meaty, their stalks made from the same material as the eye itself. The shiny, moist skin around them was pulled taut, but there was no iris, just a long, black, pupil – sharp, like a slit of nothingness. The leathery lips were drawn across the shell beneath in a permanent gruesome smile, fixed and too-large, like a grotesque circus clown. The eyes swivelled on, searching for the noise. It couldn't see me, I realized; it'd just turned its eyes towards the sound, but there was no recognition there.

I was glad I'd looked. The krik was horrifying and hideous and ugly. But after seeing it, I at least knew what we had to face. And somehow, however terrifying the krik was – and it was cripplingly awful – it was better than my imagination. The reality was bearable; the monsters of my dreams weren't.

Next to me, I could feel James shuffling round too.

'Hello, Big Boy,' he called, loudly.

The krik turned its face up towards us again.

'Watch out, Martha,' muttered James.

And he dropped the fork straight down.

With a wet, meaty sound, the prongs struck straight through the mouth slit and into the vulnerable flesh beneath. The krik stood for a moment, suspended on the end of the weapon, but then, with a shake, James pulled the fork free, and the krik peeled away, and fell to the ground beneath us.

35

So anyway, I'm not going to try and justify this next bit, because I know what we did next sounds weird. But basically, all I'm saying, is that sometimes, life can be confusing. And sometimes, you can have too many emotions and you're not thinking properly. This is especially true when you've just been involved in a fight-to-the-death scenario which you've won, but that also involved you killing an evil monster, then close-up watching it die painfully and loudly.

So we went shopping.

In our defence, we hadn't exactly planned to go shopping. I think we'd just been trying to go as far away as possible from everything and to maybe get somewhere safe, but then the shops were just there. Don't judge me, OK, but I was all about the looting, and also we wanted to look nice for when we met some other people – like those fighter people. I realize we were basically stealing. But I don't think it matters quite so much when everyone who owned the shops is probably dead, and nobody else wants to go near the town at all and take anything in case they get eaten. So, yeah. We were all pretty excited.

'I'm going to get some amazing things,' said Lana. 'I'm going to look gorgeous.'

'You already do look gorgeous,' said Kate.

'Whatever.'

'Some trainers would be nice,' I said. 'And maybe a dress. But we should probably get some really sensible stuff, I suppose.'

'Like a flamethrower?' said James.

'No. Like a diamond tiara, or the perfect shade of lipstick,' said Lana.

'Some large knives, maybe?' said James.

'Maybe. But also some underwear, and a hairbrush.'

Kate smiled.

To be honest, the shops made everything better. There was a whole street of them too, and they mostly contained clothes and shoes. A whole street just of shops with clothes and shoes in them! There were shops full of just tiny, multi-coloured baby clothes, and there were shops full of crazy, painted stilettoes and glittery ballet pumps. There were shops full of jumpers and coats and jeans and lovely, lovely dresses. Warm things and sensible things that would be the practical things to take, absolutely, but also the nicer things like silky T-shirts, make-up, toiletries and ball gowns.

'Let's split up,' said Lana. 'Let's go and find some gorgeous clothes and then meet back here and show each other what we've got.'

'Can't we go together?' said Kate. 'I don't want to be alone.'

'You can come with me,' said Lana. 'But I don't want you holding me back. I'll have to leave you behind if you're too slow.'

Kate nodded. Lana had always made it clear that that was her attitude towards life.

'Well, we're not going to be long, are we?' said James. 'We'll be quickly in and out?'

Lana just looked at him.

'And here's water,' I pointed out. 'We can have a bath.' There were a couple of circular pits in the middle of the street which had collected rainwater. The thing I liked the most about them was you could see the bottom of the pools, and you could see there was nothing bad in them. The water was greenish, but at least there was nothing in there which was going to kill me.

'What?' said Lana. 'Don't be ridiculous. I'm not washing in the middle of the street. There's a bathroom shop over there. That's where I'm going.'

She walked off first towards a large, blue shop front decorated with two faded mannequins, each wearing furry jackets.

'Oh,' said James, heading towards a shop called 'Survival Experts', and 'Outdoor Specialists'. 'Yeah, I suppose we can spend a bit of time in the shops, then.'

In the middle of the street was a large white stand on

rusting red poles. It was a map. One of those ones with a useful, 'You are here' arrow in the middle of it. At least, that bit would be useful if 'being here' wasn't one of the few things we were sure about. I grabbed Kate and pulled her towards it.

We both walked slowly because, well, it meant so much, didn't it? I guess maps have always been symbols – a way of organizing the world when it maybe isn't that organized. A fantasy of places you could go and the way things are supposed to be – as though places and things don't change. Also, the main reason I walked slowly was because I wanted Kate to figure it all out first because I wasn't sure I could remember how to read proper writing. Plus, it would mean I could blame her if she got it wrong.

Beads of moisture had leaked into the edges of the map, bubbling and warping the plastic so that it was difficult to see – the sort of reading we were used to. Kate ran her finger over the map, searching round and round, and touching the smoothness of the board. She rested her finger on the arrow for a minute before taking it away again and frowning. The lines on the map, those roads, were very straight and very perfect, unlike the jagged sunken bits of tarmac that led down to the drowned houses and the hidden streets under the water. It took us a few minutes of silence to work it all out, but I think maybe a quarter of the town as shown there was now missing. We didn't say that to each other, though.

And it took us even longer, because we were mainly trying to figure out where 'here' was, but over to the far side of the map, the side away from the sea, there was a big blue circle which somebody had drawn on to the map. It was around a black blob labelled *Castle Huw*. And here's the important bit, which I had to read twice, and then again, before I trusted I wasn't just making it up. Somebody had also written: 'Safety here. All welcome.'

'Woah!' I said, checking.

'Yes,' said Kate. She turned to grin at me then.

'Do you think that's where they are? Those fighter people?'

'I don't know. But there's somebody there. It's somewhere we can go!'

The writing looked fresh. I don't mean like it had just been done yesterday or something – but it wasn't as faded as the rest of the board. It looked like it was recent.

'It says there's safety. Imagine that. And . . . we can get there either along the road, or by following the river.'

'Yes.' Kate looked in closer at the map – but it was really clear. There were only two lines which went that way. The rest of that part of the map was green and empty. For a second it felt like the ground gave a little shiver beneath us, like we were back on the Jellyfish again and it was checking where we were, but that moment passed and the world was back to being solid. Concrete.

Suddenly it *did* seem more urgent that we shouldn't go there wearing our jellyfish rags. Now that there were other people, and somewhere to go.

Right next to us, there was a shop containing bottles and

creams and pills and things. Yes, I knew it was a chemist, but I hadn't remembered there being so many different types of medicines and soaps. I ran in, sticking to the sections which were light and near the entrance, and not venturing into the parts that were in shadow at the back. There was broken glass sprinkled over the floor, and lots of the bottles were lying around in the aisles, but towards the back of the shop I could see rows and rows of supplies still neatly stacked. I wondered, if there were people close by, why they hadn't taken these supplies. Were there so few people now that they didn't need them? Or was it that this town wasn't safe? I picked up some eyeliner, lip gloss, four toothbrushes, some hairbrushes and some toothpaste, and I left.

'Hey, idiot,' Lana called to me from a green shopfront. 'Come over here and have a bath. Come, quick.'

She was holding a bucket, full of the water from the pools.

'Come on. You can only have this much water, though, because I'm not carrying any more over. And, wait, let me measure you. I need to know what clothes size you are.' She whipped a piece of tape round my chest, and then bent forward to examine the numbers on it.

'What the . . . ?'

'Just shut up, Martha. Hold still.' She peered in close again, and then moved the tape down to my waist.

'Excellent,' she said, though I had no clue what it was about any part of my body and a tape measure which would mean praise from Lana. 'Put your toothbrushes and stuff in that rucksack over there.' She pointed towards a large yellow bag in the middle of the street, the one we'd carried the petrol cans in. 'We're going to fill just that one with clothes and things, and then we can take it in turns to carry it. Just one bag, and then the other three of us can hold the weapons to defend it.'

'To defend *us*, Lana,' I pointed out. 'It's *us* who need defending, not a bag full of clothes and toothbrushes.'

'Yes, that's what I meant,' said Lana, though her voice made it clear she didn't. I was fairly confident that if kriks attacked, she would defend the toothbrushes rather than me.

Kate emerged beaming, her wet hair glistening and sleek. She was wearing a pair of well-fitting black jeans, and a long-sleeved green T-shirt. She looked, to somebody who'd only ever seen her in rags, amazing. Simply amazing.

'We'll get some nice clothes for you, Martha,' she said. 'You just go and get washed.'

James was swaggering along the street whistling and clutching several water pistols. Two of them were so large they had straps so that he could carry them over his shoulders. He had these ones slung casually across his back. He raised another in a wave as he walked past us – a blue one with a large water chamber. He grinned and pointed it at the window behind us, pulling back the powerful-looking pump to release a jet of water which missed us by only a couple of inches. Then he turned around and fired off another couple of random shots at the empty street.

'Pow, pow!' he said. 'I'm a killing machine! Are you scared of me?'

'Nope,' I said. 'I can think of a few things that look a bit scarier than you.'

'Bet *they'll* be scared of me when these are filled with petrol. Or if they're not, then they should be.'

He squinted at one of the lampposts, took careful aim and fired.

The mirror was the strangest thing. The bath wasn't really that unfamiliar. The shampoo and soap smelt nice, which I wasn't used to, but the bath just involved getting wet and covering myself with water, and I'd done that every day on the Jellyfish whether I wanted to or not. I hadn't looked in a mirror, though.

It took me a while to work myself up to it, and I decided to have the bath first. I hadn't spent much time looking at myself naked on the Jellyfish, so that was weird. Not crazy weird, as I did know what I looked like, but it had been hard to get privacy, so it was more that I hadn't seen myself naked all in one go.

And I'd rather not talk about the colour of the water either, but if you imagine a sort of brown soup, the type with little slices of thin onions and cheese in it, well the water looked like that. No, I don't know what the floating bits in the brown water were either, but they can't have been anything good. My hair felt amazing afterwards, though: soft, and light, and silky. I loved the smooth way I felt and smelt. I know what you look like is not important, and you should judge people by what's inside and by their value as a person and that kindness and personality matter more than anything. But that's also just rubbish, isn't it?

When I was on the Jellyfish, and we had all that time to think, I had thought about what I looked like now, and I'd asked Kate and Lana, and sometimes James, to tell me. But I knew that what they said would always be based around what they thought of me and, do you know, they were always really nice. But vague. In any case, despite them telling me that I had light brown hair and freckles, I'd imagined myself anyway with long, blonde, perfectly curly hair and gorgeous green eyes. I knew that wasn't true, of course, but the thing with not knowing for definite is that you can always make your own reality. So if I wanted my reality to feature myself as an amazingly beautiful woman with extra-special ninja skills, then I could.

In the mirror I was younger than in my imagination. My face was thinner, and my lips fuller. I did have those freckles the others had kept on mentioning, and I did have that light brown hair, but it wasn't a bad face. It wasn't an ugly face, and it wasn't a gorgeous face like Kate's. It was an average, forget-table, blending-in sort of face. It felt like a stranger's face, and I knew I'd need to look at myself a lot more before I really believed it was me.

'Will you hurry up, loser?' Lana opened the door, throwing

in some clothes for me. 'Get these on quickly, and get down-stairs. I want to be at the castle before the sun goes down. Huh. You don't look too bad, do you?'

'No. I don't.'

I kept on looking at myself in the mirror while I was getting dressed, but it felt rude, like I was spying on a naked stranger.

Lana had chosen a pair of leaf-coloured jeans and a plain white T-shirt, and some red trainers. She had also chosen a pair of pants, and a bra, which had small pink birds on them. When I put the white T-shirt on top (and, yes, it took me a few minutes, because putting on a bra doesn't come naturally, OK?), you could just about make out the pattern of the birds underneath if you stared and stared, and I was glad about that. I was glad about the underwear, because it already felt special to be wearing it – not just because it was comfortable and clean, though that was good – but because it felt like I had this special secret that you couldn't know about just from looking at me.

'Come on, Martha!' called Lana. 'Let's get out of here.'

I think we all felt completely fabulous, and for the first time, standing in the middle of that deserted town, we looked like we really could be something. We didn't look like we were losers who'd been marooned on a lump of jelly wearing rags, and eating raw seaweed as a treat. We looked like we could be fighters, like we could defeat monsters.

36

On one of the trees overhanging the river there was an orange plastic bag tied to a branch. We'd stopped to stare at it, and to hope.

'They must have come this way! That's from Dr Jones's hair!' said Kate. 'They got away!'

'It's just a plastic bag,' said Lana. 'There are thousands of those.'

'It's tied in a bow though,' I pointed out. 'It hasn't got there by accident. It's a sign for us.'

'It's a rubbish sign for us,' muttered Lana. 'Literally.' But she said it quietly, and I could see she was having to stop herself from smiling. Orange plastic bags were rare, and it was unlikely the wind could have tied a bag as neatly as that – trust me, we were experts in plastic bags.

The land around the mouth of the river was flat and open and gave a good view along the coastline. There were abandoned, broken boats, and there was debris strewn along the length of the shore in amongst the sunken, sea-damaged houses near us, and the beaches and cliffs beyond. But there was no sign of the boats the Jellyfish people had been in.

I avoided looking the other way, the way we'd come. The way the Jellyfish was.

'Do you think they went up the river too then?' said Kate.

'What, instead of going out to sea again?' said Lana, her eyes wide and sarcastic.

'It would have been weird if they hadn't gone up it,' said James, ignoring Lana. 'It would have been an easy route inland for them.'

The freshwater and the seawater mingled here so you couldn't see a division between the two. I know that's what rivers do, and the whole point of them is that they flow down through land until they eventually get to the sea, but I didn't like the idea of the river and the sea joining. The water was smooth and glassy, with stagnant layers of foam and rubbish bobbing gently along the edges. It looked slow-moving and peaceful, but here and there in the brown water there were whorls of fast-swirling sediment, some with leaves or twigs caught, twisting round and round on the surface. Places where the sea was pushing against the river water, trying to get inland.

I wondered how easy it would be for other things to travel up the river – things which weren't boats. And I wondered how far up the river the saltwater went.

'Come on,' said James, 'let's walk faster.'

'I think—' said Kate.

'Oh god,' said Lana, '*stop* thinking. Please. Just shut up!'

'All I'm saying,' Kate was already sounding defensive, 'is that I think we should go back for the sheep. They're creatures too. With feelings. And I don't like that we've just left them on the Jellyfish. If I'd known that, then I wouldn't . . .'

'Wouldn't what?' said Lana. 'You're not going to say you would have stayed on the Jellyfish with them, are you? Because I know that would be a lie.'

'I just feel really sad,' said Kate. 'We didn't even leave them any grass. And I don't know if they eat fish.'

'They eat seaweed,' said James. 'They definitely eat seaweed. I saw them.'

'Oh. OK,' Kate was placated slightly.

I don't think they eat seaweed, James mouthed at me and Lana.

We'd started out in our new clothes and trainers by jogging at a distance from one another; our garden forks were in our hands, because, you know, that way if one of us got attacked, then the others would have time to get away. But we'd slowed to a walk, and were now right next to each other.

None of us looked behind us as we walked, but I could still sense the presence of the Jellyfish out there, somewhere. Maybe missing us, maybe killing the sheep, maybe still digesting our friends. I didn't want to look behind me because I knew the sea was still visible from here, and that it wouldn't take much for me to want to go back and check on how the Jellyfish was reacting. Already I felt funny being this

261

far away from the noise of the waves, like it was all too quiet.

I only sort-of remembered being this far from the sea. It felt very grown-up and responsible to have this level of freedom. It also felt scary and unreal. The thing was, there were loads of places a krik could hide. If they did hide, that is. Could they be lying down in the long grass? *Did* they lie down?

I felt an itch on my shoulder. I slapped it, wishing I'd had more for breakfast. My stomach was rumbling already. I wondered whether there would be any food for us when we arrived, or – more likely – whether we'd have to find it ourselves.

The itch was back. I slapped my shoulder again. Suddenly I realized something was touching me, stroking my shoulder, following me.

'Agggghhhhhh!' I screamed, running forward, desperately flapping my arms. I turned round gripping my fork, ready to defend myself . . . to see James holding a long piece of grass and laughing gleefully.

'You . . .' He could hardly get the words out because he was laughing so hard. He just pointed at me. 'You . . . were such an idiot. All that scanning and staring . . . Oooo look at me. I'm Martha!' He put on a high voice and did a crazy jig, waving his arms around in the air. 'I'm Martha, and I'm going out to kill kriks. Ooooo!'

'What is *that* supposed to be?' I repeated his jig back and waved my arms too. Much better than he did, I think, actually. 'Is that supposed to be an impression of me? Because it's the most crap impression I've seen. You basically just look like a demented octopus.'

'Well, you said it, Martha,' said James, with a very superior tone. 'There's very little between you at times.' He waved his arms wildly in the air. 'Martha or octopus? Martha or octopus? Which am I?'

'Oh, whatever,' I sighed. 'I don't know. Octopus?'

'Correct. Now what about this one?' He waved his arms again, this time in a swooping motion. 'Martha or octopus?'

'Me, I suppose.'

'Nah. Martha, don't be so hard on yourself. That was also an octopus.'

'Hey, idiots,' interrupted Lana, 'how far is this castle of yours anyway?'

'I'm not sure exactly,' said Kate. 'I think it's probably further than we've come so far, though. I think we've only been walking for about half an hour.'

'And what about the river? Do you think we should have crossed over it as we left the town? What if we're on the wrong side of it?'

It was a good point. It would have been useful to have more information about the directions: I didn't particularly want to arrive looking wet and muddy as well as hot and sweaty. I wanted to arrive looking calm, together, and the best I could – given that I'd been stranded on a mythological horror story for ages. Slim chance, though, particularly with

263

people waving bits of stupid grass at me.

'I guess we should probably just stick close to the river,' said Kate cheerfully. 'If we do that we'll get there eventually.'

We walked on further, but the grass was becoming long and dense. There were low, hidden layers of nettles and brambles which jagged and caught at our arms as we passed, and patches of cow parsley as big as small trees, the heads of the plants splayed out like alien umbrellas swaying above us, shielding us from the sun. The narrow path we were following was now barely even visible, and I was trying really hard not to think too much about what had made the trail in the first place. We could still see clearly over the river to the other side, but the water was muddy and I remembered all of our discussions about whether kriks needed seawater . . . or just any water. I didn't want to have the others make fun of me again, but I didn't really feel safe.

The others had all gone silent now: it was hard to talk when you were walking in single file. I tried to distance myself from Kate, who was immediately in front of me, but the only escape route would be out into the river anyway, and Lana had obviously forgotten our rules about spreading out, because she was only a foot behind me. Up ahead, James had slowed down the pace, so we were dangerously bunched together.

'What do you think we should do?' called Lana from the back. 'Is this a good way?'

'If we push through here we'll make a lot of noise,' said

James, stopping altogether.

'We've been making a lot of noise anyway. Your frigging octopus impressions weren't exactly quiet,' snapped Lana crossly. 'If we go back, we'll be going back through a place where we can't see very well . . . and where anything that's been following us will be hiding now. I think it's too risky. I think we have to go on.'

'Well, you can lead if you want, because I can't see what's in the grass, the path has gone and the ground is boggy. I don't think going on is a good idea.'

'Maybe we could push through the grass to the side and make a path up to the road?' suggested Kate.

'Oh, don't be ridiculous, Kate,' hissed Lana.

We all stood, silently, looking back and forth along the path. By stating the problems, Lana and James had made us all aware of how vulnerable we were.

'I just think,' Kate said softly, 'you're both right. Neither way is safe, but we're not safe standing here either. Maybe we could go through the river? The grass is much lower on the other side.' She looked uncertainly at the murky flow. It was about four metres wide, but so dirty it was impossible to tell the depth. Or what was underneath the surface.

There was no way I was going to risk getting into it.

'I'm going back,' I said. 'Come on, Lana, Kate. It's not that far back. Come on.'

Lana set off at a fast pace, and I could hear her trying to slow her panicked breathing. I felt really jumpy myself now. I kept half imagining I was hearing noises other than the tramping of our feet on the soil and the rustle of our legs brushing against the undergrowth. I tried not to look at the tall grass as we squeezed through, but I kept imagining movement, or darker patches of strange shadows swaying in the bushes.

I wasn't sure how far we'd come along this path before we realized there was no way through, but it all looked threatening and sinister now that I was concentrating and searching for problems. The brambles seemed spikier, the grass seemed thicker; it was full of easy hiding places – not just for the kriks, but for other more unknown, unidentified enemies. Lana started half-jogging and I could almost feel Kate's breath on her shoulders, she was so close.

'Shhhh,' came a hiss from behind. 'We're going too fast. We're making too much noise. Slow down!'

Lana nodded in acknowledgement, holding up her hand to signal that she was stopping. She turned round and put her finger to her lips. We all halted, listening. I held my breath, waiting for noise, but all I could hear was the soft brush of the reeds in the river as they rubbed gently against each other in the breeze.

'What's the plan?' whispered Lana, looking at me. 'We must be almost out of this bit now.'

'I don't know,' I whispered, leaning back so that everybody could hear. 'Maybe we should just go up to that open field in the town again and head up the hill, because then we can see the valley below and work out how to get through?'

They all nodded. Going back there meant we'd also be able to see the Jellyfish, which was something . . . I don't know . . . which was something I felt like I didn't want. But at the same time I felt like it was almost pulling us back, like it was a big white blob in our lives which we still couldn't ignore.

'Where do you think the others went?' said James. 'Do you think we might see them if . . .' He paused, turning his head to the side.

'What?' hissed Lana, tensing up again.

'Shhhhh . . .' He tilted his head further towards the direction in which we'd come, frowning as he listened.

There it was. A gentle, barely discernible rustle.

'What?' said Lana, unhooking her fork and turning back towards the seashore. 'Quick!'

And she ran. We all ran. Blindly, pushing through brambles, half tripping over tree roots, not caring about the nettle stings or the scratches from the reeds and tall grasses. The path was so narrow that I couldn't risk looking behind me to see what was coming, but I kept expecting bony clawed pincers to creep out of the undergrowth, grasping at my ankles or face.

'Hurry UP, Lana,' shouted James. 'Move!'

'I'm trying!' she screamed, panting loudly in her terror. She was running in a real panic now, her fork held out in front, waving erratically. I could no longer see clearly beyond me and I was having to concentrate in order to avoid stepping on Lana's heels. The feeling of not being in control, of being trapped between Lana and Kate, was almost overwhelming. I had to battle my instincts which so wanted me to break through the grass and go round Lana, to push her out of the way, to trample over her and break free . . . But I also knew this would take me longer. And besides there was a security in being in the middle: Lana or James would get attacked first. Actually, we should have heard James being eaten by now.

'James?' I called, 'is anything coming?'

'Nope,' he shouted back. 'And honestly, it might just have been the wind. Still hurry up, though. I'm a bit stressed here.' Despite his relaxed tone, there was a catch in his voice and he sounded breathless, which, I knew, could not just be from the distance we'd run.

Kate gave a sob.

'It's OK, Kate,' I said. 'I think it's OK. Just keep running.'

The grass and reeds seemed to be getting lower now, but they were still higher than my head and dense enough to hide an army of rabid shelled monsters. Thing is, I somehow knew they didn't. Not for any logical reason, or because James hadn't been eaten, though that definitely supported my theory; no, I could just sense a lack of the *feeling* of death.

I steadied my breathing and looked around at the landscape. We had been careless to let ourselves get into this situation. We'd been careless and wrong to rush into a world we were no longer familiar with. We'd forgotten we were in a war. And it was a war humanity was losing.

I knew then what we were going to have to do. I'd known it, I think, since we first stepped back on to land and found that it wasn't as wonderful and magical and perfect and brilliant as we'd hoped. I'd known it when being on land didn't feel safe, and when it didn't even feel quite solid beneath my feet.

I stopped running.

'We can't go to the castle yet,' I said. 'We've got to go back. We've got to kill the Jellyfish.'

37

I couldn't stop looking at James. I don't want to sound shallow, but he did look suddenly really hot. I'm not going to say I fancied him, or was attracted to him or anything, but I did really see how people could be. It was either the new clothes, or the threat of our likely death, but his freshly shaven cheeks and his neatly cut hair (well . . . neater, anyway) really brought out his cheekbones. Underneath all that dirt and wild frizz, it turned out his real hair was a dark brown, and was wavy. His face did look odd, with the tanned part on the top half and the paler section below which had been covered by his beard, and also the little cuts on it from shaving for the first time. I think I liked it more like that though, and I liked seeing his dimples when he smiled. I'll just mention that his muscles really looked good under his black T-shirt too. It's fine to mention that, because I'm just saying it, and not going on about it. It's a fact in my story at the moment, and not an opinion.

I think maybe he felt something too, because he was really

quiet as we climbed back into town. I don't mean he felt something about *me*, I just mean he felt something about the whole situation. We'd decided to stay back up on the hill for the night. There was nowhere else where we felt safe and, weirdly, it was full of sheep again. You couldn't tell that we had put any on the Jellyfish at all. James did make a couple of jokes about trying to catch them again, but other than that, he just ate a couple of cans of cat food, brushed his teeth, and lay down on the grass.

Over the cliff edge and into the sea, the Jellyfish was a calm, perfect lozenge, smoothly lying on the undulating, lightly choppy water. Its surface gleamed whitely against the red–and–amber streaks of the early evening sky, and there was no sign of the killer tentacles hidden below the surface. I think we all noticed it, but there also didn't seem to be anything moving on it at all. No sheep. No nothing. Not even a resting flock of seagulls disturbed that laser-cut polish of the surface. At this distance, it didn't look a threat at all. It didn't even look alive. The only clue was that it didn't seem to move, while the wind-speckled tips of the waves flickered all around it.

From up here the geometric dark lines of the sunken houses and the line of mottled plastic debris along the edges of the coast bordered the Jellyfish like an ornate picture frame, as though it was the focal point of the bay. As though the creature was something we were drawn to watch, that we needed to stare at, something special. But those straight lines were also a barrier, jagged man-made intrusions into the water which spiked at and attacked the waves, breaking up their power and slowing them down. Protection for the land.

'I don't want to do it,' said Lana. 'It's a stupid idea. I want to go to the castle and be safe.'

'Off you go then,' said James.

'Shut your face. You know I can't go by myself. And it'll be dark soon.'

'Well stop whinging then, because you're giving me a headache.'

'I think I might prefer not to kill it either,' said Kate. 'It's just . . . you know . . . It did feed us and it did try to look after us.'

'*How* did it try to look after us?' said James, raising his eyebrows.

'Well, OK . . . it didn't kill us then, and it could have killed us straight away.'

'It kept us there for ages, like it was playing with us, before starting to kill us. One by one,' said James.

'We have to, Kate,' I said. 'You know that.'

She nodded, miserably, staring out towards the sea.

'I don't think we would ever feel safe unless it's dead,' I added. 'We'd always know it was out here, waiting.'

It wasn't just because the Jellyfish might attack other boats, or otherwise massacre humanity – though I do feel like both of those were probably good reasons. I think it's more because it was there. Does that make sense? I don't know if it does. But I think we knew we needed to kill it because of what it was, and because of what it had done, and because of what it might do . . . and because of those dark shapes, the ones which would suddenly appear, and then slowly disappear into the jelly beneath our feet. None of us said that though. None of us talked about the *why* at all. We didn't need to.

I just knew then, and I still know now, that if we'd left it, if we'd left it there on the sea and we'd gone inland to the safety of the castle, then we sort of wouldn't have left it; and not just because I'd always have been thinking about it creeping slowly up that river, oozing and squeezing between its banks. I don't think the castle would have felt safe at all. I think the hard ground would always have felt wobbly, and those secure walls would always have felt see-through, like they might move and absorb us at any time. And I think we'd also have brought those dark shapes with us. I think they'd always have been there, beneath our feet – not quite visible, but also impossible not to see. We didn't talk about it, so I don't know if that's exactly what the others felt. But I think it might have been.

'Is it . . .' said Kate, 'does it have to be a choice between us and the Jellyfish? Is there no way we could try and live with it?'

The Jellyfish lifted one of its tentacles high out of the water, almost as though it had heard her. The ripple of white waves when it smashed back to the surface again looked peaceful from up here, rings of foam drifting out from its body in perfect concentric circles. But it reminded me of the power, of the force of the creature. Of its dominance.

'Only if we're OK about always feeling under threat,' I said.

273

'And I'm not. I want to feel safe in our world.

'I guess, back in Before I feel like people spent a lot of time pretending, and ignoring things. They didn't believe sea monsters existed even though there were loads of stories about them and loads of sailors said they'd seen them; everybody *still* pretended they didn't exist until those people were dragged under the sea and drowned. And in Before people also said there was nothing wrong with the planet even though sea levels were rising, and the climate was changing, and strange weather was happening. All the people in the world ignored the problem and waited for somebody *else* to fix the planet. But while they were waiting it just got more messed up.

'So this time, if we want things to be different, I don't think we should wait for somebody else to sort out really big problems any more, and I don't think we should pretend those problems don't exist. I think we should just do it ourselves.'

'The other Jellyfish people left though, didn't they?' said James. 'Why does it have to be us who sort it out? Couldn't we at least go and get them back to help us?' He zipped a sleeping bag up around him, wriggling down into it so that only his face was exposed.

'Losers,' said Lana. 'They're from Before. They're the adults who messed up in the first place and they're running away from it all again.

'You can stop whining on about it, Martha. I'm happy to kill the stupid Jellyfish just so we can make the world a better place

274

and everything. But I swear to god, if I get even a droplet of slime on my nice clean clothes then I'll wipe it on your face.'

'Whose face?' said James, sitting up again. 'Martha's?'

'All of yours.' Lana had started to hum under her breath, as though maybe the thought of rubbing Jellyfish mucus on our faces was making her happy. Like Kate, she was still staring out to sea, but she was looking beyond the Jellyfish, at the setting sun and the miles of shimmering water.

'I am totally in favour of ripping that massive white slime-ball into shreds,' said James, 'but by killing it we're not exactly creating a better world for jellyfish, are we?'

There was a long moment when we all contemplated this deep moral issue. Actually, being honest, it was a brief moment for me. I spent most of the time we were silent thinking about *how* we were going to kill the Jellyfish, and picturing myself with that long blonde hair and the ninja skills again. I'm pretty sure it was also brief for Lana too, because I mainly saw her squinting at the side pocket of the yellow rucksack, where she'd put a selection of different nail varnishes.

'I don't think jellyfish normally eat sheep,' said Kate.

'What?' said Lana.

'Well I don't know what they normally eat, but it's not going to be sheep, is it? And whether that, down there's, a giant jellyfish who's grown too big because of climate change, or whether it's a sea monster that's been hiding forever, it's not behaving like it normally would now, is it?'

'So?' said Lana.

'So . . . so I suppose it just shows that things are different,' said Kate. 'We have to be different now too, because the world has changed.'

'We're not going to kill the stupid thing tonight anyway,' said Lana. 'So shall we have another look at all our clothes? So we can see each other's?'

Our rucksack was completely full now, fuller than it had been with just those petrol cans inside. As Lana pulled the zip open, the clothes that had been stuffed inside spilled out.

'Oh, we do have some brilliant stuff,' said Kate, turning away from the sea and smiling again.

Lana pulled out pants from the side pockets. There were maybe thirty pairs, all brightly coloured and scrunched up small. 'These are great, aren't they?' she said. 'We've got bras as well, but I only got a few. We can go back for more if we need them.' She unzipped the main compartment. From there she pulled out another few pairs of jeans, and some leggings, but then she paused. With a dramatic flourish, she pulled out a gold dress. It was sequinned and flashed in the dying light of the sun. Then she pulled out a green one with delicate, wispy material. Finally, she pulled out a beautiful soft pink dress, shiny and perfect.

'I've got some shoes and stuff in here too,' she added.

'And James has all his survival stuff in the bottom,' said Kate.

'Yes, but just a few things like knives and torches. We

wouldn't let him bring really big stuff. He wanted to bring a blow-up boat, but we told him that was pointless as we were never getting back in the water.'

We three looked at each other then and smiled. It wasn't a happy smile, obviously, but it wasn't exactly a sad one either. From where James was lying in his new sleeping bag, the pile of water pistols at his feet, there was a little rustle as he turned away from us and pulled the covers over his face.

'Whoop!' said James, loudly. 'Game's up, people. Time for some jellyfish-killing action!'

'What?' For a moment, waking up there on the grass, it felt like the world was rocking gently back and forth, and back and forth; that there were waves beneath the surface of the earth moving us up and down as we drifted in the middle of the calm ocean. But then one of the sheep gave a loud bleat and the ground felt solid again.

'Put all your stuff back in the rucksack,' said Lana. 'And make sure it's neat. I don't want to leave anything behind.'

'What shall we do with our dirty pants?' said Kate.

'How are they dirty?' said James. 'You've only had them on a few hours. The last pair I had I wore for the whole time we were on the Jellyfish and they were fine.'

'Put them in this pocket,' said Lana, ignoring him. 'I've got washing powder too, so we can wash them when we get back this afternoon.'

Me and Kate silently put our pants in the front pocket

277

of the rucksack.

'We'll put the rucksack on the beach, by the boats, so that it's there when we get back later,' said Lana. She said the last five words very confidently.

'And the water pistols too. We might need those.' said James. 'Shall we go straight away?'

'Yes, well,' I said, 'There's not much else to do here, is there?' We smiled.

'Me and Kate will go and get as much petrol as we can. Can you two sort out the boats and get some matches?' I said.

We shared some peaches and rice pudding for our breakfast. But it was hard to properly enjoy it, knowing what we were about to go off and do. Knowing that these might be our last rice puddings, and our last peaches.

The Jellyfish was closer to shore than it had been last night and, while it wasn't obviously angry like it had been when we had been escaping, its tentacles were flailing around in a way which showed it didn't feel comfortable. On board there was a darker patch to one side. It was hard to tell what it was: seaweed, fish, sheep . . . humans. But there was a sheen to the darkness, a whiteish coating which glistened in the sunlight as the shadows shifted across the sky. Something was being eaten; something weaker than the Jellyfish was being absorbed.

Me and Kate trudged towards the nearest cars.

'All we need is a long straw,' she said.

Anyway, I'm going to cut things short at this point, because let's just say all we needed wasn't just a long straw.

Literally, I don't want to relive the 'getting petrol out of cars' story again. We needed buckets to put the petrol in; we needed a much, much longer thing than just a straw: we needed a hose. And we also, and this is the flippin' worst bit: we also needed to suck the petrol out.

By the time we'd filled four buckets – which took about twenty cars, by the way – Lana and James had arrived, and were sitting around making fun of us.

'Just shut up and help,' I said.

'I've found some sweets,' said James. 'That's valuable help. When you've finished you can have one to take the petrol taste away. And then there will be one each for when we're back from the Jellyfish.'

We went silent again at that, and filled some more of the buckets. James tipped the water in his water pistols out, in a little trickle that ran down the street. He filled them up again with the petrol from our buckets.

'And I've also got this machete,' he said suddenly, holding up a long knife. 'I found it in one of the houses. I thought we could use it . . .'

'I think we should have all the sweets now,' said Kate, bravely saying what we'd all been thinking. 'No point in waiting until we get back from the Jellyfish.'

'But what about our reward for victory?' said James.

'I don't think we'll need a reward,' I said. 'If we make it back. I mean, *when*.'

38

'Follow us,' I said. 'But not too close. Don't come within range of the tentacles.'

Kate and Lana nodded.

'Good luck, you guys,' said Kate.

'If you're back before us, can you get some food?' said Lana. 'I'm feeling hungry already.'

There wasn't much space in the two-seater rowing dinghy we'd chosen for our task, and we were lower than I would have liked to be in the water because there were tools and twelve cans of petrol arranged around us. I adjusted my feet awkwardly into the small gap we'd left in the middle. Still, space wouldn't be a problem on the return journey.

From here the Jellyfish looked calmer and almost as though it was welcoming us back, one or two tentacles rising occasionally into the air in a desultory fashion, waving at us whenever it could be bothered. Otherwise it was sitting serenely in the waters, closer into shore than normal, but then it had always liked to move around a little in the bay.

James pushed the boat away from the shore, striding through the breaking waves before climbing in.

'Are you ready?' he said.

'Yes.' I formed my face into what I hoped was a smile, but it felt like it probably came out more as a twitching grimace. James had already shoved his oars against the submerged walls, propelling us forward with a sudden spurt of speed. We both started to row.

'Why are we doing this again?' he said. 'Just remind me.'

Back on the shore, I could see Lana and Kate getting into their boat and pushing away.

'You know why. It's because we have to.'

'Do we though? Do we? Couldn't we just go off to that castle and leave it all behind us?'

'No, I don't think we could. I couldn't. Eventually we'd have to do this.'

For the first time, I started to have doubts. They weren't doubts about me though. I knew what I had to do.

'Do you want to stop? Do you want to get out and get in Lana and Kate's boat?' I said. 'To stay behind with them? It's fine if you want to.'

'No. No, I need to,' he said. 'I just . . . I think . . . if this works, I mean, if we do it . . . then I want you to know that I enjoyed my life. That time on the Jellyfish was fun. My life was fun on there. I think . . . I'm just not sure life will be so simple for us in the future. Whatever happens.'

There was a sudden high wave then; we were getting

281

further out, and we tilted down into the trough with a splash.

'Yeah. It was good,' I said. 'We were very secure, and very loved.'

'And we knew what was expected of us, and we had friendship,' he said. 'Whatever happens now, it was great being on there with you.'

He was silent for a minute.

'I need to kill it too, Martha.'

'Yes.'

I looked back towards land as we rowed further away from the shore. The view was becoming more familiar now, the world becoming the one I knew again. You could fool yourself into feeling that it was safer, happier, better from back here, out on the ocean, away from people and problems and nice clothes. But it wasn't. Nothing was safe here now – and maybe it never had been.

'It was great being there with you too, James,' I added. 'We had some really good times.'

Kate called something out to us.

'What?' I called back. 'What did you say?'

'Lana says there are five types of female body shape. Which one do you think you are?' called Kate.

'What?'

Lana held up a magazine. It had looked like they were going slower than us. It looked like Kate was doing most of the rowing.

'What?' I let out a loud sigh. It wasn't loud enough for them to hear, but it was loud enough to show James that I really didn't care about my body shape. Well, not very much. Everything had changed, but everything had needed to change. Going back to the past would kill us. Literally. The past, Before, whatever it was humans had done, or had failed to do, had killed them and changed the world. But staying in *our* past, on *our* jellyfish, would have killed us too. We couldn't stay the same; we couldn't keep doing the same things; we had to live in the new world – even if that meant killing our past.

The waves were higher now, and the rowing was much harder. I could hear James's breath between strokes as he pulled at his oars. The muscles of my arms were aching, but it was good to have something to concentrate on and, for a few minutes, as it became even more difficult to keep up with James's pace, I looked only at my paddles as they splashed awkwardly into the water, forcing us through it.

There was a suddenly flickering darkness beneath the boat. It could have been nothing, a cloud passing in front of the sun, a patch of seaweed, perhaps a shoal of fish; but then it came again, dark and deep and monstrous.

I pressed my lips together and pulled firmly on my oars again. The shoreline looked almost the way I'd remembered it now, so familiar, a fantasy of what our lives could be. The white house near the cliffs looked perfect and still untouched. From here, the scorch marks on the walls looked merely like a shadow from the cliff above, the broken windows still seemed to promise the secrets of a lost civilisation. You couldn't see the submerged houses, or the rusting, broken cars beneath the waves. You couldn't see the abandoned rubbish in the houses, or the weeds growing in living rooms. You couldn't see the shops with their magical colours and fabrics. You couldn't see the rotting dead bodies of the kriks along the beachfront.

A tentacle flickered below us again, lingering this time, searching us out.

'Are you all right, Martha?' said James, between breaths.

'Yes. I just want to get this over with.'

He pulled again, stronger this time, the little bubbles of water fizzing brightly against his oars as he cut through the murky waves.

Behind me I could feel the shifting in the light as the tentacles snaked gently around us, not touching us, but exploring and welcoming.

'There's no sheep,' called Lana. 'It's eaten them all.'

We pulled again at the oars. The feathery, small feelers were beneath us now, stroking us and rippling with their strange emotions. They dragged us in, pulling us towards the body. Then there was a sudden tug.

'Lift your oars up,' I said. 'Quick.'

There was a light bubbling sound beneath us, and the mesoglea started to ooze round the prow of the boat, pulling it in and fastening it to the edge of the Jellyfish.

James turned to me, white-faced, and gave a weak grin. 'This is definitely going to go well. There is no chance we can fail.'

I smiled back. He reached out and offered his hand. I took it, gratefully. It felt rough, and dry and . . . just nice.

'This is it, then,' he said. 'Let's do it.'

I stepped on to the mesoglea, and it gave a little under my feet in that soft way it always did, so familiar and comforting. There was that clinging thread of goo that stuck to your shoes as you took a step, and the smooth white surface. It felt like coming home.

But then James climbed on to the surface next to me, and a moment later there was that low vibration beneath the surface of the jelly. It was so subtle you could have missed it, but we were both waiting for it now. We looked at each other grimly.

'Let's go right to the middle,' said James. 'I'll start digging, but you get the cans.'

I nodded.

He unstrapped his machete and set off towards the centre, near where the Big House had been. There was no trace of it now, but there were a lot of darker patches hazily visible through the flesh of the Jellyfish. The sheep? Had the Jellyfish had a feast? Or was something else happening? For a split second I pictured us being sucked down there, sliding into that jelly, being absorbed. But then I shook off that thought and grabbed two cans of the petrol.

James had already sliced a circle into the mesoglea. It was hard going, and I could see his muscles straining as he pulled the machete through, but it had to be here, because the jelly didn't seal up so quickly in this bit of the creature. I pushed one of the shovels into the gash James had made, and started to lever it apart. With a sticky squelch, it gave a little, and I pulled away a large chunk of flesh. James put a shovel in on his side too, and started to lever there, pushing the shovel further and further into the slit. He grabbed the machete and cut at his section again. There was already sweat on his forehead, but his face looked determined. He pulled away another, larger chunk, bending down to lift it with both hands. He kicked it away across the mesoglea towards the sea. I put my shovel back in the slit and started levering.

Beneath us, the Jellyfish gave a little shiver.

I pulled away another chunk and threw it towards James's piece. 'I'm OK here,' he said. 'Go and get the rest of the petrol. Quick.' He was cutting away at the bottom of our hole now. This was already further than we'd ever managed to dig before.

I ran to the boat. Not stopping to worry about weight – because we were probably dead anyway, weren't we? – I climbed straight into it, lifting two more cans of the petrol and slinging a couple of pairs of curtains over my shoulders. I ran straight back to James and dropped them off there.

I made all the trips in a whirr of panic. You know when your head is focusing clearly on your task, but the rest of what you see is all blurry? I was in that state of adrenaline. But it was only on the last trip, when I'd already taken all the curtains, and ten of the cans, and even the matches, that I looked up at Lana and Kate. They were out of range of the tentacles, sitting there, staring at us. The pretence of the casual magazine-reading was over, and they were just watching, silently. I could see from their positions that they were riddled with tension. They had a rope tied to their boat, and the other end was tied to ours, because we'd had this mad idea that they could just pull us to safety. Even as we'd tied the rope on I think we'd all known it wouldn't work. But just then, I realized something that might.

'Cut the rope,' I shouted.

Their faces scrunched up in confusion.

'Cut the rope!'

'No,' Lana shouted back. 'Bog off.'

'Cut the rope,' I repeated. 'I've got an idea.' I could see Kate starting to cry. 'I think I can use it for something to save us,' I shouted.

Lana reached up, and I think her hands must have been shaking because it took her a few attempts to untie the rope. It fell, and quickly I gathered it in through the curious feelers. I shoved it straight into one of the cans of petrol. Some of the petrol sloshed out, over the edge, but I made sure that all of that rope was submerged before I ran back over to James.

Around him, there were piles of melting, oozing, translucent flesh, reforming themselves back into the Jellyfish. There was also a low, trembling vibration. It was constant now, a hum that you could feel right inside you. I scooped some of the piles of flesh away, throwing it back towards the sea.

James was standing inside a pit of Jellyfish blubber. The walls around him were leaning in, and were running with slow trails of glutinous liquid. A ripple ran across the surface. From the corners of my eyes, in that adrenaline fog, I could see the angry swishes of the tentacles crashing through the air.

'We've got to do it now, James.'

'Just one more.' He looked up. His hair was wet with sweat, and there was a sheen of slime over his T-shirt.

'No. Now,' I said. I passed him the machete.

He took it, and sliced in deeply, leaning down and pulling firmly through the flesh. There was another sudden rippling wave of jelly across the surface, just where I was standing. Above me, the shadow of one of the larger tentacles passed overhead, so close I felt its wind.

James jammed in his spade, levering the flesh apart. 'Now,' he said.

I jumped down, shoving in one of the curtains, and then another one. I reached over for the first can of petrol, carefully soaking all of the material.

There was another sudden whisk of cold air above us as the tentacle came back. We both ducked sharply, and for a minute it felt like I wanted to stay there, hunched inside the Jellyfish.

'Quick,' said James, and I could hear that he was panting with fear.

I grabbed the rest of the curtains and threw them down.

'Keep low,' I said.

The vibrations beneath us had turned to a rumbling menace that made even the petrol cans vibrate.

'Get out of the way,' I said to James as I started pouring two cans of petrol over the curtains. He grabbed another couple.

Thwack! The ground shook as a tentacle smashed on to

the mesoglea next to us.

We crouched down further in the pit. I undid all of the lids on the cans and tipped them so that they sloshed down on to the material. There was a pool of petrol covering the curtains now, and we were both having to clutch on to the mesoglea, exposing ourselves to the flailing tentacles, in order to avoid getting it on our shoes. I had the final can ready.

'Go,' I said. 'Go back to the boat.'

'What?'

'Go now.'

He paused.

'Trust me! Wait for me there, but get the oars ready.'

He ran. Keeping low, and still clutching his machete.

There was another sudden thwack behind me, and the ground shook again.

I pulled the rope out from the can quickly, splashes of petrol coming with it and soaking into my jeans.

There was another whooshing of wind from overhead. There was no time for thinking. I grabbed a shovel and quickly tied one end of the rope around it. Then I threw it into the petrol pool. It disappeared beneath the liquid.

I waited for the tentacles to do another swoop, and then I ran towards the boat, unfurling the petrol-soaked rope behind me. Beneath my feet, the mesoglea was roiling and rippling with urgency and confusion.

James was lying down in the boat, trying to avoid the rage of the Jellyfish, but we didn't have much longer. I leapt in, pulling out the box of matches from my back pocket. I was covered in petrol but, right then, being burnt alive seemed like a less painful way to die than being whipped across the sea by a giant tentacle.

Dropping my end of the rope on to the mesoglea, I lit a match and threw it. The rope went up immediately, a trail of flame leading towards the centre of the creature.

'Give me your machete,' I said.

The Jellyfish seemed suddenly to sense what we were doing, seemed suddenly to realize.

There was a brief lull, and the vibrations stopped, the tentacles paused in mid-air.

'Get ready,' I said.

And then it was like it breathed. A giant wave of jelly flesh rippled towards us. The tentacles rose, flicked back, their muscular strength readying for attack.

I cut into the jelly holding us to the edge. But even then, I was ready for the hit.

Then . . . there was a dull, distant thud. A boom.

'Go!' I screamed.

James started to row, and I scrabbled for my oars.

Behind us, the Jellyfish seemed to inflate, heaving up and getting bigger, and bigger.

We pulled, and pulled, and pulled. The rhythm of our terror was faster than any race you could ever imagine.

We were past the tentacles and near Kate and Lana before the first explosion happened.

39

I don't know how we got back exactly. I remember the way the Jellyfish looked, of course, its body huge: stretched thin and bulbous, the tentacles drooping, floating on the waves like ragged plastic bags. But I don't remember dragging ourselves back through the water again. That part of the story is really fuzzy.

At some point we got into the same boat as Lana and Kate, and I can remember the thudding explosions, each one inflating another side of the Jellyfish so that it bulged out awkwardly, tilting. Then the air would release and the mesoglea would shrink back, shrivelled and sagging.

We were almost at the submerged houses before the big explosion came, the one which ripped through the creature, finally tearing it apart. With a loud boom the Jellyfish ballooned out on all sides, then there was a high squeaking, whistling noise and half of the creature peeled off, as though melting away. It floated at a strange angle for a couple of seconds before dropping beneath the waves.

But Kate was determinedly facing the other way, looking at the shore and not at what was going on behind us, her shoulders hunched and flinching against the noise. 'Look,' she said, and she is the first person I definitely remember speaking. She pointed to the wavelets lapping against the shore.

There, on the edge of the water and the land, was a herd of jellyfish, small and delicate, their bodies pulsating gently with the rhythm of the water. Pale, translucent, each one had a whiter starred core, around which a perfect circle of glistening, jellied flesh danced just underneath the surface of the water. Swaying in time with each other, their tentacles flickered out below them like the strands of seaweed growing along the walls of the houses. As we pulled the boat in, one of them was thrown forward by a wave on to the old tarmac of the road; and as the water withdrew, it stayed behind. Harmless. Vulnerable. Along the shore there was a line of others, lying like blisters on the road, whitening and dying in the sunlight while in the water the rest of them waited, floating wherever the current went.

Behind us there were two larger explosions, and lumps of jelly flew through the air, scattering into the water with little raining plopping noises; but they were too far away to reach us. As they fell, they sank straight beneath the water, disappearing beneath the calm, opaque, sea.

'We've got this, haven't we?' I said. 'We can really win.'

'We've always had this,' said James. 'We've always been in

control. It's just taken us a while, that's all.'

'The stories don't end like this though, do they? The ones with the mermaids and kraken and selkies and stuff,' I said. 'They end with people happily living under the sea, peacefully, with the enemy.'

Lana was standing on the seaweed-covered wall of one of the ruined houses. She paused and looked down into the room below, wrinkling her nose.

'No, they don't,' said Kate. 'You weren't listening. They end with a wedding . . .'

James caught my eye for a second and started to laugh before looking away. He covered his mouth with his hand.

'. . . and it's a wedding between one of the sea creatures and one of the humans.'

'Well I'm not going under the sea. And I'm not marrying a flippin' krik,' said Lana. 'You can if you want, Kate. Actually, that seems like just the sort of man you'd be interested in.'

Lana kicked at one of the jellyfish, its flesh wobbling and wetly blubbery.

'At least they're big and muscular, Lana. And I bet they're really nice underneath their shell,' said Kate. Lana dipped her foot into the water and kicked a small jellyfish out on to the road. It didn't seem to make a noise as it landed, and it spread out softly, its body sinking into the tarmac.

'What happens after the wedding?' said James, still smiling. 'Do any of the stories say that bit?'

'No . . . I don't think so,' said Kate.

'Because I don't think a krik would have great conversation skills. And . . . you know . . .' He winked.

'What?'

I think we all did know, but Kate tilted her face to one side as though she was really puzzled, and Lana looked at him with a frown, daring him to say it.

'Well . . . I don't know if you could have . . . erm . . . kiss a krik. Could you?'

'Kate?' said Lana.

'How would I know? I don't want to kiss a krik! Why are you even asking me?'

'Actually, they do have a slit in their shell, in that bit that grows right over their face,' said James. 'Kate, you could kiss their shell slit and maybe touch their crabby tongue!'

We all started to laugh. Somehow, it was now just really, really funny. I mean, it wasn't funny at all of course, and we all looked around us a little bit as we were standing there, just in case, but that didn't stop the tears of comedy, or those pains in my stomach from too much laughing. The kriks were funny now. Funny.

'Come on,' I said. 'It might take us a couple of hours to get to the castle.'

I lifted up one of the garden forks; Kate and Lana bent down to grab theirs. James tucked one water pistol into the belt of his trousers, and slung another two over his shoulders.

'Shall we get changed now, do you think?' said Kate. 'I want to wear that gold dress.'

'No, I don't think so,' I said. 'We might get dirty on the way. We can get changed when we see the castle.'

'Did you pack a mirror for our make-up?' said Kate.

'No,' said Lana. 'But it's OK. We can just do each other's.'

James passed everybody a box of matches.

There was another explosion from the sea, but none of us turned round. We didn't need to see what was behind us. I reached out for James's hand, and I clasped the fork tighter in the other one. Beside me, Lana picked up the rucksack.

'This time,' I said, 'let's go along the road.'

Standing there on that sand-covered tarmac at the edge of Long Street, we could see the road stretching straight up, past the houses, into the hills beyond. The birds still circled over the fields, and the sheep still ambled across the top of the cliffs. We couldn't see where the road went, and we couldn't see the castle. But it went away from here, and away from the Jellyfish.

'Come on,' I said. 'Let's go.'

Acknowledgements

I would like to thank the staff and students of Luckley House School for the role so many of them have had in this book. I am very lucky to work in an environment where creativity is an active part of the curriculum, and where any crazy schemes I have had for promoting literacy have been so supported by staff. I appreciate the freedom and encouragement given to us by the best senior management team I've ever worked for: Jane Tudor, Sally Hills, Ian Vallance and Claire Gilding-Brant.

The English Department and library are obviously amazing (Elaine, Katie, Rachel, Liz, Darshan and Angie), but I'd particularly like to thank all the students who have inspired me to finish what started off life as just an unusual lesson resource. So many of you have helped me with your (often brutal!) criticism and I have genuinely learnt so much from writing alongside you; I hope some of it has made me a better teacher as well as having improved my writing! I'm sorry that, despite your enthusiasm for her death, Dr Jones survived. In earlier drafts, following the Year 9 vote, she did die. Dr Jones, thanks so much for your scientific advice and apologies for ignoring most of it. I hope the fact that I didn't kill you off (and also the fact that the character's nothing like you!) will mean you'll forgive me!

A particular thanks to the fabulous Rachel Leyshon for

being a brilliant editor. I've learnt so much from you and you've been so much fun to work with (I am confident there are no possible jellyfish jokes which you haven't made!). I'm also grateful for the suggestions made by Kesia Lupo and Barry Cunningham, as well as the copy-editing of Helen Jennings. My agent, Claire Wilson, has been unfailingly kind, supportive, and has also given really useful input to the book. One of the things I've realized from the experience of working on *Jelly* is how many people are involved in the publication of a book. Thanks so much to Laura Myers, Rachel Hickman and everybody in Chicken House that I haven't mentioned!

Owen has, as always, been my writing inspiration. Thanks for your willingness to discuss fictional children and worlds, and your always useful thoughts on plot and structure. Your ability to know exactly when I would like a glass of wine or a cup of tea has also helped enormously with this book.

And finally, thanks to my parents for taking me to the library every week as a child, and for only occasionally banning books from the dinner table. I value your continued support, which, amongst other things, has included buying me the entire Booker Prize shortlist every year on my birthday for the past twenty years! I am so grateful.